A Holiday Yarn

A Holiday Yarn

A SEASIDE KNITTERS MYSTERY

Sally Goldenbaum

AN OBSIDIAN MYSTERY

OBSIDIAN

Published by New American Library, a division of Penguin Group (USA) Inc., 75 Hudson Street, New York, New York 10014, USA · Penguin Group (Canada), 90 Eglinton Avenue East, Suite 700, Toronto, Ontario M4P 2Y3, Canada (a division of Pearson Penguin Canada Inc.) · Penguin Books Ltd., 80 Strand, London WC2R 0RL, England · Penguin Ireland, 25 St. Stephen's Green, Dublin 2, Ireland (a division of Penguin Books Ltd.) · Penguin Group (Australia), 250 Camberwell Road, Camberwell, Victoria 3124, Australia (a division of Pearson Australia Group Pty. Ltd.) · Penguin Books India Pvt. Ltd., 11 Community Centre, Panchsheel Park, New Delhi - 110 017, India · Penguin Group (NZ), 67 Apollo Drive, Rosedale, North Shore 0632, · New Zealand (a division of Pearson New Zealand Ltd.) · Penguin Books (South Africa) (Pty.) Ltd., 24 Sturdee Avenue, Rosebank, Johannesburg 2196, South Africa

Penguin Books Ltd., Registered Offices:
80 Strand, London WC2R 0RL, England

First published by Obsidian, an imprint of New American Library,
a division of Penguin Group (USA) Inc.

First Printing, November 2010
1 3 5 7 9 10 8 6 4 2

Copyright © Sally Goldenbaum, 2010

OBSIDIAN and logo are trademarks of Penguin Group (USA) Inc.

LIBRARY OF CONGRESS CATALOGING-IN-PUBLICATION DATA:

Goldenbaum, Sally.
A holiday yarn: a seaside knitters mystery/Sally Goldenbaum.
p. cm.
ISBN 978-0-451-23158-1
1. Knitters (Persons)—Fiction. 2. Murder—Investigation—Fiction. 3. City and town life—Massachusetts—Fiction. 4. Bed and breakfast accommodations—Fiction. I. Title.
PS3557.O35937H65   2010
813'.54—dc22   2010026734

Set in Palatino • Designed by Elke Sigal

Printed in the United States of America

For Don

Acknowledgments

First, my thanks to Sandy McDonald and her family, who started KasCare and built the amazing community that contributes to the blankets and garments that warm the children of South Africa. In *Moon Spinners*, the Seaside Knitters are happy to join these generous knitters and others who contribute to the knit-a-square project. Learn more about KasCare at www .kascare.org.

And additional thanks:

To the gracious, generous, and insightful readers of the Seaside Knitters mysteries whose e-mails often keep me going during a long writing day.

To the people of Cape Ann, who have provided me with the inspiration that fuels the Seaside Knitters and the people of Sea Harbor.

To novelist Mary Stuart, whose novel first introduced me to the Moon Spinners myth.

To my steadfast and very special friends, who still read my e-mails, even though I may be inviting them to another book signing.

To my first writing partner and lifelong friend, Adrienne

Staff, whose friendship helped launch me into the world of fiction writing. And my coffee shop, porch-writing partner, Nancy Pickard—mystery-writing mentor and dear friend.

And to Todd and Laila, Aria and John, Danny and Claudia, who have built Web sites, proofread, designed bookmarks, promoted and researched and dished out bountiful amounts of encouragement—and brought four incredible grandchildren into our lives.

Chapter 1

*I*n the confusing days that followed, one thing that would stand out in Nell's mind was that each member of the Thursday night knitting group had talked to Pamela Pisano that day. An unlikely event, considering that Pamela didn't fit into the normal order of their lives. The conversations varied, but all four knitters remembered hearing her say—with some conviction, they'd agreed—that her cousin Mary Pisano was crazy. Certifiably crazy, she'd said to one of them.

More than the insult to her friend, what stuck in Nell's mind with profound irony was what Pamela had said to her next. She'd spoken the words with authority, although that in itself wasn't unusual—almost everything that came out of Pamela Pisano's mouth had an overtone of authority.

But the words had an ominous tone, with a tinge of warning. Not only was Mary Pisano crazy, she'd told Nell, but her turning the ancestral home into a bed-and-breakfast would come to one end, and one end only: it would kill her.

And then she'd repeated two of the words, leaning forward in the chair until a slice of her golden hair moved in slow motion against her cheek: "Kill her."

. . .

Nell and Pamela had met that Thursday morning in Polly Farrell's Canary Cove Tea Shoppe. The meeting was purely by chance.

Nell had gotten an early start to her day, leaving home before her husband had finished reading the paper and had his second cup of coffee.

It was early morning, and the frozen air was so still that Nell could hear her heartbeat beneath her fleece hoodie. The delicious quiet filled her with a visceral kind of peace. And only on crisp winter days when the town was blanketed in snow and the summer people were long gone did it happen quite this way.

"Summer vacationers don't sleep," was her husband, Ben's, explanation of the difference in the town's mood. "It's because vacationers' days here are short, limited, and those folks need to absorb every minute of Sea Harbor magic while they have a chance."

Nell understood that. She loved summer, too—the sun-drenched days, the smell of grilled swordfish on the deck, the carefree ambience and frivolous laughter and morning runs along the long sandy beaches.

But winter quiet was special, contemplative. Fewer visitors came to town, and everyone "stretched out" as Birdie Favazza described it. There was room to breathe. To throw your arms and your spirit open to the winter air without toppling a sunbather or bicyclist or tourist.

Nell pulled a woolen hat down over her ears and braced herself as the cold air hit her face. She breathed in the scent of snow and broke into a slow jog down her hill and onto Harbor Road. The town of Sea Harbor lay at her feet like a picture postcard, its winding streets as intricate as a lacy winter shawl.

She took in a deep breath and smiled as the exhale caused a white plume to rise in front of her face.

She loved this town.

At the bottom of the hill Nell turned east, toward the strip of road that led to the Canary Cove Art Colony and Polly's Tea Shoppe.

A quiet corner table. A hot cup of cinnamon tea, a buttery scone. And then a jog home and a hot shower.

Pure indulgence.

Traffic was minimal: another jogger here or there, moms out pushing strollers, their babies bundled up like tiny Eskimos, and an occasional car. The gallery owners were just beginning to pull up their blinds and unlock their doors.

Rebecca Early waved at Nell through a window display of sparkling beads. Nell waved back. She slowed slightly, unable to resist the beauty of the display—dripping rounds of lampwork glass in magnificent colors. Crimson ovals, brilliant green and gold drops hung from boughs of holly and fir. She made a mental note to come back later with a gift list in hand. Rebecca was one of Nell's favorite artists on Canary Cove Road, and she never failed to have the perfect earrings to match Izzy's eyes or a necklace that Birdie would find intriguing and unique.

Nell moved on to Polly's shop and hurried through the wreathed door, out of the brisk wind that had turned her high round cheeks a bright crimson.

"Snow's in the air," Polly announced from behind the counter as she waved over the heads of customers and above the crooning of Bing Crosby dreaming about a white Christmas. "I'll have your tea in a jiffy, Nell. And today's cranberry scones are to die for."

Nell waved her agreement, then spied an empty table in the corner and settled down into a pool of sunshine. She unzipped her hoodie, pulled off her mittens, and began to rub blood and feeling back into her hands.

Looking up, she saw Pamela Pisano standing at the counter. Beautiful, elegant, aristocratic—or so some Sea Harbor folks said. And then they'd chuckle, knowing that the woman's grand-father, a humble man, would scoff at any hint of pretension in his family.

Her platinum hair was unnaturally straight, as smooth as sea silk, and cut in a severe wedge that slanted toward her face, bringing attention to prominent cheekbones and a straight, per-fect nose. She was medium in stature, though the stiletto heels of her boots brought her up to Nell's height.

Balancing a teacup in her gloved hand, she looked at Nell, smiled in recognition, and walked over to the corner table. "It's nice to see you, Nell." Pamela Pisano's voice was a blend of En-glish boarding school and Boston Brahmin, mixed with a touch of who she really was—a Sea Harbor native.

Nell smiled back. The successful editor who'd graduated from the local high school, then Tufts, and went on to control her family's fashion magazine intrigued her. She was doing a good job, from what Nell heard. Nell motioned to the empty chair, but Pamela had already pulled it out. She sat down, shrugging out of her fur jacket and stripping off tight leather gloves.

Nell watched the purposeful movements. Self-assured. Graceful. The body language of a successful woman.

"I haven't seen you for a while. You look lovely." Nell tilted her head and looked at her closely. "But something's different. Your hair, perhaps?"

Pamela's fingers tapped her forehead lightly. "No. Botox and a chemical peel." She stroked her smooth cheeks with long, narrow fingers. "We do features on these things, so I wanted to see how it worked. I can't say I see a noticeable difference."

"That's probably because you've inherited the Pisano gene for perfect skin. You have as much need for face work as I have for mud wrestling."

Pamela's laugh was light and practiced—and wrinkle free.

She sipped her tea and looked around the shop. "This place is quaint. New?"

"About a year old. You should spend more time here. Sea Harbor is growing."

"I may—I've made an offer on a place on Sea Harbor Point. This town is a nice getaway from the frantic world of magazines. Of course, there's a downside—running into family at every turn in the road."

Nell chuckled. That was certainly true. Everyone in town knew at least one Pisano. And though some of the younger generation left town to run Enzo Pisano's newspapers or magazines in other parts of New England, they always came back— Sea Harbor ties were as strong as fishing lines. Sea Harbor was home. And even if allegiances weakened over the years, the annual Pisano family meeting always lured them back.

Nell suspected that this year the meeting—following the death of the family patriarch—which had started days ago, held additional importance. Family holdings were being scrutinized and discussed with strong opinions and self-interest.

Pamela looked through the window as if evaluating her hometown. "Sea Harbor is a sleepy place compared to New York and Boston, but there's entertainment anywhere you go. All you have to do is look for it. Even here."

Nell smiled and nodded, although she wasn't at all sure what she was agreeing to. The look in Pamela's eyes didn't seem to indicate the kind of entertainment she equated with Sea Harbor. But then, the nearly twenty-year difference in their ages would certainly account for different tastes.

"Your cousin Mary tells me you're meeting in Enzo's old home. How's that going?"

"Yes, we're all there, gathered around the dining table, being polite, mostly, and acting like we like one another more than we really do. We're almost finished. A late meeting today should be it. We're having to close some publications, consolidate, but nothing too disastrous."

"I hear *Fashion Monthly* is in fine shape, though. The issues I've seen have been lovely."

Pamela accepted the praise for her *Vogue*-like magazine graciously.

"Are you staying in town for a while?"

"For the holidays. I'll spend time with my mother at the nursing home. This year will be difficult for her without Grandfather Enzo."

Nell had known Dolores Pisano in better years, when her mind was clear and her sense of humor contagious. She was a lovely woman.

"Our grandfather was a powerful man," Pamela said, "but he wasn't always reasonable in later years—just like my mother. His grasp of the business had slipped."

"I never saw that side of Enzo. I saw him dancing at the yacht club a few days before his heart attack—and he was always out on the water, fishing and sailing. He was a vital, active man. One of a kind. The whole town misses him."

"That's because he poured money into Sea Harbor. Money has a way of making people miss you."

"There's no question that he was generous, but he was also entertaining, a wonderful conversationalist, and a good friend to many of us."

Nell paused. Why was she justifying this wonderful man to his own granddaughter? She stopped talking, focused on the buttery scone Polly had set before her, and sought an easier topic. "What do you think of Ravenswood-by-the-Sea? I know it's not finished, but I think it's lovely."

Pamela's perfect lips twitched slightly, and she looked at Nell as if she had lost her mind. "It's definitely unfinished. But overlooking that fact, it's awful."

"I'm not sure what you mean. The parts I've seen are beautiful. Enzo would love the life and laughter Mary will bring back into his home."

"By housing strangers in a bed-and-breakfast? It's degrading, Nell. She might as well have turned it into a tavern. And she won't even be living there herself—"

"But she'll hire a full-time manager, she said. I think her husband thought the house a bit overwhelming."

"Exactly. And if she isn't up to living in it, she should have acknowledged that."

"But her plan makes sense, don't you think? The estate is huge, with all those bedrooms, a carriage house, acres of land. What were the options? People aren't living in mansions anymore."

But Pamela continued, her words pouring out in a stream as if they'd been bottled up for too long. "Her decisions aren't thought out. Housing strangers. Getting decorating advice from some Sea Harbor twit who doesn't know the first thing about design. And then there's that mangy dog. The humane thing would have been to euthanize it when Grandfather died—people do that. But not Mary. She kept it, and she lets it run wild in that home."

Nell winced at the mention of Georgia, Mary's anything-but-mangy dog. Mary had coaxed the part poodle, part retriever mix back to life after Enzo died. Georgia was now her shadow, and she and her husband, Ed, adored the dog. She was a great companion for Mary when Ed was out on his fishing boat for weeks at a time. She could see there was no convincing Pamela that a dog was man's best friend. Maybe she'd have a better chance on the decorating front.

"Mary wanted Ravenswood-by-the-Sea to look as much like the original estate as possible," Nell explained. "Nancy Hughes was director of the historical museum and has access to a library of old photos. She's smart and very generous with her time and expertise. She's a huge help to Mary."

"Mary is probably paying her a fortune."

Nell shook her head. "Nancy's husband left her well-off. She's doing this because she loves old houses." Then she added for good measure, "And she has excellent taste."

Nell wasn't sure that was entirely true, but she suddenly had a compulsion to protect Mary and her choices. Nancy was smart and capable and liked being a part of a project the whole town was interested in. It filled a void in her life.

Pamela rested her arms on the table, her long fingers tapping the surface. "My grandfather wanted me to have the Ravenswood estate—that's the truth, no matter what my greedy cousins say. Somehow Mary convinced him otherwise. This kind of greed and deception seems to run in the Pisano family, Nell. Beware. Mary wanted my house—and my cousin Agnes wanted my fashion magazine. Agnes, with a face like a horse, editor of a fashion magazine?" Pamela sighed.

Nell was silent. The last place in the world she wanted to be was in the middle of a Pisano family squabble. She looked around to see whether anyone was listening. People were busy chatting, enjoying Polly's muffins and scones. She refocused on Pamela's strong words. Maybe Pamela was the better choice for the fashion magazine; Enzo must have thought so. But she knew for a fact that Mary had not coerced Enzo Pisano into giving her anything. Mary liked her life just as it was—writing her chatty column for the newspaper, dancing the night away with her fisherman husband when she could lure him off his boat. Walking with Georgia. Enzo had practically forced the house on Mary, telling her that she was the only family member with enough sense to do the right thing with it. And he'd left it up to Mary to decide what that right thing was.

For this week, Mary had decided the right thing was hosting the family meeting there, although she had confessed to Nell why she had done it: guilt. Mary was well aware that her grandfather's leaving the home to her was a thorn in some of her cousins' sides. "Maybe hosting the gruesome meeting will eliminate a little of the tension."

"As nice as Mary is," Pamela continued, "she didn't inherit the Pisano brains. She doesn't think things through, like that silly column she writes, chatting about things that are often none of her business. It's an embarrassment, just like the bed-and-breakfast will be. I don't know how I got into this family. There are times I think I'm adopted."

Nell held back a smile. "Well, maybe it's a small-town thing—we like her column. She makes people feel good—or not good, if that's what they deserve. Mary has a sense of humor. She's perceptive."

Pamela laughed. "'Crazy' is the word family members use. And this ridiculous decision about my grandfather's estate will prove it. It's insane. And it's going to kill her; you mark my words."

She paused, then spoke a little louder in case Nell might miss her message over the background chatter and Christmas music.

"Kill her," she said. This time she looked at Nell intently, waiting for her response.

"Mary has more energy than a teenager. There's no need to worry about that."

Pamela dismissed Nell's comment with a toss of her head.

Every hair remained in place, the sharp angle of platinum still aimed at one smooth, sculpted cheek. She finished her tea silently.

Outside, the wind blew and a loose awning flapped against the window. Nell wondered when the snow would come. They'd had one good snow a week earlier that had set the holiday mood, covering yards and flower beds, delighting children as they dug out their sleds and ice skates and built igloos in their front yards. It excited the Harbor Road merchants too, as the snow was luring holiday shoppers out in full force. Another snow would be coming soon; she could feel it in her bones.

A shadow blocked the sunlight, and Nell looked up to see Tommy Porter, his chin tucked against the front of his police uniform. He was looking into the shop, oblivious of Nell.

Reflected in the blackness of his dark glasses, Nell could see Pamela's face. She was looking back at Tommy with a disinterested look on her face. Disinterested, but with a touch of amusement.

Another policeman walked up, and Tommy spun around, startled, as if he'd been caught doing something against regulations. He managed a laugh at whatever his partner said, then followed him down the street without a backward glance.

"Not one of my fans," Pamela said, watching Tommy walk away. She pushed back her chair. "His brother Eddie and I had a good time one summer—for a while, anyway." She stood and pulled on her fur jacket. "I was so young then. Young and foolish."

She was talking mostly to herself, but the end of her sentence had turned hard. Foolish. Not a word one assigned easily to Pamela Pisano.

Pamela slipped on her leather gloves and pushed the memory away. "I'll give Mary credit for one thing—she hired some entertaining men to work around that place. Somehow, I didn't think she had it in her. It has certainly eased the pain." She smiled then, a careful smile that allowed no crease, and waved good-bye to Nell. "It was lovely seeing you," she said, the words trailing over her shoulder as she turned and moved toward the door, her head high, her slender body silhouetted against the winter light.

Just outside the door she stopped and lifted a cigarette to her lips, her head turning both ways, as if expecting someone to appear with a lighter. Her smile was in place, practiced.

Two young mothers were pushing strollers down the street and stopped to look at the Alfa Romeo parked at the curb. Sleek and polished. Just like the woman standing beside it. They looked at Pamela with the same envy, then stepped aside as she strode to the driver's-side door.

Across the street, Ham Brewster was unlocking the door to his gallery. He glanced across the street at the car and the woman beside it.

Although Pamela pretended not to notice, Nell suspected she was acutely aware of every admiring glance, like models on a runway or celebrities before a camera, whose images become defined by photographs.

Pamela touched the door handle, then looked over the car and down the road. She pushed her sunglasses to the top of her head, apparently pleased with what she saw.

Slipping her keys back into her bag, she stepped up onto the curb and strode purposefully down the street, a playful smile lifting her lips.

Chapter 2

"She came in to take a class," Mae Anderson told Nell later that day. "She was mad as a wet hen when Izzy showed her the class schedule. It didn't suit her fancy. 'Who in heaven's name would want to knit baby clothes?' That was what she said. My answer was, 'Who wouldn't?' They're making those cute little cuddle wraps for kids in Africa. Now, who in their right mind wouldn't want to do that?"

Izzy's store manager was counting out receipts for the Seaside Knitting Studio as she talked, her rimless glasses balanced precariously on the end of her long nose. Mae wore a thick red sweater with sleigh bells all over it—her December uniform, Izzy called it. Her thin eyebrows lifted occasionally to emphasize a word.

"Who wouldn't do what?" Izzy mumbled around a plastic bag of needle protectors that she held between her teeth. She was kneeling on the hardwood floor on the other side of the main room in the knitting studio, slipping packets on a rotating display stand. A thick midthigh cable sweater engulfed her narrow shoulders and hips and kept her warm against the store's drafts.

Nell looked over at her niece. "Mae said Pamela Pisano was in. She's making the rounds. I had tea with her this morning."

"Why would you do that?" Izzy asked. She sat back on her legs and eyed the display, adjusting a wayward packet.

"Why, indeed." Mae closed up the computer and locked the drawer beneath the checkout counter. "It's a wonder she doesn't break both legs with those fancy boots she wears."

"She has beautiful clothes; that's true. It's important to her job, I suppose. If she dressed like I do, she'd lose readers." Nell grinned at Mae's grumpiness and tried to force a smile from the store manager. "She's interesting."

"Pretentious," Mae muttered.

Cass stuck her head around the corner from the small galley kitchen. "Not to mention that she wears fur. *Animal* fur. Did you check out that white jacket?" Smelling food, Cass hurried over and relieved Nell of two white bags that held their dinner.

"Seriously, Aunt Nell, I thought you were running this morning. Did you have tea with Pamela Pisano on purpose?" Izzy asked.

Nell laughed. "Come on, now. Where's the Christmas spirit? She's not a bad person."

"That's debatable," Mae said. "Besides being mad as a hatter about all the baby-clothes knitting classes, she was appalled that we didn't offer a special class for lefties."

Izzy laughed. "Maybe she's right. Maybe I should schedule a class for left-handed knitters. They're forgotten sometimes."

"Fiddlesticks," Mae said. She straightened a sprig of mistletoe hanging above her computer.

"Well, let's give her a break," Nell said. "Her job must be stressful."

"Humph." Mae pulled a heavy black purse from beneath the counter. "How many men has this 'nice' woman left stranded in the mess of her affairs? But enough of her. I'm leaving. Tonight's my Sweet Adeline rehearsal—women's barbershop harmony at its finest. We've been booked for several tree lightings, and we're getting very good, if I do say so myself." Mae's long face broke into a wide smile, and she began jiggling her skinny hips, humming "Jingle Bell Rock" on her way to the door.

Door chimes announced Birdie Favazza's arrival. She gave the dancing figure a surprised look and broke into delighted laughter. "I think there's potential for you, dear Mae. Maybe you'd like to join my tap-dancing class? Or the Rockettes, perhaps?"

Mae threw her head back in a throaty laugh as she made a dancing exit, her laughter floating behind her.

Birdie slipped off her backpack and looked around at the store. "Izzy, this is amazing. A holiday wonderland."

Izzy grinned. "You like it? Mae would have had me spray-painting the whole place red and green, with talking elves and animated Santas bobbing around every corner. I restrained her a little."

Nell walked over to a table with a wooden sleigh piled high with glittery yarn. She remembered the sleigh from Izzy's parents' Kansas City home. The memory came back with surprising force—Izzy and her brothers, their eyes huge as they tumbled down the stairs on Christmas morning, greeted by an enormous tree and piles of brightly wrapped presents.

Izzy had her own tree in the yarn shop, in the middle of the room. The branches were heavy with dozens of small socks, booties, hats, and scarves that customers had knit up for Father Northcutt's homeless shelter.

Nell looked into the children's room—the Magic Room, customers called it. In one corner stood a rocking reindeer that Angus McPherron had carved for Izzy. The old man had even painted the nose red, a concession just for her, he said, since painting the beautiful pine seemed disrespectful. Candy canes strung on a red velvet ribbon circled the room, and red and green plaid cushions invited small bodies to settle down with a book or toy truck.

"Birdie's right. It's a fairyland," Nell said.

"Great. I'm glad you like it. But enough with the decorations," Izzy said. "If we don't feed Cass soon, she'll start eating them."

Cass echoed the sentiment loudly, and they followed one another down three steps into the familiar comfort of the back room. Izzy had already started a fire in the old stone fireplace in the corner, and Purl, the shop cat, was settled on a love seat in front of the dancing flames. From small speakers up near the ceiling, Andrea Bocelli sang about the holidays in soft, tender tones.

"Salve for my soul," Birdie murmured. She settled in next to Purl and pulled a ball of emerald green mohair from her bag.

"Wow. Amazing color." Cass walked over for a closer look.

"It's from Mary's blanket." Birdie pulled the finished blanket from a plastic bag at her feet—a soft, lacy blend, with deep blues woven into the patchwork design and a hint of rose edging the squares.

Izzy nearly dropped the wineglasses. "It's gorgeous. A knit quilt."

They'd been admiring it in stages for weeks, but the finished blanket was the sea itself, rolling and renewing—smooth, vibrant waves of color.

"Mary couldn't have imagined anything this elegant when she asked us to knit blankets for her B and B. You're a hard act to follow, Birdie."

Cass filled the wineglasses and passed them around. "The ocean looked like that this week. It's the winter light—it was so amazing, we took Sam back out to take photographs."

"Sam?" Izzy looked up. "He . . . he was so busy last week. But that's good that he took the time. I hope he got some great shots."

Izzy's tone was odd. Sam was always out photographing

something beautiful or interesting or arresting—it's what an award-winning photographer did. Before Nell could comment, Izzy wiped away the concern with a quick smile. She picked up a glass of wine and took a sip.

Birdie folded the afghan back into its bag. "I told Mary we'd drop this off tonight, Nell, just to give her an idea of what's coming. With all those relatives around, she needs something lovely to look at."

"Good idea. I think they're taking a toll on her. She missed writing her column two days in a row."

"My brother Pete hung out with a few of the Pisanos at the Gull this week," Cass said. "They know how to party up a storm, he says. I don't think Pamela hangs out with them, though—only when she has to."

Birdie laughed. "Somehow I can't see Pamela Pisano in the Gull. I ran into her at city hall today. She said today's the last gathering of the clan. It was said with great relief."

Nell lifted the lid from the soup tureen and set it aside. Steam spiraled up, filling the room with the scent of garlic and wine, fresh thyme and parsley and butter. Nell changed her mother's bouillabaisse recipe each time she made it, adding this or that. A splash of Muscadet, a pinch of saffron. Ever-changing soup, just like life.

"Pamela wields a mighty sword at those meetings, I'd suspect," she said, stirring the soup with a wooden spoon.

"She wields something; I'm sure of that," Birdie said. "My sympathies are with dear Mary, surrounded by all those relatives wanting to make sure they get their share of the newspaper or magazine world that Enzo owned. Or whatever it is they do at those meetings."

Izzy brought in a basket of warm rolls, and Nell motioned everyone to the table. "Please don't let it get cold."

In minutes, soup bowls were filled and favorite chairs

claimed as they settled around the fire, glasses of wine and heaping bowls of bouillabaisse on the coffee table. For a few minutes the only sounds in the room were the crooning of the Italian tenor and the gentle slurping of Nell's latest version of the French soup.

Birdie wiped a flake of parsley from the corner of her mouth and put down her spoon. "Ah. The best yet."

Nell smiled. It wouldn't be bouillabaisse without Birdie's predictable response. "Did Pamela end up buying any yarn? It's odd we all seemed to bump into her today."

"I'm not sure. She said she might do a feature on contemporary knitting fashions in her magazine—that's why she wanted to take a class. She said it would give her a better feeling for how to plan it. And it'd be cool if she mentioned us. The only classes that fit her schedule, though, were for knitting baby sweaters. It didn't make her happy." Izzy shrugged.

"I think she's anti-kid," Cass said. "But she has a point—you *do* have a lot of baby classes, Iz. Is the old clock ticking?"

"People like knitting baby things at holiday time; that's all. I have a scarf class, too. And a socks class, so there." Izzy tossed a ball of yarn at Cass. "Pamela will find other ways to occupy her time while she's here, I'm sure. She said there were some—and I quote—'hot bodies' over at the B and B, which helped make the time pass."

"Pamela has always loved men," Birdie said. She began casting on stitches.

"Fodder for a TV reality show maybe?" Izzy said. "Housewives of Sea Harbor, beware."

"Batten down the hatches." Cass laughed. "She touches Danny Brandley, and she'll find herself in a lobster trap."

Nell laughed. "It's good she has something to occupy her. She's definitely not happy about Mary's opening a B and B."

"Frankly, she's not alone," Birdie said. "Some of my neighbors are ready to throttle Mary—and Pamela has encouraged them. She attended a meeting the other night at Henrietta O'Neal's. Henrietta is sure that once the B and B opens, sin, promiscuity, and a tavern in the carriage house are sure to follow. She's quite furious about the whole thing. I didn't know she had that much steam in her eighty-year-old body, but she's raising a nor'easter over this."

"People can be uncomfortable having strangers in their neighborhoods," Nell said. "The Pisano estate is so large, though, I don't imagine the neighbors will even know when guests are there."

"Well, it certainly won't bother me, and I'm one of the closest neighbors. I think I need to have a talk with Henrietta and set her straight."

"Pamela seemed to think Mary wasn't up to running a guest home. She said it will *kill* Mary," Nell said.

"She said that to me, too. A strange choice of words. Mary is as strong as an ox. A good fisherman's wife—and she's quite young by my standards. What, mid-forties? Running a bed-and-breakfast might kill Pamela, but not Mary." Birdie carried her empty bowl to the table and brought back a fresh bottle of wine.

"Birdie's right. She's doing a terrific job on Enzo's house." Nell collected the other bowls and took them into the kitchen alcove, then retrieved her knitting bag from the bookcase.

Izzy lifted her blanket from a basket near the fireplace and stretched it across her knees. "I'm getting there. What do you think, Aunt Nell?"

Nell slipped on her glasses and examined the blocks of color—rich gold, some with a hint of green, a touch of rose and lavender that Izzy had expertly knit into a wavy design. She could imagine a tired guest wrapped up in the impossibly soft alpaca wool blend, wanting to settle down for a long winter's nap. "It's beautiful," she said.

Mary Pisano's vision imagined each bedroom in Ravenswood-by-the-Sea with its own ambience, its own color theme, and each room would have an inviting, unique blanket at the end of the bed. Thanks to the Seaside Knitters and a few friends, her vision was nearing reality.

As the fire burned low, talk turned away from the Pisanos to the first holiday parties of the season, Christmas pageants, food collections, and the growing pile of cuddles, tiny baby buntings ready to send off to mothers in South Africa.

Birdie held up the beginnings of her cuddle—a small, soft yarn envelope, big enough to hold a tiny baby. They'd all knit a few over the next few weeks and send them to Soweto to cuddle babies to sleep. "And now," she said, covering a yawn, "my time has come. An early night for me, my dears."

Nell agreed. They'd leave now and deliver Mary's blanket, and she might be home before Ben fell asleep.

"Go, both of you," Izzy urged. "Cass and I will clean up—and then we're off to a holiday party at the Ocean's Edge."

"And don't worry one split second about the rest of this soup, Nell," Cass called across the room. "I'll see that it finds a loving home."

Nell laughed. Nearly all Thursday night dinners ended up in Cass's tiny refrigerator, feeding the lobster fisherwoman for at least a few days before she had to start opening her stash of canned beans. She wrapped a scarf around her neck and slipped into her coat. "Have fun, you two. Is Sam meeting you, Iz?"

Izzy didn't answer. Instead, she busied herself changing the music selection on her iPod, as if it were somehow critically important that Andrea Bocelli give equal time to Norah Jones.

Nell looked for a movement of Izzy's narrow shoulders. A smile. A shrug. When nothing came, she forced the frown from her face and followed Birdie out the door and into the winter night.

Chapter 3

$\mathcal{A}$ brisk wind ruffled Birdie's hair and sent it flying in all directions—a flurry of white. She tugged a knit hat tightly down over her ears and breathed in the frosty night air.

"Christmas," she said softly.

"Christmas," Nell repeated. They stood still for a moment, side by side, Nell's tall and slender frame shadowing her diminutive friend. Though nearly twenty years separated them in age, their friendship defied the difference. They were each other's rocks.

Birdie hooked her arm through Nell's, the blanket tucked beneath her other arm, and they walked slowly across to the car.

"It's so peaceful." Birdie's breath rose when she talked, feathery spirals in the black night.

All along Harbor Road, garlands of greenery turned gaslights into festive posts. Tiny white lights outlined doors, and store windows were filled with Santas and elves, sweet dolls and toy soldiers standing guard. Soft holiday music filtered onto the sidewalk from Archie's Bookstore, his contribution to Harbor Road's holiday spirit.

Nell glanced down toward the tavern on the corner. A steady

stream of people hurried through the door, out of the cold and into the hot, noisy interior.

"Jake and Andy Risso are doing a good business tonight at the Gull."

Birdie climbed into the front seat of Nell's car. "Mary said most of the family is gathering at the Rissos' bar tonight—their grand finale. Good. We'll get her to ourselves. Maybe get some juicy Pisano gossip."

The route to Ravenswood Road wound past the harbor and the Ocean's Edge restaurant, then up a hill, circling a children's park before it merged into the stately treed neighborhood in which Birdie lived.

Nell remembered the first time Izzy had seen the Ravenswood area—when she was small and her parents had brought her and her brothers to Sea Harbor for a summer vacation—she said it looked like a forest turning into a town. More trees than houses to a child's eye, though, in fact, many of the homes were hidden discretely behind low stone walls and thick stands of white pine, cedar, and eastern hemlock.

The oldest neighborhood in Sea Harbor, Ravenswood was once home to sea captains and wealthy businessmen whose money came from granite quarries and fishing fleets, or Bostonians who built elegant summer places up on the hill. Some homes still remained with the original families; others had been sold, remodeled, and updated into elegant permanent homes. Christmas decorations matched the houses, stately and grand— lovely strands of white lights twisted through the tallest of trees, enormous wreaths with red bows fastened to driveway posts, candles in long mullioned windows. A giant star that glowed atop a pine tree must have taken a crane to find a home at such heights.

Nell slowed, then turned into a wide drive. In the distance was a discreet white sign bordered and freshly painted.

RAVENSWOOD-BY-THE-SEA, it read.

Ahead was Enzo Pisano's family home, proud and welcoming, a Sea Harbor landmark for longer than anyone could remember. Enzo's father, a celebrated sea captain, had built the house for his bride a century before—and now, thanks to Mary, it shined as brightly as it had decades earlier.

"It's a Norman Rockwell painting," Birdie said. "And it keeps getting better. I think it's perfect, and then Mary finds something else to make it even more beautiful."

Nell pulled into the brick parking area. They slipped out of the car and walked up a winding pathway to the front porch. Every window held a wreath; every post was wrapped in fresh greenery. Small white lights outlined the towering pines. "It's so quiet. Mary's expecting us, right?"

Birdie nodded. "Although it would be understandable if she forgot, considering the week she's had."

They walked up the steps. A wide porch stretched across the front of the house, from one side to the other. It was lined with rocking chairs, ghosts in the Christmas light, their arms and seats high with untouched snow.

Nell tried the door. It was locked. She pressed the doorbell and stepped back, listening to the bell echo through the still house.

"This would be a lovely place for a wedding," Nell mused.

Birdie raised her eyebrows. "Do you have anyone in mind?"

Nell peered through the frosty bay window, letting Birdie's question hang in the icy air. She tried not to think of Izzy and Sam's future—their business was their business.

"And face it, Nell," Ben had said not long ago. "Izzy may not want to get married. Maybe not ever. She might be perfectly content with her life the way it is. She has a career, great friends."

And he was right. At least about her not interfering. But Izzy wanted Sam—and a houseful of babies. Nell was sure of it, no matter what Ben said. It was something men didn't always intuit as well as women.

"I don't think Mary's here," Birdie said.

Nell pulled her coat tight. "That's strange. You'd think there'd be a stray Pisano hanging around somewhere."

"Maybe Kevin is. He may not be able to hear the bell in the kitchen."

"Kevin?"

"Kevin Sullivan—Moira's boy. That sweet chef from the Ocean's Edge. Mary managed to steal him for a week to cook for her family. We could leave the blanket with him."

"Okay," Nell whispered, then laughed at herself. "How silly. What's the matter with us, whispering? We're not in a morgue."

They began walking along the porch toward the side of the house and had nearly reached the corner when they were stopped in their tracks. A raucous, frantic barking rolled around the corner, followed instantly by a large, snowy dog. It slid to a stop in front of Birdie, then stood on its hind legs and planted both front paws soundly on her narrow shoulders.

Birdie folded up beneath the weight, the blanket falling to the side, and the dog landed happily on top of her, greedily licking her face with its pink tongue.

Nell grabbed the dog's collar and tugged, but the dog refused to leave the comfort of Birdie's tiny body.

Straining against the dog's weight, Birdie managed to balance herself on one arm. She wrapped the other around the curly hundred pounds of shivering pup. "It's all right, Georgia," she said calmly. "You're fine, sweet pup. And so am I—not that you've asked."

The words seemed to work magic, and Nell managed to

extricate Birdie from Georgia's bulk, helping her to her feet. Birdie brushed off the snow and leaned over the dog. "What in heaven's name are you doing out here, Georgia?"

Georgia's tail hit the wooden floor in response.

"Mary must be here somewhere, Nell," Birdie said. "Georgia won't go outside without her. She's like a toddler with mommy attachment."

Birdie reached down and scratched the dog's curly blond head. "Georgia's finally gotten to a point where she lets me hold her leash when Mary and I walk together, but it's taken a while. She grieved for Enzo for a long, long time, but Mary finally won her heart." She looked down at the dog. "You silly sweetheart, you. Now, let's go find your mother."

They walked around the corner of the house, Georgia pressed closely to Birdie's side.

Beyond the porch, meandering paths and the property's natural outcropping of granite boulders, towering pines, and thick woods turned the grounds into a perfect place to hike or rest or absorb nature's soothing magic.

But tonight it all looked ghostly, like the rocking chairs, covered in snow.

Nell looked up at the carriage house in the distance. Soft panels of gauze fell over the dark windows.

She stopped, frowned. Then looked up again.

Georgia barked.

"What's wrong?"

"Is someone staying in the carriage house?"

"Maybe. I think most of the rooms are being used while the family is here. Why?" Birdie looked up.

"I thought I saw the curtain moving."

They stood silently, staring at the windows. The curtains were still.

Georgia's tail lifted.

"I'm seeing things." Nell tried to block out the sudden shiver that rippled up and down her arms. She thought she'd seen a light, too. But it must have been a reflection from one of the security lights.

They walked along the back of the house, pausing at a set of French doors. Birdie and Nell peered inside. A low light in the corner revealed bookshelves, a fireplace. A library table. Birdie tried the door. Locked.

"This doesn't make sense. Mary wouldn't go off and leave Georgia outside. She must be here somewhere." They passed a windowless door to a utility room, then walked on toward the far end of the house.

They looked through the kitchen windows. Low appliance lights—clocks and timers and control buttons—cast eerie shadows across the floor.

"There's no one here."

Birdie sighed. "I've led you on a goose chase." She hugged the wrapped afghan to her chest. "I don't know if it's the weather or something in the air, but I don't like being here like this, without Mary."

Nell felt it, too. The estate looked different at night. Mysterious somehow. Foreboding. She looked back at the shadowy woods and the towering pines that rustled in the winter breeze. The tingling sound was eerie against the black night.

Nell looked up at the carriage house again. "Maybe in the confusion of people leaving, Mary forgot. Not a catastrophe."

"Or the others may have insisted she join them at the Gull."

But that didn't explain an abandoned Georgia.

"I say we take Georgia with us and run by the Gull," Nell said. "One of the Pisanos will know where she is."

They began walking toward the porch steps, skirting a pile of cigarette butts that formed a shallow pit in the soft snow.

"Messy," Nell said, noting the debris.

Birdie tsked in disgust. She leaned down and scratched Georgia's head. "Come on, sweetie; let's find Mary."

Georgia's heavy tail thudded in agreement, but as they walked toward the steps, the dog pulled back and planted herself soundly on the porch.

"Come on, girl."

Georgia barked, then threw her curly head back and yowled into the black air, a plaintive sound.

Birdie looped her finger beneath Georgia's collar and spoke firmly. "Come, Georgia. Now."

Ahead of them, the wind had mounded snow into the corner where the railings met, piling it high.

It was powdery, thick, and high enough to build a snow fort.

Georgia growled.

Nell's brows pulled together. She looked at Birdie, a step behind her. "What is that?" She pointed toward a smooth stretch of snow leading to the bank.

Birdie took a step closer. Dark marks marred the smooth snow.

Georgia pressed against her leg. Her growl was throaty now, a mournful, wounded cry.

"It's okay, girl," Birdie said, patting her head.

At first glance, the marks in the snow looked like tracks.

"An animal?" Birdie offered. "Maybe that's why Georgia is spooked."

"No," Nell said. "I think they're words."

They moved closer, and the lines took clear form. Words etched into the crusty snow with the tip of a finger or stick. Two simple words.

I'm sorry.

"I'm sorry?" Nell said aloud. Frowning, she moved beyond the words to the steep drift.

At closer range, they could see shadows in the snow, a life-size imprint.

"Oh, lord."

Nell lifted one hand to her mouth. With the other, she grasped Birdie's arm so tightly that Birdie squirmed beneath the pressure.

Running along the surface of the corner drift was a narrow red river, winding over the pile of snow like a strand of holiday yarn.

Wordlessly, Nell and Birdie took a step closer, hoping that it was, indeed, a loose strand of yarn that the wind or a playful gull had dropped on Mary Pisano's back porch.

But it wasn't the work of a gull or the wind or someone's knitting gone astray.

The two women stood side by side, breath trapped in their chests, staring into the shadowy snowbank.

Behind them, the wind picked up and the whistling through the pines grew louder, more strident.

In front of them, the motionless form was as still as the night, cradled there in the hollow of snow. Arms and legs spread playfully, as if making a snow angel.

But no laughter filled the night, and there was no movement to the limbs, no fan of an angel's wings.

In the cold, blue shadows, a woman's body lay cushioned in a bed of pure snow.

Come play, her outstretched arms might have said.

But her hands held a different message. One pointed toward the steps, as if seeking direction.

The other, wrapped around the handle of a small black pistol, spoke of finding it.

Chapter 4

$\mathcal{N}$ell sat in an oversized chair near the front window of M.J.'s Hair Salon, one ear tuned to the din of early-morning conversation. Voices rose and fell over the steady hum of hair dryers and the gentle swoosh of a broom. An occasional gasp told Nell that the morning paper was being opened, then passed from chair to chair. She looked out the window, wanting to block out the wave of sadness ebbing and flowing around her.

As she and Birdie had done endless times the night before, she replayed the conversations they had both had that day— Pamela Pisano's cultured voice portending her cousin's death. *The bed-and-breakfast will kill her,* she had said to more than one of the knitters. *Kill her.*

But she had been sorely wrong.

Dead wrong.

Nell felt certain that at that precise moment, a photograph on the front page of the *Sea Harbor Gazette* held the entire town captive—in coffee shops or warm, safe kitchens, in beauty salons or on the commuter train.

Had it not been so awful, the photo might have been considered art. Something from a minimalist exhibit she and Ben had seen recently in Boston at the ICA, perhaps.

Pamela Pisano's white fox coat was resting in the snow. An interesting composition in whites, except for the winding red river that flowed from the folds of her hood and down over the snow to the porch floor. The headline was simple and to the point:

EDITOR OF NATIONAL FASHION MAGAZINE
DIES OF GUNSHOT WOUND AT FAMILY HOME

Poor Mary. Nell and Ben had read the hastily written news report at the breakfast table an hour earlier. It said little, leaving readers to fill in the blanks, which they would eagerly do. But the true burden of the horrible event would rest on Mary—the rumors, the curiosity seekers who would wander the grounds of the lovely bed-and-breakfast to see what they could see, the neighbors who would be sure it was a sign to close down the guesthouse before the first paying customer rested head on downy pillow.

The police had called the death a probable suicide. The gun was in Pamela's hand. The words in the snow were significant— a suicide note, one of the officers on the scene was quoted as calling it. *I'm sorry*, Pamela had written.

But when Mary had finally shown up the night before, she had managed to push her grief aside and answer the police chief without hesitation when he'd asked about Pamela's state of mind.

"I can't imagine my cousin taking her own life, ever. She thought too much of herself to ever do such a thing."

Mary had uttered the words with tears streaming down her small cheeks, her sadness mixed with regret and anguish and disbelief.

Birdie had wrapped Mary's shivering body in the new afghan, and Georgia, pressed against her side, had provided additional warmth.

Mary didn't intend for the words to be mean or judgmental. It was simply a fact, as Mary saw it. And she never talked around things, a trait her newspaper column gave testimony to.

Mary wasn't alone in her opinion. Everyone in Sea Harbor knew the controversial fashion editor and probably had an opinion about her. But suicide generated so many questions, Nell thought. Not the least of which was doubt over how well we really know a person, especially someone like Pamela Pisano, whose appearance and position seemed to define her to the public—but few knew the private person.

Chief Jerry Thompson said that they'd consider everything, of course, and not discount Mary's opinion. But the initial findings indicated that she had, in fact, taken her own life.

Nell rested her head against the back of the chair. She was momentarily lulled by the hum of the hair dryers in the distance, the soothing sounds of running water in the shampoo alcove, and soft voices that rose and fell in the lavender-scented air.

Such an ordinary thing to do . . . on such an un-ordinary day. A trim to even the ends of her hair before the bevy of holiday gatherings began. Maybe a splash of color, a highlight or two.

She had thought about canceling her appointment.

"Why would you do that?" Ben asked earlier as he poured coffee for them. What could Nell do to change events? To alter the unraveling of the day?

Nothing. That was what. Nothing at all. She tried to call Mary, but she didn't pick up. Nell left a message. She was there to help if help was needed. There would certainly be plenty going on at Ravenswood-by-the-Sea. Plenty of hovering family members. Plenty of lawyers, executors. Sometimes even friends could be in the way at such times.

So Nell had bundled up, slipped into furry boots, and walked along the snowy streets to Harbor Road and the comfort of M.J.'s Salon.

She had always considered waiting in M.J.'s a gift and often got there early, a treat to herself. An interlude in her life, free of phones, of writing grants, planning talks, of household chores, of responsibilities. With the recent renovation, M.J. had tried to rename the salon "Pleasure," but the name didn't stick. Some thought the name a bit risqué. Others, like Nell, simply couldn't change old habits, and M.J.'s Hair Salon it remained. But risqué or not, Nell thought, the attempted name fit what M.J. offered to her customers. Pleasure and, even more important, escape.

Today that was especially true. She knew that wherever she went, she'd be reminded of last night's events. Although the paper didn't mention her name or Birdie's, people would know they were the ones who had found Pamela's body. Somehow, in that mysterious way small towns work, people would know.

And there'd be endless questions, suppositions, talk. People would wonder in sad tones about the gorgeous, wealthy editor who had everything the world had to offer. And who had ended her life alone. In a snowbank.

Suicide. Nell's college friend Shelly Archer had taken her own life at the beginning of their senior year. It had haunted Nell for years.

She and her friends had analyzed Shelly's death endlessly, hoping for a shred of understanding, for some comfort that reason might bring to them. They'd been angry, hurt, devastated. Furious at Shelly that she hadn't allowed them in, given them a chance to help her, as if their own anger would lessen their sadness. And then they had broken down and grieved the unfathomable loss of someone they thought they knew so well.

Nell had been with Pamela Pisano hours before she died. Had she missed a sign? A plea for help?

But nothing in the conversation bespoke a woman in pain.

Nell sipped her coffee, then closed her eyes and thought of the fashion editor in her expensive coat and her tall boots, walking out of the tea shop. She'd held her head high, and she'd been smiling, as if anticipating that something good was about to happen. That was the look Nell remembered.

Something good. Something pleasurable.

Nell set her coffee down and looked out the window, focusing on the bright sunshine reflecting off the snow along Harbor Road. People walked by quickly, collars turned up, heads leaning into the wind. She spotted Mary Halloran, Cass' mother, heading to work at Our Lady of the Seas.

Mary spotted Nell and waved, then paused briefly at the window. She lifted her shoulders slightly in a gesture of helplessness, then followed it up with a sad smile.

An acknowledgment of the death. Nell nodded back, then closed her eyes and settled back into the soft chair. *Relax*, she ordered herself.

That's what the waiting area of the salon was about. M.J. had added comfortable chairs, small tables piled high with current magazines, and displays of handmade jewelry and purses from local artists. A small bookshelf was crammed with used paperbacks. Across from it, a bar was built into the wall with coffee, water, tea, and later in the day, wine.

The background chatter fell away, and soft music began to fill Nell's soul and ease away the tension. A magazine slipped from her fingers.

"Aunt Nell!"

Nell's eyes shot open.

Cass and Izzy stood on either side of the chair, staring down at her.

"Are you all right?" Izzy asked.

Nell took a breath. "I . . . I'm fine. Just dozing, I guess. What are you two doing here?" Nell pushed herself forward in the chair and tried to clear her head.

Izzy and Cass sank onto a couch.

"It's just seeing you like that, with your eyes closed—"

"You've been staring at the picture in the morning paper. I'm very much alive, Izzy, dear."

The front door opened, bringing in a gust of cold air. Birdie walked into the salon lounge and dropped her backpack to the floor. She slipped out of her puffy down coat and walked over to her friends. "Mae said I'd find you all here. 'A gathering of the minds,' she said."

Izzy laughed. "A gathering of friends works better for me. I should be helping her open, but I wanted to be sure you were okay—*both* of you. This is awful. I can't get my mind around it. Here we spent the evening discussing this woman, and now she's dead. And you two were *there*."

"We're fine, sweetie," Nell assured her. "But poor Mary isn't."

"'A single gunshot. No signs of struggle,'" Izzy said. "At least that's what Mae said."

"I wonder how she knows that." The fact that Pamela hadn't struggled and seemed to simply slip down into a dead, snow-cushioned sleep had been obvious to Nell and Birdie. The snow around her was untouched. But the news story hadn't gotten into that much detail.

"Her sister works with Esther Gibson in the police dispatch office."

"That explains it." Esther, a thirty-year veteran of the dispatch office, always knew things before anyone else—sometimes, Ben often teased the white-haired woman, even before they happened.

"The paper didn't say much else," Cass said. "So . . . what do you two know?"

"Not very much," Nell said.

"We went to the Ocean's Edge after you left last night," Cass said. "Mary was there. She and Nancy were making some final design decisions for the carriage house and had lost track of time, I guess. When she saw us, Mary was frantic—she realized she was supposed to be meeting you. She rushed out, leaving poor Nancy with a pile of papers and an unfinished bottle of wine."

Mary had told her and Birdie as much when she arrived. The meeting with Nancy had started late, and they'd had a few glasses of wine.

"The stars weren't lined up right," was how Mary had put it. And Nell knew what she meant. If only she'd stayed at the Ravenswood house longer, or returned sooner, then maybe. They were recriminations that even she and Birdie had felt. What if they'd left Izzy's earlier? What if?

"Mary arrived to a driveway lined with police cars and an ambulance. At first, she thought one of us had fallen on the ice," Nell said.

"A far better option," Birdie said.

"Where were all the Pisanos? Were you there by yourselves?"

Birdie nodded. "They had a predinner meeting, late afternoon. Then they headed to the Gull Tavern to celebrate the fact that they'd finished yet another annual family meeting without killing one another."

"So they all went to the Gull . . . except for Pamela?"

"Pamela would have considered the Gull a bit crass," Birdie said.

" 'Dirty' was the word she used," Cass said. "I told her my brother Pete was playing, but she told me Pete wasn't her type, as if I were trying to fix her up."

Izzy managed a small laugh. "Can you imagine sweet, huggable Pete with Pamela?"

"Mary said she had other plans, though she didn't say what they were. I don't think she liked hanging around some of the cousins any more than she had to," Birdie said. "She didn't mince words when talking about her family."

That was true. Nell thought about Pamela's less-than-pleasant descriptions of Agnes and Mary.

"I can't imagine Agnes went to the Gull, either," Birdie said.

"She probably went home. She has a lovely place over near Rockport," Nell said.

A familiar voice floated in from the busy salon.

"So, ladies, you've heard the news?"

Laura Danvers stood on the step to the service room. The young society leader's hair was separated into foil-wrapped plackets, and her narrow shoulders were draped in a smock. She held a bottle of spring water in one hand.

"Suicide—that's what they're saying."

Nell nodded.

"I've read that suicide around the holidays is not uncommon." Laura took a drink from her water bottle.

"But tragic, no matter when it happens," Birdie said.

Concern shadowed Laura's face. "Yes, of course. Absolutely tragic. But somehow we need to make sure this doesn't weigh us all down. We need to . . . to move on and get beyond this dreadful . . . happening."

"Move on?" Cass repeated.

"What I mean is, it's the holidays. It's time to be with our families and friends, to be joyous and grateful for what we have. And, well, I guess what I'm saying is that I hope all of you will still be at our holiday party tomorrow night. Elliott and I talked—and we think we need to keep to our plans—"

Laura looked genuinely sad, but determined, Nell thought. She had her mother's tenacity and diplomacy. The young civic leader would go far.

"Of course we'll be there, dear," Birdie said, easing the moment. "It will be lovely and a needed distraction."

"It's a nice idea to hold it at the historical museum. The

party will bring people's attention back to one of our town's treasures," Nell said.

Izzy assured Laura that she'd be there, too, with or without Sam. She stood and picked up her bag, and Cass followed, telling Laura that she and Danny Brandley would be there—"with bells on," she added.

They were off, Izzy to the yarn shop for a busy day of classes and Christmas sales, and Cass to don her warmest wintry slicker, brave the ocean air, and check on the lobster traps that she and her brother, Pete, owned.

Nell watched them leave, wondering why Sam might not come to the party. Of course he would; he was very good about attending these affairs—even when he'd rather be off skiing or taking photographs or talking to Ben about sailboats. Sam had a knack for fitting in anywhere he went, a photographer's gift, she supposed. His awards for capturing people's raw emotion certainly spoke to the comfort and trust people placed in him.

She tucked away a reminder to ask Ben whether he knew what was up with Sam Perry.

"Pamela Pisano was going to come to the party," Laura said. Her tone changed, her voice edged with disappointment. "I invited her weeks ago when I heard she'd be in town. She was looking forward to it and was bringing a photographer to take photos of the museum and the holiday dresses. It would make a good angle for a magazine story, Pamela told me. A small-town holiday party that highlights a community landmark."

A young woman wearing a skinny skirt and clunky shoes came up behind Laura and tapped her on the shoulder. "Time to rinse," she said with a cheery smile.

Laura turned to follow her, then looked back and said sadly, "She even told me what she was going to wear—a new Versace."

Nell watched the young woman walk back into the maze of hair dryers, mirrors, and rotating chairs.

Of course. That was it—the cause for the regret and slight irritation she had heard in Laura's voice. She wasn't coldhearted. But it would have been an amazing coup for her party to be featured in Pamela's popular national magazine, not to mention the attention it would bring to the museum. It was a huge disappointment to Laura, even in light of the tragic circumstances that would prevent it from happening.

A waving hand called to her. M.J.'s assistant. Time to go.

Only later, during the gentle wash and neck massage that turned her body to liquid calm, did she replay Laura's conversation in her mind. But it wasn't the hostess' regret that pulled Nell out of her massage stupor.

It was Pamela's commitment to the holiday party. Her promises to Laura. Choosing a dress. She'd even talked about buying a condo.

Exactly how many commitments and plans did one make—how many slots on a social calendar fill—before taking one's own life?

Chapter 5

$\mathcal{N}$ell dressed warmly for Laura Danvers' party Saturday night. She liked the lovely feel of silky, sleeveless dresses, but she also liked to be warm. The silvery wool dress she took from her closet had long sleeves and a scoop neckline and flowed to her ankles, perfect for combating the drafts that old buildings were noted for.

Slipping into a long black coat, Nell wondered briefly whether the chill that permeated her bones was weather induced—or came from somewhere else. An hour with Mary Pisano at the small, unpretentious home she shared with Ed Ambrose, her fisherman husband, had revealed little news regarding Pamela's death. She'd been fine at the meeting that afternoon, Mary had said. Her usual argumentative self.

Try as she might, Nell couldn't extricate the image from her mind—the single trickle of blood warning onlookers that it wasn't sleep that held the beautiful woman immobile in the snow.

"Let it go, Nellie," Ben urged, holding open the door to his car. "Just for tonight." His lips touched her cheek as she slid onto the seat. A comforting kiss.

Nell nodded, smiled. *Let it go. Let it go.* The words swung back and forth, a pendulum in her head. She climbed into the car and turned on the radio, hoping for the sounds of a symphony or jazz, a trumpet solo to warm the chilly air.

But Nell knew deep down that it would take more than music or Ben's words to shake her free of the image of Pamela's cold body. And it wasn't just because of the obvious—finding a dead body. The whole experience had disoriented her. Confused her thinking. She wouldn't have been able to put words to the reason if Ben had asked her why, but she knew it to be true.

Ben turned a knob on the dashboard and warm air circled around her. But inside, Nell shivered.

As the poet said, there were miles to go before they slept.

The Sea Harbor Historical Museum was located in an old house just off Harbor Road and across the street from a small park. Four brick pathways crisscrossed the square, converging at a small gazebo at its center. As if dressed for a party, tree branches along the pathways were draped with thousands of tiny Christmas lights, and hundreds of luminaries lined the pathways, their flickering candlelight lighting partygoers' steps to the museum.

For the past few years, Laura and her banker husband had hosted the first big party of the season in their spacious home out on Sea Harbor Point, and each year Laura used the occasion to benefit a Sea Harbor need. This year Laura was determined to highlight the historical society building and to encourage residents to support needed repairs, staff hirings, and the acquisition of new exhibits and books.

"If anyone can bring attention to this old building, Laura Danvers can," Nell said as she and Ben walked across the street. Izzy and Birdie followed close behind.

The three-story structure shimmered like a winter jewel with two enormous wreaths on the double doors and electric candles in every window. A shutter that just last week had been hanging loose was fastened tightly, ready for a party.

Even though the roof needed repairs, and here and there paint flaked from the eaves, the building was beautiful—a New England Colonial built a century before as a vacation home for a wealthy Boston businessman and his large family. Over the years, the home had gone through additions and changes and had finally been added to the historic registry and turned into a museum. It now housed exhibits, an impressive library, staff offices, and a paneled hall for events—especially festive tonight for Laura and Elliott's party.

The double doors opened, and several teenage helpers dressed in holiday finery took their coats and pointed them toward the main hall.

Laura stood in the wide opening, composed, welcoming, and in a beautiful emerald green dress covered with tiny pearls.

She hugged Nell tightly. "Thanks for coming. I knew you wouldn't let me down."

"Of course not. And you haven't let us down, either. This is magnificent." She looked into the hall, brimming with guests and alive with color and lights.

At the far end, with faces bright and free of the world's worries, a choir of young boys and girls stood in a semicircle, their small bodies as straight as the candlesticks they clutched in their hands. Their sweet voices rose into the air as a single silvery sound, their mouths perfect ovals as they sang about coming home for Christmas and walking in a winter wonderland.

"A wonderland. That's what you've created, Laura. You've done yourself proud," Birdie said.

Alongside the singers, a tree nearly touched the high ceiling. It was covered with ornaments made and donated by Canary Cove artists. Each one reminded guests of their heritage—small wooden mermaids and lobster buoys, crocheted starfish and ceramic lobsters, and whales and sailboats. Tiny wreaths fashioned from yarn in Willow Adams' unique style. And all for sale, a tasteful lettered signed told them. Proceeds to benefit the Sea Harbor Historic Museum.

On another wall, leaping flames in a huge old fireplace cast warm shadows across the room and lit round, smiling faces as the choir finished a number and bowed in unison, beaming at the applause. Small hands waved vigorously to proud parents.

Waiters, balancing trays of champagne and wine, pastry-wrapped olives, and small seafood quiches, moved through the festive crowd.

"Sam left a message he'd meet us here," Izzy said, looking around the crowded room. She stood to the side, nervously fingering a lacy knit shawl around her bare shoulders. Beneath, a shimmering dress flowed over her narrow hips to the floor. Her eyes moved from group to group, looking for the sandy-haired photographer.

"If he said he'd be here, Izzy, he will be," Nell said.

Izzy didn't seem to hear her aunt's ready assurance. She stood apart, smiling politely at neighbors and friends, her mind clearly elsewhere.

Harry and Margaret Garozzo walked by, the ruddy-faced deli owner holding his wife's arm with unusual tenderness.

The season gets to all of us, Nell thought, *even dear, gruff Harry.*

As if reading her mind, Harry stopped and gave Nell a brief, awkward hug. His baker's arm was huge on her narrow shoulder. "Sad time for Mary," he said softly, nodding his large head. Harry's wide forehead was dotted with tiny drops of perspiration, as if he had just been toiling in his kitchen deli, baking his famous rustic Italian bread. He wiped it away with the sleeve of his dark suit. "We dropped off some platters today."

Nell nodded. Of course Harry would take food over— probably his specialty for unexpected gatherings—an enormous platter of prosciutto, plenty of imported cheeses, and his famous capicola—more food than the Pisanos would ever eat. Food said, *I care.*

And blustery Harry Garozzo cared.

Ben handed glasses of champagne to Birdie, Nell, and Izzy. "To family, to friends," he said, lifting his glass. Then he waved toward the bar and added, "And to *more* friends."

Sam, Cass, and Danny Brandley waved back and immediately wove their way through the crowd to the small group. Sam moved directly to Izzy's side, cradling her waist with his arm and drawing her close. He whispered something in her ear.

Izzy smiled, a slow flush traveling up her cheeks.

Ben leaned his head toward Nell. "I can feel the relief traveling through your body like earthquake tremors when those two are in good spirits. You're hopeless."

Nell pressed closer. "You're right—I'm a hopeless, interfering aunt. It's in my genes, right there in that stringy little chromosome. And there's nothing you or I or the man in the moon can do about it." She touched one finger to his lips. "So there."

Ben took the hand that touched his lips and kissed her fingertips. "And I suppose it's one of the many things I love about you—sometimes, anyway."

Nell drew her hand away and urged him to mingle. She pointed toward Jerry Thompson standing across the room staring down a baron of beef. "Maybe the chief will have some news. . . . "

Nell wandered off to congratulate Nancy Hughes on how lovely the museum looked. Although cutbacks had slashed the former director's hours to just a few, Nell felt sure that Nancy was responsible for the museum's festive flair tonight—and had probably purchased half the decorations herself.

Nancy stood alone near the fireplace. She looked happy as she watched the sea of color and life move across the room.

"We all agree; it's beautiful." Nell walked up and stood beside her. "And I suspect you had a lot to do with this."

"It's lovely, isn't it?"

Nell touched the edge of the loose, wavy scarf looped around Nancy's neck. It moved in slow motion down the length of her simple red dress, the loops of the lace intricate and artful. Nancy certainly knew her way around a skein of cashmere. "You're amazing, Nancy. You do many good things. Knitting, organizing, and if I might venture a guess, you probably fixed those broken shutters yourself."

"It keeps me sane, Nell," Nancy said. "It fills a void. And anything I do at this museum is definitely a labor of love. I've loved working here." She rested one hand on a polished glass cabinet that held artifacts from an ancient shipwreck. "Dean loved the museum, too—he was proud of what we did here. He used to tease me when I'd bring my toolbox to work to mend a display case or fix a broken step or saw branches off the trees out back, but beneath the teasing was pride. I always knew that. "

Nell nodded and watched a familiar sadness fill Nancy's eyes. Dean Hughes had been a handsome, successful lawyer. Not only had his needless death a few years before cut a successful career short; it had left a bereft wife dealing with the worst kind of pain.

"If there are such things as saints, Nancy Hughes is certainly one of them," Birdie had declared not long ago. "Her job at the museum is diminished; then her husband leaves her in such an awful way—and how does she respond? She volunteers for every known cause in Sea Harbor. Given the same circumstances, I would shrivel up and turn into a prune."

Birdie, of course, would do nothing of the kind. Widowed herself in her late twenties, she had done more for the town of Sea Harbor than any one person alive. Although she'd married several more times after Sonny Favazza died, Birdie had kept his memory alive, and the Favazza wealth had been put to good use, never squandered.

But Nancy's generous spirit was certainly admirable. Suicide could destroy more lives than the deceased's. Somehow Nancy had risen from the ashes and devoted herself to others—and fortunately had the funds to support her efforts. Dean Hughes had made sure that with him or without him, she was well taken care of.

She thought of all the Pisanos dealing right now with the same painful emotions, a family member gone—by choice.

Nancy straightened a candle in a brass holder. "Laura's done a good thing here. She is so talented and energetic."

"Speaking of talent and energy, Mary says you're the reason Ravenswood-by-the-Sea is becoming a reality."

"Another labor of love. I love being in that grand house, bringing it to life. Mary's a gem to work with."

Nell watched Nancy's smile slip away. In the beauty and festive mood of their surroundings, it was easy to forget the sad occurrence just across town.

"It's been a dreadful week for Mary. One more day and that family of hers would have been gone. We could have gone back to our work without their constant interference. If only . . . If I hadn't kept Mary so long that night . . . "

Nell shushed her. "Tragedies always bring about a list of 'if only's.' You know that better than anyone. And you know what a waste of energy that kind of thinking is. No one could have done anything. If it hadn't happened that night, it might have been the next. Or next week. We can't control other people's lives or what they do with them. We just can't."

"You're right. It took me a long time to accept that. But what will be, will be, and sometimes there isn't anything you can do about it."

"There you are." Laura Danvers swept over to the two

women, the elegant folds of her satin gown floating down to the floor. Emerald green earrings dangled nearly to her bare shoulders. She tucked her arm in Nancy's.

"I need to steal Nancy away, Nell. Father Northcutt has a question about a Winslow Homer painting, and Nancy knows far more than I do in that department. She's our resident expert tonight."

Nell watched them walk away, the elegant hostess and the quiet librarian, an unlikely pair, but both feeling equally maternal tonight toward the museum they'd festooned in holiday finery, bringing all its ancient artifacts to life.

Nell stayed by the fire a moment longer, enjoying the warmth. Standing in the shadow of the enormous tree, warmed by the fire, she felt nearly invisible. The museum ghost. The thought pleased her, and she sipped her glass of champagne, her eyes smiling as the evening unfolded around her.

The children, having finished their medley, had been bundled off to home and bed. In their place, a string combo sat on straight-backed chairs, filling the air with a perfect mixture of holiday music and classic jazz. Friends and neighbors greeted one another, their faces bright with expectation, holiday dresses sparkling and elegant. Laura had invited nearly half the town, it looked to Nell, and they'd brought with them the feeling of Christmas.

No matter what lay outside their doors or at the other end of town or was hidden for the night in police and coroner's reports, tonight was a festive night.

Conversations sometimes erupted in hoots of laughter, sometimes in soft smiles. And when tones lowered to a whisper and expressions grew serious, Nell knew they were acknowledging Pamela Pisano's suicide. *Tragic.* The word fell off lips. *So sad for her mother*, the older set acknowledged.

And the family. And what about the fate of her cousin Mary's bed-and-breakfast?

Why? How?

Guests would need to mention it, of course, in the way tragedies required. And then it would cease to be the elephant in the room and the guests could set it aside, move on to happier talk—Santa's arrival at the pier, the opening of the skating rink, the lighting of the town Christmas tree, and choir concerts scattered all around Cape Ann like glorious snowflakes, softening the night and brightening the season.

In one corner of the room, a photo and book exhibit detailing the birth and growth of Sea Harbor in the late 1700s drew a crowd. Nell watched her friend Archie Brandley wander over, then saw his eyes dance with delight as he saw donated books from his own bookstore acknowledged and handsomely displayed.

Archie's forty-year-old son Danny had recently moved back to Sea Harbor to work on a book of his own. "My son the novelist," Archie proudly whispered to customers in his store. Nell spotted Danny, dancing with Cass Halloran near the floor-to-ceiling windows. Cass dancing. She smiled. The tomboy fisherman turned elegant. And elegant she was, her slinky black dress matching the mass of hair that cascaded around her shoulders. Who knew? Danny Brandley's return to town had added a new dimension to Cass' life.

Izzy and Sam hovered near the doors to the library, their heads leaning in toward each other, their world reduced to just the two of them. Their faces were serious, deliberate, as if the problems of the world were being solved right there in the Sea Harbor Historical Museum.

A few steps away, Ben and Birdie stood in front of a table that groaned with spinach crepes and smoked ham, thin slices of cheese and turkey and pasta dishes, a baron of beef. They were talking with Ham and Jane Brewster. Nell noticed that Ben's plate was piled high with carpaccio, hunks of French bread, and chunks of Brie. Not his daily fare, but a holiday indulgence, Nell reminded herself. Let him enjoy it—his heart would be fine.

Looking at her husband from a distance, Nell's heart still reacted. It wasn't with that wild rush that ran straight through every inch of her body when she'd see the tall, gangly graduate student coming toward her across Harvard Yard. But a quieter rush, like fresh springwater, coursing through her body, waking her spirit and her senses. It was a softer flow of desire, but one enriched by nearly forty years of sharing life's moments and intimacies.

"You think you're invisible, but you're not." Jane Brewster gave Nell a warm hug. "From that sexy smile lighting your eyes, I dare not offer money for your thoughts."

Nell chuckled.

"This is a great spot for people watching." Jane settled in beside her, her back against the wall. The giant Christmas tree and mantel on either side shadowed the two friends. "Maybe people will think we're ornaments."

A minute later Birdie joined them. "A lovely party. But I need a slight break from being charming. Do you have room for one more in your little cave?"

"You can be an old grouch with us," Jane said. "Problem is, I don't think you know how."

Birdie laughed and looked over the crowd. "People are having fun, don't you think? We all needed something like this to end this week."

A waitress walked by, and Jane stopped her with a wide smile, lifted martinis from the tray, and passed them around. "And something like this." She slipped a lock of salt-and-pepper hair behind her ear and peered into the delicate glass. "Not Ben's, for sure, but it will do."

Jane Brewster and her husband, Ham, had been friends of the Endicotts for longer than either couple could remember. The

Brewsters had come upon Sea Harbor by accident in the late sixties, looking for Woodstock-type action and instead finding a sleepy harbor town perfect for growing an artists' colony. And so they had, buying a small patch of land and opening a gallery that featured not only Jane's ceramics and Ham's paintings, but also the work of other artists they had lured to the area. Years later, the area was thriving, encouraged and supported by not only townsfolk, but artists from the notable Rocky Neck colony over in Gloucester. "Artists help one another," Ham explained. And it had certainly been true in growing Canary Cove into a Sea Harbor tourist attraction.

"I stopped over at Mary and Ed's today," Jane began. She paused and took a sip of her martini. "They were alone—I don't know what happened to the rest of the Pisanos—but Mary seemed grateful they weren't there."

"It's a sad time for that whole family. They may not have all gotten along, but having Pamela die so young and so unexpectedly is a tragedy—and I know they're feeling it deeply."

They stood quietly, sipping their martinis in the comfortable way old friendships allowed, their thoughts moving from a body in the snow, to the diminutive newspaper columnist, to the festive party playing out around them.

People moved about the room as if performing in an extravagantly choreographed movie. Elegantly dressed guests moved past them; couples drifted over to a small dance floor. And everywhere people chatted and drank and ate, happy to be in a warm, lovely place, happy to be alive.

"Pamela had planned on coming tonight," Nell said, admiring a parade of designer gowns moving across the room on toned bodies. "She was bringing one of her magazine's photographers from New York. Laura was thrilled about the possibility of being in *Fashion Monthly*."

"It would have been a nice thing for the museum," Birdie

said. "And a generous gesture on Pamela's part. I'm sure she had invitations to dozens of holiday parties all around New York and Boston."

"And now a holiday party is the last thing any of the Pisanos will be thinking of."

"Pamela is being cremated. A private service, Mary said," Birdie told them.

"Everyone in town knew who Pamela was. She was in and out of here often enough, and she often left things in her wake—like crushed relationships. But I don't think she had many friends, at least not here."

They all knew that was an understatement, but they let it rest. Everyone knew *of* Pamela because she was a "personality." An editor people found difficult to work for, or so said the rumor mill. And a beautiful woman who loved men.

Jane set down her glass and folded her arms around a silky blue stole. Hand-painted flowers in golds and greens detailed the ends of the fabric, and Nell knew without asking that Jane had made it herself and painted the tiny images with great care and talent. "Mary doesn't think Pamela's death was a suicide," Jane said.

Nell and Birdie were silent, playing with the thought that had finally been voiced. Pamela's dying was so neat. The words in the snow. Even the place. A snowbank and a back porch didn't seem a likely place for Pamela to end her life.

Pamela had seemed happy in Polly's Tea Shoppe, not distressed or depressed.

Nell had mentioned it to Ben as they'd dressed for the party.

"Sometimes people about to commit suicide are happy," he'd reminded her. "Their pain—or whatever is driving them to it—is about to end."

But Pamela hadn't seemed happy in *that* way, though Nell couldn't articulate it to Ben. No. It didn't fit—none of it.

So Ben had tried being circumspect, the practical one. "Let's wait until Jerry releases his report," he had said. Chief Jerry Thompson was good at his job, he reminded Nell pointedly. He was the expert.

"I don't think anyone wants to take that thinking to the next step," Birdie finally said. "That's the thing. We want to be singing of white Christmases and decorating trees. We don't want to be thinking 'What if Pamela didn't commit suicide?'"

"But what if?" Jane urged.

The words fell to the floor, untouched. No one wanted to push this further; Birdie was right. And there was no reason to do so. At least not tonight.

Nell watched Ben off in the corner, talking to Jerry Thompson. She wondered whether they were talking about Pamela. She had been surprised earlier to see the police chief there, but then realized that was silly. A death didn't require round-the-clock duty.

Their heads were bent, two tall, graying men, their conversation protected by the huddle of their bodies.

"What's going on?" Birdie set her martini glass down on a small table and pointed toward the dance floor. Her thin white brows were pulled together.

A tall, skinny man whom Nell didn't recognize was setting up a portable spotlight, plugging an extension cord into its base. A young woman stood nearby, holding a pad of paper. Nearby, Laura Danvers, her face flushed, stood with her husband, her arms linked around his waist. Her beautiful Donna Karan gown flowed to the floor.

The photographer pointed to a spot on the floor, and Laura and Elliott Danvers moved to it, positioning themselves. The flash of a bulb captured the moment, and Nell looked again at the photographer. It wasn't anyone local; she was sure of that.

And the equipment was elaborate, not the usual *Sea Harbor Gazette* digital one-shot.

"Look," Birdie said, her voice so low, Nell could barely hear her.

She followed the point of Birdie's finger.

On the other side of the lighting equipment, a woman gave instructions to the photographer, then to the couple in the spotlight, then to the assistant taking notes. Even from a distance, her movements were authoritative, precise.

She was a tall, big-boned woman, with her hair pulled back and fastened tightly at the base of her neck. A glitter of diamonds surrounded the bun, and a sequined dress fell from her square shoulders, moving uncomfortably over her hips to the floor.

Although she wasn't overweight, everything about the woman was long and strong—her body, her nose, her cheeks, her chin. The elegant dress looked strangely out of place, as if it had been made for a model but purchased by someone unfamiliar with the art of dressing glamorously.

The woman turned slightly, and Nell's eyes widened in surprise.

Pamela's unkind words in the tea shop crept, unbidden, into Nell's mind.

A face like a horse, she had said.

Defying her dead cousin's unfair words, Agnes Pisano stood tall and proud next to the photographer, oblivious to onlookers. Her fingers clutched a large leather notebook with the words *Fashion Monthly* flowing across the front in gold script, and *Editor in Chief* printed beneath.

Chapter 6

They stood in the shadow of the Christmas tree, watching the unusual vignette play out in front of them.

Laura Danvers was the talent scout, pointing out women in designer dresses, men in Armani, couples and people with ties to the museum. Agnes was the producer, nodding and pointing and speaking to the young woman beside her, who dutifully recorded names and notes. Beside them, the skinny photographer checked the lighting and exposure with each new shot.

Laura waved Nancy Hughes over to the group, and a shot was snapped of Laura and a reluctant Nancy. Then one of Agnes herself, standing between the Danverses, her arm around Laura's waist, Elliott Danvers looking handsome and accustomed to having his photo taken. Next the mayor and his wife were ushered over, the details of her Vera Wang dress pointed out, and more photos taken of an array of beautiful gowns and equally beautiful women.

"Interesting," Birdie said.

"Birdie, you can say more in one word than anyone I know."

Birdie laughed. She picked up her small evening bag and looped the gold chain over her arm. "What do you make of it?

Agnes seems to be picking up where Pamela left off and not letting any dust gather in the process."

Agnes was one of the few Pisanos who lived in Sea Harbor full-time. A writer, she worked remotely, contributing to several of the Pisano periodicals. She lived alone in a lovely home near the sea, and those who knew her thought her to be pleasant, plain, and intelligent. The Agnes before them was a different person entirely.

"Perhaps we're misjudging," Nell said. "Since Pamela had committed to attending the party, Laura may have asked Agnes to fill in for her, though I admit, it would be an odd request to impose on a grieving family member."

But Agnes Pisano didn't appear to be grieving. Her face was flushed and her eyes alive with the air of someone who was exactly where she wanted to be.

"The three muses," Ben said, coming up beside the women.

Ham Brewster and Jerry Thompson, Sea Harbor's chief of police, were behind him.

"You three should be in line over there," Ham said. He looked across the room. "Why are you hiding?"

Jane silenced him with a nudge to his side. "What do you suppose Agnes is doing here?" Jane asked.

"It looks like she's organizing some photos for her deceased cousin's magazine," Jerry Thompson said.

The chief's voice revealed nothing, but Nell noticed the deep furrow in his brow. His eyes remained fixed on the photo shoot.

"But . . . well, why?" Jane asked.

"I imagine a lot of people are asking that," Nell murmured.

Ben nodded. "Her timing's not great."

Nell shook off a feeling of discomfort. She looked over at Agnes, but the image was blurred. What Nell saw instead was the image that had stayed with her day and night.

Pamela Pisano—still and lifeless in a white bed of snow.

Her palms faced the sky, and the fingers of one hand wrapped around the black grip of a pistol, its sight pointed to the right, to the words in the snow.

I'm sorry.

Nell squeezed her eyes shut, then opened them again.

The image was still there.

A feeling of foreboding wrapped around her. She shivered.

"Cold?" Standing behind her, Ben spoke quietly. He wrapped an arm around her shoulders and drew her close.

"Low blood sugar." Nell forced a smile to her face.

"Easy solution for that. How about a piece of lemon and amaretto cheesecake?" His voice took on a dramatic flow. "Dribbled with melted Belgian chocolate and brandy, dusted with powdered sugar and toasted walnuts?" His brows lifted enticingly.

Birdie laughed. "If you ever tire of being the unofficial business and legal consultant for the entire town," she said, "I would suggest you try the Food Network. They might have a spot for someone like you."

Ben laughed and pointed toward a tray of desserts sitting on a glass-topped coffee table ringed with comfortable chairs. He began leading the group toward it.

Nell fell in step beside Jerry Thompson. "I'm glad you were able to come tonight, Jerry. These are tough days. A dose of good food and friends can be a good thing."

"You're right about the friends and food. And about the tough days. But it'll come together."

At five foot eight, Nell didn't usually have to look too far up to face male companions, but the chief of police, a basketball player in college, towered over her. Behind his height and strong frame, though, he was a gentle soul. Tonight he seemed relieved to be ordinary, to be himself—a gentle man.

"I hope so," Nell said.

"Not a good time of year for this sort of thing."

The way he said "this sort of thing" made Nell look up again, but Jerry's eyes were unreadable. Again, the uncomfortable feeling passed through her.

It was then, when Nell pulled her gaze away from the pensive look in Jerry's eyes, that she spotted Tommy Porter, his policeman's uniform a contrast to the glittering jewels and long satin gowns around him. He stood just inside the door, scanning the crowd.

"I think your quiet evening may be coming to an end," Nell said to Jerry, nodding toward the young policeman.

At the same time, Tommy spotted his boss and lifted one hand in the air.

Nell looked at Tommy, and as if he had answers written across his face, she knew what had been bothering her for the past twenty-four hours.

A collision of images came together in a split second, wound up as neatly as a ball of yarn.

She and Birdie, standing over Pamela's frozen body.

Pamela's hand reaching out, as if to grab the railing, an escape.

And in her other hand, a revolver pointing to the right, to the words written in the snow.

I'm sorry.

And playing beneath the clean white images of her mind were the words of Mae Anderson. *She was appalled that we didn't offer a special class for lefties.*

Pamela Pisano—like her cousin Mary and her grandfather Enzo, like Ben Endicott and Julia Roberts, Bill Clinton and Barack Obama, and a tenth of the population—was left-handed. If she had wanted to kill herself, she would surely have used the hand most likely to accomplish the task. Her left hand.

Chapter 7

$\mathcal{T}$he reporter who stood behind Tommy was excused from the small group that had gathered in the museum's front office. Nancy Hughes unlocked its door and ushered them in, switching on lights and offering to have coffee sent in.

Jerry had suggested Ben join him. He mumbled something about legal things. But the real reason, they knew, was because Ben could handle people and the press with a finesse that bad news sometimes required. And in addition to the young local reporter standing behind Tommy Porter, there was one from Boston waiting in the wings.

When Ben returned to the party a short while later, the desserts were gone, but Ham Brewster had wisely filled a tray of brandy snifters and carried it over to the small gathering of friends.

"It wasn't a suicide?" Nell asked softly. "She didn't kill herself?"

"Not likely. Not that way, anyway," Ben said. "A left-handed person—especially one not used to shooting guns, which we don't think Pamela was—would have used their strongest hand. It doesn't make a lot of sense not to."

"How do reporters manage to find out things so quickly?"

Cass asked. "I saw Ned Myers lurking in the shadows, looking like the cat that ate the canary."

"It's a good story for them," Danny Brandley said. He sat beside Cass, one hand resting on her knee. A former reporter, Danny spoke with authority. His research for a new mystery novel only added to his cache of information. "Pamela Pisano's name is newsworthy. The suicide angle in itself would sell newspapers. This is even bigger."

"Maybe it was an accident?" Nell asked.

"Even if it was, that opens up a whole lot of other questions— why was she out there with a gun, for starters?" Ham said.

Ben nodded. "The left-handed thing was noticed quickly in the morgue. And the entry angle of the bullet was wrong, even if she'd been right-handed."

"Murder," Nell said softly.

Such an ugly word. Not a holiday word, not an anytime-of-year word.

All around them, partygoers moved on and off the dance floor, to the bar, laughing and dancing and sharing the joy of the night.

"It wasn't completely a surprise. The suicide was too neat," Ben said. "Mary never believed it."

Too neat. Too convenient. But that meant someone had clearly intended to murder Pamela. And wanted people to think it was a suicide.

I'm sorry, the words had read. Who was sorry? Nell wondered now. For what?

She looked around, suddenly aware that the group was smaller than usual. "Where's Izzy?"

Cass looked up. "Home."

"Sam?"

"He took her."

Nell looked hard at Cass. Words usually fell more readily from her mouth. "Why did she leave without telling us?"

Cass shrugged.

"She had a good reason, I'm sure," Birdie said. "Probably a busy day in the shop, and Sam looked tired, too. She didn't want to interrupt us with good-byes."

Nell was forced to drop the subject.

Feeling the weight of the evening's news, Ben suggested that he was winding down, too, and perhaps they'd want to follow Izzy's lead.

Laura Danvers was effusive in her good-byes and suggested they all reserve their copies of *Fashion Monthly* soon. "They'll fly off the shelves," she said, hugging Nell tightly.

No doubt. But it might not be because of Laura's Donna Karan dress or the Alberta Ferretti strapless gown that hugged Beatrice Scaglia. Or the pink peacock look that brought the photographer's attention to the mayor's wife.

It would be for a far less festive reason, as the next day's *Sea Harbor Gazette* would boldly detail.

It seemed like a lifetime later when Ben and Nell finally turned out the lights and settled beneath the down comforter. "What's going on in that head of yours?" Ben leaned up on one elbow.

A low light behind Nell outlined her shape beneath the blanket. "You," she said.

"An interesting place to be, inside your head." He ran one hand down the shape of her hip.

"Not so interesting. I'm just glad to have you here beside me."

Ben leaned one arm across Nell and switched off the light, then pulled her close. "This whole mess is awful, no matter how you cut it, but the contrast with all that happiness tonight, the music and food and laughter, is jarring, obscene in a way."

She nodded against his shoulder. "The holidays are a difficult time for some people, anyway. Even in the best of times. Now this, layered on top."

"Nell, you're a big stew of emotions tonight. They're written across you in neon letters."

Nell shifted slightly, resting her head on his shoulder. "I know. A part of me is so sad for the Pisano family. For Pamela. It's not fair she died like this. And a part of me is angry. It's not fair to Mary and what this will do to her, to the bed-and-breakfast."

"And beneath it all you're worried about Izzy. And she wasn't murdered or hurt. Her life here is a good one, intact, full of nice people."

Nell was quiet. She watched the shadows of moonlight fall across their bed and onto the wall, a hazy outline of snowy pine branches moving in slow motion. She thought about the way she and Ben crawled so easily inside each other's heads and hearts. It was decades in the making, but there it was. It made keeping secrets difficult.

Ben knew she was worried about Izzy; of course he did. They both loved Izzy like the daughter they never had, and were forever grateful to Caroline Chambers for sharing her daughter with them in a lifetime embrace.

"Izzy is a wise and amazing woman," Ben murmured beside her.

His breath was warm on her cheek. Nell closed her eyes. *Yes, she is.* And that would be enough for Ben, even if he sensed something not quite right. Izzy would handle it. It was a difference between them, a chasm that even all these years of marriage couldn't breach. A male-female difference, maybe. She would forever be the mother bear, ready to right all wrongs, to fight for her young—even those loaned to her by her sister.

Ben, on the other hand, would rationalize the situation, analyze it until he was comfortable that it would be handled wisely. And then he would let it go.

She rolled her head on the pillow until she was looking at the familiar profile of his face.

Ben's breathing slowed, then fell into the comforting rhythm of sleep. His chest rose and fell. His mouth fell open.

Next to him, Nell sighed. And then she began counting, and as the night slipped away, a whole farmyard of sheep moved before her closed eyelids.

Chapter 8

A holiday cookie exchange was such a normal, sane thing to do that Izzy called Nell to see whether she should cancel Monday's gathering.

"The papers are filled with stories about Pamela Pisano. Not just the *Sea Harbor Gazette*—the *Globe* is all over it," Izzy said. "It's on everyone's minds. A cookie exchange seems so . . . I don't know, so frivolous."

"Maybe that's exactly why you shouldn't cancel it, Iz."

The knitting groups that Izzy's shop hosted loved the holiday season—the warmth and delicious colors of yarn piled high in baskets all over the store, Izzy's hot chocolate, the fire in the back room, and the festive gatherings of knitting, eating, chatting, and music. It was safe and happy. It was good.

The phone was silent for so long that Nell wondered whether Izzy had hung up on her.

"Iz?"

"I'm thinking."

"Would you like to think at Annabelle's? Ben and I were about to drive over for brunch. Birdie will probably be there. Mae can open up the studio for you today."

Again her words were met with heavy silence. *Disturbing*

silence, Nell thought, but Ben would have countered her if she'd said that out loud. *You can't hear emotions in silence, Nellie*, he'd say.

But she could. Some silences were peaceful, like sitting in the family room with Ben at night, reading. Or on Birdie's deck during a snowfall, bundled up, just the two of them and two glasses of wine, the ocean stretched out in front of them and snow silencing the world. No words. Just peace.

Some were awful, like the silence after bad news falls from the sky. The silence when staring at a dead body in the snow.

And some were disturbing. Like the silence on Izzy's phone call.

"All right," Izzy said finally, and the click of the phone echoed in Nell's ear.

Nell half expected Sam to follow Izzy out of her tiny house when she and Ben drove up to the curb. He'd push a shaggy lock of hair back from his forehead as he greeted them, and his slow, lopsided smile would warm the cold air.

But Izzy was alone, her down jacket zipped up to her chin and a thick knit cap pulled down over her ears. Her multicolored hair fell from beneath the cap and around her shoulders like a cape.

"A goat-cheese frittata with spinach and roasted peppers—fresh basil sprinkled on top. Maybe some avocado slices and a dollop of sour cream on the side. That's what I want," she said, climbing into the backseat. "Oh, and fried potatoes, too."

Well, at least Izzy had an appetite. When Nell and Ben were negotiating their relationship—an odd word that strangely fit the process those many years ago—she sometimes found it difficult to eat. Her heart seemed to take over her whole body, leaving little room for anything else. She was head over heels in love—but determined that it be a fully responsible, equal relationship. Not that Ben would have settled for anything else himself. But it was the sixties, a turbulent, changing time, and if only for her own self-respect and that of women everywhere, she needed to make her points, be clear on her feelings about relationships, equality. Looking back, it all seemed unnecessary. But at the time it was critical.

Beside her Ben was laughing, his eyes meeting Izzy's in the rearview mirror. "Well, then, Izzy, you shall have it. Nothing is too extravagant for my favorite niece."

Izzy laughed, too, and the ride over the narrow road to Canary Cove and Annabelle's Sweet Petunia restaurant went by quickly—and happily.

In the winter, with summer people gone, Annabelle restricted her restaurant hours to just a couple of days a week. But Sunday mornings were sacred. And she risked a revolt from Sea Harbor residents should the Sweet Petunia not open its doors that day.

"It's not quite the same without our Stella at the desk," Nell said to Annabelle as the plump owner took their coats.

"She's my baby. And in college now, can you believe it?" Annabelle wore her well-deserved pride for her children on her sleeve. Starting her own business after her husband died at sea, being mother and father to four kids and putting them all through college, was not for the faint of heart. Annabelle grabbed three menus. "So, where's our Birdie?"

"She's not here?"

"I haven't seen hide nor hair of her. She's usually here before the blueberry scones are out of the oven. But the Favazza home is right over there near the Pisano place, isn't it?"

"Yes."

"Well, that's it, then. All this terrible news about that place is disturbing people's routines. It's terrible."

Disturbing routines. Murder had a way of doing that. Yes.

Nell followed Ben and Izzy as Annabelle led them over to a table near the windows.

"Maybe she overslept," Nell said, sitting down and turning over her coffee cup. She looked around the room, half expecting Birdie to be following them.

Sometimes Birdie woke up in the middle of the night, then slept later the next morning to make up for it. It was Sonny who did it, she claimed. Her long-deceased husband would nudge her from bed, and she'd retreat to his den at the top of the house. The small room that had been Sonny's sanctuary was still filled with his pipes and books and leather-topped desk. The smell of cherry tobacco rose from the leather chair when Birdie curled up in it and welcomed the familiar comfort of its creases. She'd breathe in the smell of him, and then she'd feel his arms around her, warming her.

A large brass telescope on a wooden stand was positioned in the middle of the mullioned windows, its scope aimed out toward the sea. It was always ready to take one beyond the harbor or across the town. Birdie claimed she never used it, but Nell knew differently. Twice the older woman had spotted fires in the middle of the night, and who knew how many teenage beach parties she'd discovered in the early-morning hours?

"We'll keep her coffee cup ready in case she joins us," Ben said, his hand on the back of the chair.

Father Northcutt was sitting with Beatrice and Sal Scaglia at a sunny corner table. He looked up and waved at Ben.

Ben waved back and said to Nell, "Seeing the good padre reminds me that I have a check for him. Back in a minute."

"Where's Sam?" Nell asked when Ben was out of earshot.

"Oh, you know Sam. Independent. He's off on an adventure." Izzy stirred an unusual amount of cream into her coffee, then looked up and offered Nell a smile.

But the smile came only from her lips. Her eyes were another matter.

"To take photographs?"

"No." Izzy pulled a piece of knitting from a large bag. It was a colorful square, a wooly stockinette weave of reds, yellows, and pale greens. A deep blue ribbing bordered the four sides. "It's the Knit-a-Square project," she said, holding it up. "Just needs the ends woven in. Next I start on a KasCuddle."

Nell smiled. They'd be doing more squares at the cookie exchange, sending them off to South Africa, where the KasCare volunteers at the church would work them up into blankets and sweaters for children with AIDS. Izzy had become inspired by photos of the amazing blankets produced for the needy families, and in months she had the whole town knitting squares for Aunt Ronda and her workers in South Africa.

"So Sam's gone somewhere mysterious, but not to take photographs," Nell said, reluctant to drop the subject. "Maybe he's Christmas shopping."

The suggestion wasn't lost on Izzy. She frowned at Nell. Then she set her square down on the table and looked intently at Nell.

"I know you're concerned—please don't be. It's just one of those things. Sam is acting strange. Maybe it's our relationship. Maybe we've gotten too close and he's scared. Like wondering what's next for us. I haven't put pressure on him—I'm not even sure that I want to talk about what's next. But Sam seems to be pulling away."

Izzy caught her bottom lip between her teeth the way Nell remembered her doing when she was young, spending summers with Ben and Nell on Cape Ann, and life wasn't going smoothly. The grown-up Izzy showed hurt in her eyes, as well.

She tried to mask it with a casual shrug of her shoulders.

Nell waited.

"Midlife crisis maybe? Who knows?" Izzy welcomed the distraction of Jenny, the waitress, wanting their order.

"He's only thirty-nine," Nell said softly, more to herself than to Izzy. She ordered for herself and Ben, and sat back, sipping her coffee and watching her niece while she ordered the special frittata.

There was an opinion, pushing against her lips, trying to get out, but she held it back. Izzy *was* ready to talk about the next step in her relationship, even if she didn't realize it herself. Nell could see it in Izzy's eyes when she looked at Sam. She could hear it in her voice when she held Liz Palazola-Santos' new baby boy in her arms or knit up a cuddle for the babies in Africa. She could even see it in the wistful look on her face when she unpacked a new load of fingerling yarn in soft greens and pinks and light blues.

And she had heard it loud and clear when Izzy had asked Nell on her wedding anniversary what being married to Ben Endicott meant to her after all these years. *Life*, she'd answered without thinking. *It meant life.*

Sam was another story. Nell knew he loved Izzy. Everyone knew it. What began as a surprise encounter with his best friend's little sister had slowly evolved into something far more. And before long, the photographer had bought a house overlooking the ocean, traveled less, and had slipped into Izzy's life effortlessly, as if there had always been an Izzy and Sam.

Until now.

Nell wouldn't tell Izzy, but she'd noticed Sam's odd behavior herself. At the past Friday night supper at the Endicotts' he had seemed like a bystander, standing on the fringe and looking in. Most of the time, he was looking at Izzy, and his eyes held the same longing she'd seen there before. But there was something else there now, something—as hard as she tried—Nell couldn't put her finger on.

"When your uncle and I were processing our relationship, we had to make some compromises," she finally said. The words sounded hollow, meaningless when they left her lips.

"Processing?" Izzy drew her brows together. "Aunt Nell, processing is what you do with meat—in a plant."

Nell lifted one shoulder; a small smile lifted her lips. "I suppose. I only meant that important decisions sometimes take time and care and understanding. Sometimes patience, too."

Izzy sipped her coffee and looked out the windows at the ocean several blocks away. With the trees stripped of leaves, and the restaurant high on Canary Cove Hill, the ocean seemed close. A perfect backdrop for the sleepy art colony nestled in between.

"I don't know," she said finally, cupping her chin in her hand. "There's something going on. He went to Colorado this morning."

Nell frowned. "Colorado? Why?" Sam was raised in Colorado but spent much of his youth in Kansas, either in school or spending summers at Nell's sister's ranch. The whole family— except for the adolescent Izzy, who considered boys an odd species back then—loved Sam. And they more than made up for a family he didn't really have.

"I don't know why. He said he had to see a man about a horse. But not to worry. He said he'd be back."

"Of course he will."

"The thing is . . . "

Izzy looked directly at Nell, and her brown eyes revealed what the "thing" was before the words came.

"I love Sam Perry," Izzy said. "But he's closed off a part of himself from me. He loves me. I know that. But I don't know why he's doing this. And I don't know what to do about it. I've always known what to do in my life; you know that. College. Law school. Quitting a law practice. Opening a yarn store.

"But now I don't. And I have a shop to run, dozens of women wanting to make baby booties and sweaters and scarves. I have orders to fill and a roof to fix." She paused just long enough to blink away the tears gathering in her eyes. "It isn't right for him to shut me out like this," she said softly. "It isn't right."

Nell had no answer, and they fell silent, tucking away the moment as Jenny came back with heaping platters of Annabelle's special egg creations. She set the plates down in front of them just as Ben pulled out his chair and joined them.

Ben's eyes lit up. A ring of breakfast sausages surrounded Ben's cheesy eggs. Chunks of curry-spiced sweet potatoes poked out of the eggs from between thin slivers of fresh lemony chard. A layer of sour cream coated the top like new-fallen snow.

"I think I'm in love with Annabelle Palazola," Ben said. His smile was huge as he dropped his folded *New York Times* on the empty chair and happily dug into the creamy frittata.

Ben attacked food like he attacked life, Nell thought, watching the eggs disappear. With great pleasure and fine sensibilities. One of a myriad of reasons why she'd married him.

A vibration in her pocket pulled Nell's attention away from food. She looked down at the number. "It's Birdie," she said as she lifted the phone to her ear.

The conversation was brief. "Of course . . . Certainly . . . We'll be there soon."

She slipped the phone back into her pocket.

"Birdie is with Mary Pisano at Ravenswood-by-the-Sea. She asked us to stop by when we're finished here."

"Problems?"

"She didn't say. But it wasn't really a request as much as a directive, not Birdie's usual way—although she did say we could finish breakfast first." Nell paused, thinking back over the conversation. "I thought Mary would be with the family today, considering everything, but it's just as well she's with Birdie."

"Father Northcutt said he was with the family late last night when they heard the news. They were pretty shook up. Suicide in a family is difficult. There's guilt. Confusion. A murder is a whole different story."

"I'm sure the police will want to talk to all of them."

Ben nodded. "Father Larry said the relatives had all come together surprisingly fast on who might want Pamela dead."

Nell and Izzy waited.

"Someone from the industry. A competitor. Pamela had made some sizable enemies in the industry and had even suggested that Pisano Publications give her an allowance for bodyguard protection."

"Jeez," Izzy said.

"Yes. But I suppose it'd be a relief if it were true. This could be wrapped up neatly in record time."

Like a Christmas present, Nell thought. Nice and neat with a bow on top.

But life rarely took that path. And all businesses had competition, but publishing rivals didn't kill one another off like movie gangsters did.

Satisfied there were no traces of anything edible left on his plate, Ben took out his wallet and left several bills on the table. They slipped back into their winter coats and gathered up knitting bags and purses.

Nell looked over and waved at Father Northcutt. She smiled at Sal and Beatrice. A younger man sitting in the fourth chair was looking out the window, frowning. A folded-up newspaper sat in front of him.

"Who's the good-looking guy with the Scaglias?" Izzy asked to Ben's back.

"A relative," Ben said over his shoulder. "Troy or Terry.

Something like that. His brother is married to Beatrice's sister. The guy is a model. But he lost his last job in the city, so he's doing odd jobs for the Scaglias and some handiwork for Father Larry's church. Sal and Beatrice are putting him up for a while until he gets his life together."

"That's nice of them," Nell said.

"Apparently Beatrice's brother-in-law is contributing a hunk of money to her political campaign. There was some incentive."

"With looks like that, he should be modeling, not doing odd jobs," Izzy said.

Nell looked back and caught the man's profile. Grecian-like, a strong, straight nose and chin, with thick blond hair pulled back in a ponytail. He was good-looking, she agreed, though even from a distance she could see lines and the results of too much tanning.

Nell turned away, then stopped and looked back again.

"What's wrong?" Izzy asked.

"I've seen him somewhere."

"He's been here a few weeks. You've probably seen him around town," Ben said.

Nell looked again. Where had it been? Somewhere that mattered. But her memory refused to clear, and the niggling thought stayed there like an irritating fly, just on the edges of her consciousness.

Silly, she thought. She shouldn't let it bother her. There were far more important things on her plate than a man she'd never been introduced to.

Even one as good-looking as Troy or Terry, or whoever he was.

Chapter 9

The parking lot at the Ravenswood-by-the-Sea bed-and-breakfast was remarkably peaceful when they pulled in. It looked like a normal afternoon, the street quiet, just as Ravenswood Road and the lovely neighborhood tended to be.

Mary's little blue Honda was parked in the half-moon drive. Another car that Nell didn't recognize was parked on the other side of the bricked area, just in front of the pathway to the carriage house. But there were no flashing lights or yellow tape closing off the drive. No police hovering over the area. No curiosity seekers.

"The police just left," Mary explained as she ushered them in the front door. Georgia, the floppy goldendoodle, bounced beside her, her curly head and tail bobbing a welcome.

"They've been here for hours. It's such a mess. So awful. They're asking a million questions. Who would want to kill Pamela?" Her blue eyes filled her tear-stained face.

Then she waved the air in front of her as if erasing the thought and answered her own question. "Well, me, I suppose. And lots of other people. Pamela was a handful. But of course we wouldn't have done it, not really." She shook her head of dark curls. "Come back to the kitchen."

The large kitchen was a shining mass of stainless steel with a butcher-block island that ran down the center like a fault line. The enormous Viking stove held a teakettle that whistled as they walked through the door. A mix of cinnamon, butter, and rising yeast dough filled the warm air with homespun odors.

Birdie sat on a stool at the island. At the sink, a dark-haired man in a T-shirt and jeans was scouring pots. His muscular back spoke of skiing, bike riding, or heavy lifting.

A plaid, well-used dog bed and bowl of water sat beneath the small kitchen desk. Georgia immediately curled up on the bed.

"Cinnamon rolls," Birdie said, pointing to a bowl of dough still sitting on the island. "Comfort food."

"I'd recognize that delicious aroma anywhere." Nell looked over to the sink. "So, Kevin, you're the chef that Mary stole away from Ocean's Edge?"

Kevin Sullivan turned around. "Guilty." The serious look that lengthened his face softened, and he managed a grin. "Mary needed someone to keep that mess of a family fed. She's a friend. She asks, I come." He waved a hello to Izzy as she slid onto the stool next to Birdie.

"Your cinnamon rolls alone will bring guests to this place, Kev," Izzy said. "Good move, Mary."

Mary put a hand on the young man's well-muscled arm, her fingers barely spanning the top. "I wouldn't survive without him. He's chief cook and therapist."

Kevin laughed. "I've been called lots of things, but that's a new one."

"Well, it's true." Mary turned toward the others. "Things are a mess around here, as you might imagine. The police are tramping all over the place. The neighbors are in an uproar. Look at this."

Mary scooped up a stack of tattered posters and passed them around.

CLOSED.

HOUSE OF MURDER.

EVIL LIVES HERE.

"They were all along the roadside, up and down Ravenswood Road, like those political signs we put out for elections. Kevin saw them on his morning jog, and he and Birdie tore them down."

"I knew some of the neighbors weren't thrilled with the guesthouse idea, but this?" Nell frowned at the posters. "This is mean."

"Someone wants the B and B closed down," Ben said.

"Before it even opens." Mary lifted her small body up onto a stool. She settled her sneakers on the rung and leaned her elbows on the island top. "I suppose they think a murder occurring on the back porch might scare guests away."

"They might be right," Ben said, a concerned look pulling his brows together. "But this is a nasty trick."

Mary sighed. Less than five feet tall, Mary Pisano often boasted about buying her clothes in the juniors department of Macy's. Nell thought she bought her spirit there, too. In her mid-forties, Mary was as energetic as a teenager. In addition to cheering up the town with her chatty "About Town" column, Mary was a collector of needy creatures—birds with broken wings, baby rabbits, lost souls. Her door was never closed. Nell suspected it was a way of staving off loneliness when her fisherman husband was at sea for long stretches. But it was more than that—it was who she was. And right now she was someone deeply concerned about her sister's murder, which had occurred just outside her back door.

"The real crime with these posters is using a tragedy to promote a cause," Ben said.

"Pamela's death," Izzy said.

"Her murder. A cheap thing to do, using that to keep the B and B from opening. Did you show these to the police?"

"She did," Kevin said. He wiped his hands on a towel, put on oven mitts, and pulled a tray of cinnamon rolls from the oven.

"They didn't seem interested," Mary said. "I understand. The bigger issue, of course, is finding whoever killed Pamela."

"What happened to the business-associate suspect?"

"That's the neat-and-clean solution my cousins proposed. They happen to dislike one of Pamela's competitors intensely. But it's ridiculous to think some Fortune Five Hundred company sent someone to Sea Harbor to kill Pamela. Mostly, the family just wants this whole thing to go away. It's not good for business."

For the next few minutes, the only sound in the kitchen was that of warm cinnamon rolls being passed around the island and the contented licking of fingers.

Finally Ben asked, "Did Jerry mention other suspects?"

Mary shook her head.

Kevin watched Mary, then spoke, his brown eyes still on his boss. "They asked me a lot of questions. Mary wants to pretend it didn't matter."

"Why?" Ben helped himself to another roll.

"Because Pamela hung out in the kitchen a lot the first few days she was here. She'd go out back to smoke, then come back in here and hang out."

"So?" Izzy asked, puzzled. "I'd hang out in here, too, if you were popping out cinnamon rolls like this every day."

Kevin was quiet. His eyes turned hard.

Mary pulled her body up as straight as the pine tree outside the kitchen window. "It wasn't for the food. Cousin Pamela liked younger men. Handsome men. She had the hots for Kevin, you might say."

Nell held back a smile. It was a good thing that Mary hadn't decided on politics as a career. Diplomacy wasn't her forte. She looked over at Kevin, who was clearly embarrassed by the conversation. But surely it wasn't the first time someone had come on to him. He was a ruggedly handsome man. "Pamela had good taste. But I'm not sure why that would be an issue. Whether you reciprocated or not."

"He didn't," Mary said sharply. Embarrassed at the tone of her own voice, she gave a short laugh. "Sorry. I shouldn't be so outspoken, but I brought Kevin into this horrible mess. And we need to find out who the true perpetrator is and get Kevin out of the picture. He shouldn't have to suffer such indignities." She slapped one hand down on the island.

Georgia jumped, then settled back down.

Sometimes Mary Pisano seemed years older than she was. It wasn't because of her looks, though years of being a fisherman's wife—and those early years of helping her Ed down on the docks—had tanned her skin, along with adding a few sun-kissed furrows to her forehead. It was the way she put things, as if she had lived her youth in Jane Austen's day. It was the way she looked at the world. An Elizabeth Bennett, perhaps, with a touch of Emma thrown in. An arranger of lives, a role she took on with some frequency in her newspaper column.

"So you set the police straight, Kevin?" Ben asked.

"Of course he did," Mary answered quickly. "He had no interest whatsoever in Pamela. None. Zilch. I warned you about her, didn't I, Kevin?" She spun her head around to look at him, then went on. "Finally I told Pamela to stay out of my kitchen. I told her I wasn't paying Kevin for her to distract him, and, besides, I reminded her, he was almost ten years younger than she. I told her he'd quit if she didn't stop bothering him, and then where would we be? Kevin's food was the one thing that kept everyone from killing each other during those meetings." A bright flush covered her cheeks as emotions spilled out of her.

Georgia scratched at the door.

"So what's the problem?" Ben said. He walked toward the door to let the dog out.

Mary waved him away. "Georgia won't go out unless one of us says it's okay—Kevin, me, Nancy—someone she knows and loves. Silly pup."

"I'll let her out," Kevin strode across the kitchen and disappeared through the door with Georgia close behind.

Ben picked up the thread of conversation. "If Kevin and Pamela had nothing to do with each other, why would the police care?"

"The police sometimes have a difficult time believing that someone would push a beautiful woman like Pamela away. But they would." She shook her head. "Anyone who values his self-respect would. And besides that, until they find the real murderer, they'll be bothering Kevin and me and lord knows who else around here. That's the problem. As long as there are questions in people's minds and fear in the community, whoever made up these posters will be using it against the opening of the bed-and-breakfast. And that's a real problem."

"So we all have motivation to keep our eyes and ears open. Right?" Birdie asked. Her brows lifted into wispy bangs.

A sudden banging outside drew their attention to the door.

Kevin walked back in with the dog. "It's just the painter. He finally showed up."

Mary nodded. "I don't mind if he's late. As long as he comes."

Kevin shrugged.

The noise changed from a banging sound to heavy boots stomping up the back porch stairs.

"There's still some work to be done before we officially open," Mary explained. She paused.

Nell read into the pause and knew that the words "if we open" were dangling from Mary's lips. She held them back and continued.

"One of the guys is doing the painting touch-ups. He's a good painter and needs the extra money."

Nell looked through the kitchen windows. A metal ladder was hoisted across one of them, banging against the house. Next a gloved hand grasped a rung.

She squinted against the late-afternoon light. A man leaned over and picked up a bucket of paint.

His profile filled the windowpane.

That's it, she thought, her memory finally clearing. She'd seen him right here one day when she and Izzy had stopped to talk about colors for the quilts with Mary and Nancy Hughes.

As the man pulled himself upright, he glanced in the kitchen window and caught Nell staring at him.

It happened quickly, before Nell could look away.

He seemed amused, and a sly smile curved his lips. It was the smile of someone used to being looked at, admired. Of someone who knew exactly how people responded to him.

He winked.

Nell felt shivers travel up and down her arms.

For the second time that day, she found herself pulling her stare away from the ponytailed man.

Troy DeLuca. The model, as Izzy had said.

And, so it seemed, Mary Pisano's painter.

When she looked back, he was gone, the slight shaking of the ladder the only sign that he'd been there at all.

Chapter 10

They had stayed longer than they'd intended at Ravenswood-by-the-Sea, but the time had been well spent. Both Mary and Kevin needed to talk.

"It doesn't make sense to me that the police are concentrating on Kevin," Nell said. She followed Ben into the warmth of their kitchen, glad to be home. Sunday evenings were for settling in, for soup and bread and the comfort of Ben.

"He's kind of a quiet guy, but it was clear to me he had no use for Pamela," Ben said.

"I don't think he was alone in his feelings."

"No. But they need to talk to everyone. Who knows? Jerry will probably be calling you again. You spent time with Pamela that day."

Nell thought about Ben's comment while he retreated to his den and she busied herself in the kitchen, switching on lights and taking a pot of homemade soup from the refrigerator. She lit a burner beneath the soup and stirred it absently, mixing mushrooms and tofu with the wine-flavored base.

She and Birdie had been questioned the night of the murder, of course. But what would she say to Chief Thompson if he questioned her about earlier that day? Nothing of interest or importance, certainly.

She and Pamela had met by chance, and she hadn't found the time with Pamela unpleasant. The opposite, in fact. She was interesting and opinionated, and Nell found the combination a nice one, no matter what others thought.

She didn't know why Pamela had been over in Canary Cove that morning, but she herself was there, wasn't she? And without a good reason, other than Polly's scones—which were worth traveling much farther than Canary Cove for.

And then she remembered the ending of the conversation, and sweet Tommy Porter's face as he looked at Pamela Pisano through the tea-shop window.

It was an understandable look. His brother was one of the many notches in Pamela's belt. Played with and tossed aside.

At the time, it had meant nothing.

But now?

And the look on Pamela's face, when she abandoned her car and walked on down the street. Her face lifted in greeting?

She wrapped the croissants in foil and put them in the warming oven.

Ordinary gestures that suddenly took on more ominous meanings.

Nell looked out the window at the fading light. That was the thing about winter that she didn't like—the early onset of darkness.

Gaslights outlined small piles of snow lining the flagstone walkway in the backyard. The snow looked gray in the low light, the gray of old snow.

Christmas lights turned on beyond the woods that filled the back of their property—the Endicott Woods, as they'd been called for a generation. They blinked behind the waving branches of the trees along Sand Beach Drive.

Nell imagined sweet young voices singing about Rudolph and Frosty. She and Ben had seen the carolers on their way home—a Brownie troop walking from house to house, their eyes filled with Christmas. Their young voices holding hope, promise, and peace.

But it was hard to hear the joy and innocence, though she knew it was there.

That's what murder did to a town.

It masked its innocence.

Chapter 11

$\mathcal{T}$he Monday cookie exchange, scheduled to start as the work-day wound down, had already begun when Nell walked into Izzy's yarn shop. Voices, music, and laughter floated up the steps from the back room.

Mae Anderson's niece, Jillian, covered her ears.

"Can you believe, like, how noisy they are, Miz Endicott? And they say teens squeal. Hah!"

Nell laughed. "But they're good sounds, right, Jill?"

"I guess. Though if I hear 'Winter Wonderland' one more time, I will, like, scream." The young salesclerk slipped a skein of yarn and receipt into a store bag and handed it to a customer. Then she leaned across the checkout counter, her long brown hair falling across her face as it came up close to Nell's.

"It's awful, isn't it? Like, I love Kevin Sullivan. He's the coolest guy in the whole world. He coached our swim team last summer. No way he could have killed that lady. You don't think he did it, do you?"

Nell stepped back, startled. It was a scant thirty-six hours since the police report was released. And just a day after Kevin had been questioned—not even officially—just the normal run-down with people who might have seen something. What kind of texting or tweeting passed rumors around that quickly?

"No, Jillian, I don't think Kevin Sullivan had anything to do with it. Where did you hear such silly talk?"

"My friend Ace is working over at the B and B, helping get it ready. He shovels snow and stuff. He's kinda lazy, but Miz Pisano hired him anyway. I think she felt sorry for him because he needs the money. Anyway, he says the police were questioning Kevin. He saw them through the window. Kevin looked worried, Ace said. And he saw Kevin yelling at the lady one day. But, hey, I yell at my sister all the time, but I wouldn't, like, kill her."

Nell shook her head. Well, it was a relief that the suspicion was so superficial. That kind of ungrounded gossip would hopefully turn into discarded rumor by tomorrow.

But when she headed back to the rear of the shop, an undefined weight pressed down on Nell's shoulders. The heaviness of concern for friends and neighbors, for good people whose lives could get caught up in circumstances and tossed around like a ship in a winter storm. She brushed away the feelings as best she could and smiled into the room filled with yarn and food and friendship and the delicious smells of snickerdoodles and gingerbread cookies.

"Look at this, Aunt Nell," Izzy called out. "One hundred and fifty squares ready to go to Soweto." She waved a fist in the air. "Woo-hoo, knitters!"

Cheers rippled through the crowd. Nell wove her way to the wooden table in the middle of the room. Piled high were stacks of colorful eight-inch squares, one more beautiful than the next. Izzy's devoted clientele took to the knit-a-square project for the group called KasCare with the same zeal and dedication they used to knit up cashmere sweaters and lacy silk shawls. Some of the squares had intricate cables going up the center; others boasted soft primary colors, knit in solids or fanciful designs.

Nell imagined the beautiful children in Africa—their huge eyes and round, dark faces—cuddling beneath the blankets knit from the patches, warm and wrapped in the love that went along with every piece.

"Terrific, right?" Izzy said. "I can't believe that people have taken the time to do this in the middle of the holiday rush."

"It's the perfect time to think of someone else." Nell fingered a square bordered with jungle animals knit in primary colors.

Across the room, Beatrice Scaglia waved to Izzy that she needed help. Nell watched the councilwoman demand Izzy's full attention, her fingers flapping a square in the air.

Beatrice was complicated, but over the years, Nell had decided that her heart—if not her actions—was nearly always in the right place. Taking in her unemployed relative for one thing. After her chance encounter with him the day before, Nell wasn't sure she'd be so generous. There was something about Troy De-Luca that put her on edge. Perhaps his cocky air, though Nell admitted to Birdie later that the cockiness might have been colored by her own embarrassment at being caught staring at him.

"I've gained ten pounds just by walking into this room," Cass whispered beside her. "Check it out, Nell. Ben will be in hog heaven when you go home tonight. Danny wanted to come to knit, but I wouldn't let him. He'd eat too much."

A floor-to-ceiling bookcase ran along one wall in the back room of Izzy's shop. Normally it was littered with skeins of yarn and knitting gadgets, patterns, framed photographs, and CDs, but today the counter that separated the bookshelves from the cabinets below was filled from end to end with platters of home-made holiday cookies—from decorated Santas and buttery spritz blossoms, to chocolate peanut butter drops and cinnamon-sugar sticks. A linen-lined basket at the end was brimming with choco-late coin cookies for Hanukkah, each one wrapped in gold foil. Izzy had taken a few cookies from each plate and placed them on a tray for nibbling while knitting. Before leaving, they'd all walk the cookie-lined path and fill their take-home baskets with the rest.

"I'm always amazed and inspired at the creative things busy people come up with," Nell said, squeezing her own platter in between a plate of macaroons and frosted reindeer, complete with cherry noses.

"And even some not-so-creative people—but certainly enterprising—like me." Cass pointed to a plate of red lobster-shaped Christmas cookies. "Harry Garozzo made them for me," she whispered, then slipped away to help Izzy pass out scrap yarn for new squares.

Nell laughed and looked back at the array of sweets. How interesting, the abundant comfort that homemade cookies could bring to a room. Eggs, butter, flour—medicine of the gods. She looked around the room, at heads bowed sharing family news, fingers reverently touching soft yarn, smiles flittering across lined faces.

In the midst of it, Izzy moved from group to group, her long, lean body bending to offer praise for a newly finished square. Her fingers pointing out a fresh design. A pat on the shoulder. She offered warm cider or soft drinks, a glass of wine or cup of coffee. The perfect hostess. But it wasn't a role she played. It was simply Izzy.

"Our Izzy looks tired," Birdie said, coming up to Nell and motioning her over to the window seat where Purl was saving their places, the long tabby body stretching from one pillow onto the next.

Nell nodded. "Tired. Or concerned."

"Or both."

Birdie handed Nell a glass of hot cider, and the two settled down on plush pillows, their backs to the window framing the winter sea, with Purl now curled into a ball between them.

Birdie pulled her thick red sweater around her. "What's going on with Isabel?"

"It involves Sam, but I haven't been able to make sense of it. Three weeks ago Sam and Izzy both had that magical look of expectation, of wonder, or so it seemed to me. And I don't think it was from holiday decorations or the mayor lighting the Christmas tree, or the music. It was more than that, an intimate something that was hard to define. I truly half expected an announcement."

"And now?"

"I don't know. They seem to have issues."

"Of the heart." Birdie's small white head moved with her words, and her eyes sought out Izzy. "It's difficult when our emotions are being tugged in such disparate directions. Love. Murder. They simply don't fit well in the same house."

Birdie had intended to speak the words softly, but the hardness of "murder" carried the word far enough to pull Rebecca Early's attention away from her knit square.

The jewelry artist leaned over the arm of a leather chair, bringing her head close to Nell and Birdie. "I saw her the day she was killed. She was as close to me as the two of you."

Rebecca's silky blond hair fell over her shoulder, and her brows pulled together. "It's awful. No one deserves an end like that; I don't care who they are or what they've done."

"You saw Pamela that morning?"

"Yes, not too long after I spotted you, Nell, heading to Polly's for one of her amazing scones, I supposed. A short while after that Pamela stopped in the gallery."

Nell remembered Pamela changing directions, heading down the sidewalk. She assumed Pamela had seen someone she wanted to talk to. "Did she seem okay?"

There it was again. That irrational desire to pull out a reason, an emotion, something that would make sense of a woman being happy and ordinary and alive. And hours later, murdered.

"I've gone over the conversation often—believe me. She seemed happy, in that overconfident way of hers. Pamela comes to my studio whenever she's in town—she loves jewelry, and I always hoped she'd find something to feature in *Fashion Monthly*. I'm not much of a self-promoter, but I jumped in this time and asked her if she would consider using some of my jewelry in an issue. She was interested. She tried a few things on. A necklace and some of those long drop earrings that I've made for you, Nell."

"Did she buy them?" Birdie asked.

Rebecca nodded. "She bought several things. I would have given them to her if it meant they'd show up in her magazine."

"Maybe they'll show up anyway. Her cousin Agnes seems to be filling in at the helm, from what we can gather."

"Agnes Pisano? Oh, my, that's a surprise. I don't exactly see Agnes as being very fashion conscious."

"Maybe it's just an interim thing. So what did she pick out?"

"Well, not as much as she might have if we hadn't been interrupted."

"More customers?"

"No, that blond guy who's been staying with the Scaglias followed her in. They had been talking on the sidewalk earlier. He was upset; I could tell. A vein in his overly tan forehead was throbbing, but he was smiling, trying to be nice."

"He was upset with Pamela?"

"Well, I'm not sure. Their conversation didn't make a lot of sense to me, probably because part of it had occurred on the sidewalk. He was almost ingratiating himself to Pamela, I thought. He kept saying he'd be perfect, and he'd do anything she wanted." Rebecca chuckled. "And this was all with me standing there behind a felt pad filled with necklaces.

"Pamela kind of ignored him at first. She picked up more earrings, a couple of necklaces, and put them in her 'to purchase' pile. But he kept after her, nudging her, flirting one minute, coaxing the next. All the while, the vein was throbbing. At first she was more patient than I'd have been. But then she finally told him to stop. She turned and looked him right in the eye, her hands out in front of her as if she were warding him off. He had *other talents*, she said—in a suggestive way, I thought. Then kind of laughed, you know, in a teasing way. And then she told him he needed to face the hard truth. He was too old—over the hill, was how she put it—to be in any reputable fashion magazine. It was time to put him out to pasture, she said. And that was that."

"Over the hill? Out to pasture? Ouch. That must have hurt."

"His face was as red as Birdie's sweater, but he tried to hold it in. He swallowed hard and began flirting again, touching her, brushing up against her. He's a real lothario, that one. He came on to me the other day; can you believe that?"

Of course they could believe it. Rebecca was one of the most beautiful women in Sea Harbor. A willowy blond artist with skin like an angel's. But her relationship with Melanie Foster, a new fiber artist in town, seemed to be going well. Troy DeLuca wouldn't have stood a chance for all sorts of reasons.

"He's younger than Pamela, though I don't suppose that matters. But Pamela is so classy and sophisticated. This guy—for all his good looks—is definitely not that. There's something a bit . . . sleazy."

Nell didn't know Troy DeLuca at all, but Rebecca's feelings mirrored her own.

"I got the feeling Pamela was playing with the guy. Flirting with him, but making fun of him at the same time, assuming, maybe, that he was too dumb to realize it."

"How unpleasant," Birdie said. She picked up her knit square.

"Maybe he thought he could still convince her, using a different approach. They left together, even after she'd insulted him right to his face."

In front of the room, Izzy was holding up more squares. Rebecca turned back to listen and watch.

"Pamela probably met Troy at Ravenswood-by-the-Sea," Birdie said. "The crew has been there every day."

"I wonder how well she knew him."

The words hung heavy in the air.

"You're talking about Troy."

Nell looked up.

Beatrice Scaglia was standing near a coat tree, her knitting bag hanging from her shoulder. She was pulling on a pair of leather gloves. "I didn't mean to eavesdrop, but I heard 'blond ponytail,' and since one is living in my house, I picked up on it." Beatrice managed a smile. "What's he done?"

"Nothing, Beatrice, nothing," Nell said. She hadn't the faintest idea what Troy had done or not done, but Beatrice seemed to need an answer. "It seems your houseguest is sociable; that's all. For being a newcomer, he's meeting people just fine."

"Sociable? He's that, yes." Beatrice slipped her purse over her shoulder. "He's the youngest in his family. Spoiled rotten, if you ask me. He's gotten by so far on his looks—lots of modeling jobs when he was younger. But at thirty-five, he's getting rejected for jobs. And his temper doesn't help him through such things easily. He's a hothead. He told off a Boston agency and smashed a camera to emphasize his point. Sal and I are suggesting to him that there might be other ways to get through life, rather than relying on one's body tone and looks. Something more lasting, perhaps?"

Birdie chuckled. "That sounds like good advice. It's nice of you and Sal to help him out."

"It looks like he's lined up some jobs," Nell said. "I saw him at the old Pisano place a couple times."

Beatrice sighed. "Mary was nice to hire him. I think Sal and I are beginning to impose too heavily on our friends and neighbors—they're starting to walk the other way when they see us coming. But Mary says he's a decent painter, so I guess that's working out. But who knows what will happen now?"

"What do you mean?"

"What's going to happen to the bed-and-breakfast? Henrietta O'Neal showed up at a council meeting and accused us of taking money to allow Mary to get the ordinances she needed to fix the place up. I thought she was going to poke a hole straight through me with that walking stick of hers. The accusations are ridiculous, of course. But Henrietta can cause trouble—she's richer than sin and one of the feistiest eighty-year-olds I've ever met."

Beatrice's face colored slightly as she talked. She tapped one skinny heel on the floor nervously. "Now she's saying the place is haunted. The devil at work. That's why Pamela Pisano was murdered. The devil did it."

"Henrietta lives alone," Nell said. "It probably frightens her, the thought of murder in her own neighborhood."

"It isn't pleasant for any of us," Birdie said. "But it will be solved soon."

Beatrice's face softened in relief. Somehow, if Birdie Favazza said it would be solved soon, it would be. She pulled her keys from her purse. "Yes," she said firmly, as if nailing the coffin shut. "It will be."

Nell watched the councilwoman walk off, a wicker basket filled with an assortment of cookies hanging from one arm and her knitting bag from the other. But the usual tilt to her head was missing, and she lacked the spring in her step.

Pamela Pisano's murder was taking its toll, even in the middle of a festive Sea Harbor cookie exchange.

Chapter 12

 $\mathcal{N}$ ell looked around the nearly empty room and pulled a broom out of Izzy's utility closet. She began sweeping up cookie crumbs and stray pieces of cut yarn.

Outside, the sky was darkening and a strong wind rattled the windows.

"I'm glad you didn't cancel the cookie exchange, Izzy, no matter what's going on around us. People enjoyed themselves, the cookies were fantastic, and Ben will be overjoyed when I walk in with twenty different kinds of sinful delights. I think he looks forward to this annual gathering more than I do. And having everyone knit a square was a perfect complement to the festivity."

Izzy began packing the finished squares into boxes. "You were right. It takes people's minds off the ugly things."

"Let's toast to that." Cass pulled several glasses from the cupboard and uncorked a bottle of red wine she'd taken from beneath the counter. "People had a good time, but I'm not sure they entirely forgot about the ugly. There was plenty of talk going on."

Nell had heard it, too, and not just Rebecca's story. With each comment, the portrait of Pamela Pisano, fashion editor, became more extravagant, with deep reds and purples covering over the classy, if a bit arrogant, woman that Nell suspected might be closer to the truth. The talk troubled her. There were pieces missing in the picture being painted about Pamela's murder, and once rumors took root, they could so easily mask truths.

"I suppose it's easier to accept murder if the person deserved it somehow," Birdie said. "But that's wrongheaded. No one deserves murder."

"But the truth is," Cass said, "Pamela Pisano could be mean. Even though she didn't live here year-round, she hurt people who do live here. People we care about. Even her own cousins, like Mary and Agnes."

"And don't forget Tommy Porter's older brother," Izzy said.

"Trotting Eddie all over town, all that public affection, then tossing him aside so publicly—that was cruel." Cass straddled a wooden chair, wrapping her arms around its back and sipping her wine. "I remember it well because it was the summer Pete and I officially started our business, and Eddie was helping us for a while. Four years ago or so."

"Well, the way it ended was better than if she'd married him and then ran off," Nell suggested.

"Tommy doesn't think Pamela had any intention of marrying him. Eddie Porter is great-looking. Fun. Pamela was here that whole summer, moving her mom into the nursing home. Bored. Tommy thinks Eddie simply helped her pass the days. She was playing with him, and Eddie pretty much knew it, but he was having fun, too. The odd part, as I remember it, was how she stopped so abruptly, then got really secretive. Rumors were she was having a 'secret' affair. But it wasn't her usual modus operandi. Her usual way was what she did with Eddie, playing with him for the world to see."

Playing with him. "That's how Rebecca described Pamela's

interaction with Troy DeLuca," Nell said. She dumped the crumbs into a wastebasket and put the broom away.

"The blond painter?" Cass asked. "How'd she know him?" She took a Christmas mint from the basket on Izzy's table and popped it into her mouth.

There were probably dozens of blond painters on Cape Ann. But everyone already knew that "the" blond painter referred to Beatrice Scaglia's relative.

"He's part of the crew working on the bed-and-breakfast," Nell said.

"He'd be hard to miss," Izzy said. "Maybe he made the Pisano family meeting more palatable for Pamela."

Nell repeated Rebecca's encounter with Troy and Pamela. "Who knows?"

"I wonder if the police have made a connection between Troy and Pamela. They'd want to talk to Troy, I'd think." Birdie picked up Purl and rubbed her cheeks.

"If they haven't, I suspect they will. They've already put sweet Kevin Sullivan on the hot seat," Izzy said.

"What?" Cass said, annoyance coloring her words. "Kevin couldn't hurt a fly."

"No, but he worked for Mary," Nell said. "They probably just wanted to make sure he hadn't seen something that might be important."

But Kevin wasn't there that night—even though Birdie had thought he would be, getting ready for breakfast the next day. Where was he? And where was everyone else? The emptiness of the house preyed on her, a house that just hours before had been bustling with people. The staff. Workmen. The Pisanos. Then no one.

Except for a lonely dog, cold and frightened, and a dead body in a snowbank.

And a murderer. Yes, there would have been a murderer there, too.

A familiar chill ran up and down her arms. She thought of Mary's distress and the look in Kevin's eyes. Mary needed resolution to this soon. They all did.

The rattling of the alley door caused them all to jump.

Darkness had snuck up on them. Outside a cold wind rattled windows, and crusts of snow blew up against the side of the old building. Izzy pulled the curtain back from the window in the door, frowned, then opened it. "Come in. Hurry."

Sam and Ben stepped in, along with a bone-chilling breeze.

Izzy quickly pushed the door shut behind them.

"We saw the lights," Sam explained. He kissed Izzy on the cheek. "Miss me?"

"We've been busy," she said, wiggling out of his embrace. She pushed strands of streaked honey blond hair from her eyes.

"Looks like it," Sam said, eyeing the wineglasses.

Nell watched the exchange. Poor Sam. Not much of a welcome home. She watched Izzy's face. A forced bright smile betrayed the message in her eyes. She looked so much like her mother, Caroline, at that instant—hiding every inch of vulnerability beneath a protective facade that dared anyone to broach it. *Stay away*, the look said. *Don't touch.*

Nell's younger sister had perfected that look, and she threw it away only when she had her own three children and realized children didn't allow facades.

"Sam and I were thinking you gals might like to grab a burger down at the Gull," Ben said. "My treat."

"The Gull?" Nell hesitated. The Gull had decent bar food, but it also had packed crowds of noisy drinkers, screaming-loud music, and the distinctive smell of fishermen who, unlike Cass, didn't always shower after being out on the water.

"The Fractured Fish are playing," Sam said.

"That settles it, then," said Birdie, getting out of her chair. Purl jumped to the floor. "I haven't seen Peter Halloran play in weeks. Besides, we've finished this bottle of wine."

As expected, the Gull was packed, the bar two deep, the ledge and stools along the window filled shoulder to shoulder with hungry customers devouring baskets of calamari and fried oysters, burgers and sweet potato fries, and a rapidly accumulating line of empty beer bottles filling the countertop.

From his post behind the bar, Jake Risso spotted the group.

"Hey, you guys." He waved one hairy arm over the heads of customers and with the other motioned for a waiter to wipe off a messy table in the corner.

"Haven't seen you in here in forever. Welcome to my humble abode." He came around the bar, wiping his hand on a rag, his balding head shiny with perspiration.

"Jake, there was never anything humble about you," Nell said, laughing. "But thanks for getting us a table. Makes us feel like royalty."

Jake's raucous laugh made barely a dent in the noisy bar. He leaned into the middle of the group, talking loudly. "The kids are about to start their first set. Your brother's quite a singer, Cass. You enjoy. I'll send over some sustenance and libations."

Across the room on a small raised platform, Pete Halloran stood with one foot lifted onto a chair, tuning his guitar. Next to him, Merry Jackson flipped her long blond ponytail and waved at her husband, Hank. As co-owners of the Artist's Palate Bar & Grill in Canary Cove, Hank and Merry didn't spend much time in the Gull, but playing her keyboard with the Fractured Fish trumped nearly anything. Merry loved to be onstage, and her older husband loved watching her. Andy Risso, Jake's son, sat behind three drums, twirling a stick in his hand. His face was serious, his eyes on a list of songs scribbled on a piece of scrap paper, his long hair trailing down his back. And on each of their heads, attracting nearly as much attention as the Gull's famous calamari, was a garishly loud, beautifully knit fish hat.

Cass pointed and broke into laughter. "I told you they'd love them."

Dead fish hats. Cass had found the pattern on Knitty.com. And before the first north wind had pushed summer into memory, the knitters had worked up four stylish hats. With face openings where fish mouths would be and bright colored gills flapping along the sides, the hats became the Fractured Fish's winter uniform.

Pete looked over at his friends and bowed dramatically. The fish on his head seemed to wink at them from round white eyes with an "X" in the middle.

In minutes the music had begun, and cover songs ranging from Beatles hits to John Mayer's latest album filled the room. Izzy and Cass had lured Danny Brandley away from the bar, and the mystery writer sat next to them, one arm looped around Cass' shoulders. Nell was squeezed between Sam and Ben, barely able to get her hands free to reach the basket of sweet potato fries. She turned toward Sam.

"How was your trip to Colorado?"

Sam kept his eyes on the band, his face neutral. He nodded, offered a slight smile.

"Good skiing?"

"No skiing. Family business. Had to check on some things."

Nell sipped her beer, protected by the noise and crowd. No chance for awkward silences. Sam was raised near the Colorado-Kansas border, but that's about all any of them knew about his foster family. Even Nell's sister and brother-in-law, who adored Sam and had practically adopted him once he started spending weeks each summer at their ranch, knew little. The fact that he was a great kid and kept Izzy's brother Jack out of trouble was enough for them. Caroline and Craig Chambers had met the couple who had raised Sam once—a nice older couple, Caroline told Nell. They had a farm not too far from the ranch. And they were fine with Sam spending most of his summers helping out on the Chambers' ranch, even when he was a kid of eleven or twelve.

"Did you see Izzy's parents while you were there?" Nell knew he hadn't. It was winter—her sister and Craig were at their home in Kansas City, where Nell and Caroline had been raised. But it was conversation. Perhaps it would lead somewhere.

"Nope," Sam answered, chewing on a piece of calamari. "It was a quick trip." He washed it down with a swig of beer.

On his other side, Birdie leaned into the conversation, her small body dwarfed by Sam's winter jacket. "Well, we're glad your trip was short," she said. "We're glad you're back, Sam."

Sam looked from one woman to the other, then allowed a crooked smile and spoke just loud enough for the two of them to hear. "You guys are like family. And you worry like family. But don't. No need for worry."

Later, when they drove Birdie home, Nell said Sam had added an "I hope" to the end of his sentence, but Birdie said she hadn't picked up on that.

In her own mind, Nell was positive that's what he'd said. "No need for worry, *I hope*."

But the barroom conversation was brought to an abrupt end after that, because while Sam pried himself out from between the two women to get another pitcher of beer, Pete Halloran and Merry, sounding a bit like Judy Garland, began belting out the Fractured Fish's rendition of "Have Yourself a Merry Little Christmas." Catching the spirit, the crowd began singing along and looking for spare sprigs of mistletoe hanging from the tavern's ceiling. People hugged one another and swayed back and forth.

The words to the holiday song always brought tears to Nell's eyes. The refrain "Have yourself a merry little Christmas" wrapped around her like a knit shawl, hugging her tight, holding her, just like Ben did at that moment.

Nell leaned into his shoulder and softly hummed the melody as Merry Jackson poured her whole heart and soul into the words:

Let your hearts be light.

From now on, our troubles will be out of sight.

Ben slipped a loose strand of Nell's hair behind her ear. Then he whispered close, answering Nell's thoughts as if she'd shouted them from the stage. "Maybe they're not out of sight yet, but soon, dear Nellie. Soon."

$\mathcal{T}$wo days later, the bells at Our Lady of the Seas tolled mournfully.

All through town, people paused in the middle of eating breakfast or watching the morning news. They pulled their eyes away from the morning paper or stood silent in the line at Coffee's, the only sound in the shop the hiss of the espresso machine.

It was instinctive, spontaneous, the reverence due to the dead.

Nell pulled her eyes away from the *Sea Harbor Gazette* and looked toward the window, as if she could see the bells in the hilltop steeple and the Pisano family, gathered together in the beautiful old church. "It's a shame they kept the funeral so private. People need closure," Nell said.

"It was for the mother," Ben said. "The family thought it would be best to have a small service, nothing afterward. The police haven't released Pamela's body yet, but Father Larry put together something meaningful, I'm sure. It makes sense."

"She's being cremated," Izzy piped up from her place beside the island. She sat on top of a kitchen stool pouring half-and-half into a large coffee mug.

Ben had heard that, too. He grabbed a pair of oven mitts and pulled a tray of blueberry scones from the oven.

"How was your run, Iz? Good?" Nell asked, shifting the conversation to a brighter note. Having Izzy sitting in their kitchen in the middle of the week, her cheeks pink from the wind and her eyes bright, was a welcome antidote to the funeral dirge being sung just a few blocks away.

"Good," Izzy answered, her eyes glued to the flaky scone Ben slipped onto a plate and pushed over to her. Her slender legs were wrapped in long, lined running pants, a yellow Lycra jacket still warming her arms.

"I don't know how you run along the ocean when it's this cold." Nell took off her reading glasses and pushed them to the top of her head. "It makes me cold to think about it."

"We ran up in Sam's neighborhood, not right on the beach. There are enough trees to block the wind."

Nell felt Ben's quick look. *No questions*, it said. Nell smiled at her husband and dutifully held back.

But she knew Ben held the same concerns, even if he expressed them differently. While driving home the night before, Ben admitted that Sam had been unusually quiet at the Gull. He and Izzy had left together, but there was tension between them. They'd all felt it.

Birdie had loudly declared the topic off-limits and shushed them into silence. Having buried several husbands, she felt she knew a little about lovers' secrets, she said.

But later, in the privacy of the Endicott bedroom, secrets of loved ones could be explored delicately.

"Why can't they just talk it out and move on?" Nell had whispered into the darkness.

Ben had laughed and turned on his side, his large arm pulling her into the curve of his body.

And then Nell laughed, too.

So easy to say. So difficult to do.

Nell had let it go—and allowed the warmth of Ben's body to lull her to sleep.

Things looked better that morning. Izzy seemed fine—even without the interference of her aunt. Perhaps Izzy and Sam had done exactly that—talked it out, whatever "it" was, and moved on. Maybe it wasn't so difficult after all.

"Listen to this," Izzy said, leaning over the newspaper. She read aloud:

ABOUT TOWN — SEA HARBOR, SAFE HARBOR
by Mary Pisano

The sadness of losing our beloved Pamela has been made bearable by you, the people of Sea Harbor, and for that we give great thanks. What was frightening and difficult has been eased by the comfort and loving goodwill of our friends and neighbors, and by the amazing Sea Harbor Police Department, ever vigilant, always professional.

We are comforted by the knowledge that the lost soul who brought this sadness into our lives has probably moved on, far away from Sea Harbor. A stranger who knew us not, but whose irrational act took a life.

We put our trust and our safety into our wonderful men in blue as we move forward with all of you into the joy of this holiday season, celebrating family and friends in this most amazing safe haven—our town—our sea. Our safe Sea Harbor.

"Mary's back," Nell said.

"Out of sight, out of mind—is that what she's saying?" Ben

asked. "Surely she doesn't believe that someone wandered into the Pisano backyard, shot her cousin, then moved on."

"It's her way of trying to calm everyone's fears. She's removing the murder from Sea Harbor by putting a stranger's face on the horrible act."

"And getting rid of the stranger," Izzy said.

"It's what Mary wishes were true."

Ben refilled mugs around the island. "Neat and tidy. Mary has a knack for that, but she's also a realist, and there's no way she believes it herself. I'll be interested to hear what Chief Thompson thinks about her theory."

Cell phone chimes joined the conversation. "That's probably Mae, trying to track you down," Nell said, rummaging through a stack of papers on the counter, looking for her phone.

"No. Mae officially barred me from the knitting studio on Wednesdays. At least occasionally. It's usually our slow day, and she's insisting I stay out of her hair unless I'm teaching a class. She can be a real bulldog."

"Good for Mae," Nell said. She glanced down at Birdie's number and pressed the talk button.

Birdie started talking before Nell could squeeze in more than a "Hi."

Izzy tried to catch the gist of the conversation, but the few words Nell was allowed to utter brought little explanation.

"The poor thing."

"She'll freeze to death. . . . "

And finally, "Of course. We'll be there right away, Birdie."

Nell and Izzy parked on the side of the driveway and walked through the snow toward the unlikely duo.

Birdie, bundled up in a heavy brown coat with a hood that

covered everything but her eyes, her red nose, and her mouth, stood next to the Ravenswood-by-the-Sea sign.

Next to her, a round, determined body in a white snowsuit stood in a foot of snow holding a can of red spray paint, one finger resting on the nozzle, a walking stick in the other hand. Running across the sign was a crimson diagonal, the broad sweep of paint reaching from one corner to the other.

Henrietta O'Neal's face was frozen in a fierce look, determined to spray one more line to complete her "X."

"You could get arrested, Henrietta," Birdie was saying. "This is private property."

Henrietta would have none of it. "It used to be private property. Enzo Pisano's private property. Now it's a travesty to his name, a commercial den of iniquity. A death trap. A haven for murderers." She paused long enough to wave hello to Nell and Izzy, then continued. "The devil's hideaway, tainted by murder."

"Oh, hush, Henrietta," Birdie said, shivering.

Henrietta glared back at her. "So you called in reinforcements, did you? That's fine and dandy, but it won't get you anywhere, Bernadette Favazza."

"You're going to freeze to death out here," Nell said.

"Back at you, Nell," Henrietta scolded. Her voice was strong and fierce, belying her eighty years. "And you, Isabel Chambers, you should be at that shop of yours ordering the yarn for my new sweater, not tramping around in this snow. You'll catch your death of cold, sweetheart."

"Why are you ruining Mary's new sign?" Nell asked.

"Why do you think? To keep people away. To rid this place of evil spirits. Mary Pisano isn't in her right mind. We don't need this in the neighborhood. We don't want this. Strangers tromping around, doing lord knows what. It's shameful. Disgraceful. Enzo must be rolling over in his grave, God rest his soul."

Izzy eased the can of paint out of Henrietta's hand while

Birdie and Nell each took one of her arms, guiding her away from the sign.

A car turned into the drive, slowed at the sight of the three women, and then came to a quick stop. Mary Pisano and Nancy Hughes tumbled out and hurried toward them.

"What are you doing here?" Mary asked. Her eyes moved to the sign and widened at the red paint.

"Your lovely sign," Nancy cried. "What's happened?"

"I did it." Henrietta planted her feet in the snow and pulled herself up to her nearly five feet. Her eyes flashed.

"Why?" Mary asked.

"You cannot open this bed-and-breakfast, Mary Pisano. I forbid it."

"Let's go inside and talk about it, get you out of the cold," Mary said reasonably. She began leading the group back to the driveway. Birdie cradled Henrietta's elbow in the palm of her hand.

Henrietta walked compliantly across the snowy yard until they reached the drive. Then, suddenly, she shook herself free of Birdie's hold, grabbed the can of red paint from Izzy, and stomped down the driveway toward the road, her short legs spinning and her elbows moving back and forth with unstoppable determination. She jabbed her walking stick into the crust of snow with each step.

"Will she be all right?" Nancy asked.

Birdie nodded. "Henrietta walks a couple miles a day, even in this crazy weather. She can't do stairs, but she could walk from here to California if she had a mind to. She'll be fine." She looked at Mary sadly. "But I'm afraid your sign won't."

"Troy can fix it." Mary watched Henrietta turn at the end of the drive and disappear up Ravenswood Road. "I just wonder what's next on her list of things to do to me." She picked up some protest posters that Henrietta had left behind and began to walk toward the house. "Nancy spotted her yesterday going up and down Harbor Road, handing these out to all the merchants."

"Which they will all ignore," Nell said. "Almost everyone is behind your project, Mary. Archie said it will bring new customers into the bookstore, and Harry and all the other shop and restaurant owners feel the same way. People will have a place for their relatives to stay. We've needed a small, lovely bed-and-breakfast here for a long time. Rockport is filled with charming places. We need some of our own."

Mary squeezed Nell's arm in a silent thank you. "Come," she said. "A cup of herbal tea will help shake off the bad spirits, imagined and otherwise." She rummaged through her purse for her key. "I don't think I'm thinking very clearly today."

"That's understandable," Nancy said. She pulled a key from her own bag and unlocked the door. They walked into the large entryway, welcomed by a leaping Georgia, who ran between Nancy and Mary, licking hands and happily wagging her tail.

It wasn't until they were settled into the comfortable chairs in the living room with teacups and a pot of cinnamon-orange tea nearby that Nell remembered where Mary had spent the morning. It wasn't just the ruined sign that had caused the sadness in her eyes. "Mary, I'd almost forgotten what you've already been through today. The funeral . . . "

Mary waved away Nell's words. "It's over. Father Northcutt did a lovely job of putting together a service without a body, and my aunt Dolores—Pamela's mother—handled it well, though I don't know how much she understood. It was short and sweet, what everyone wanted."

"So you can get back to leading your lives."

"I hope. There are still things to work out about Pamela's magazine."

"Rumor has it that Agnes is taking over," Birdie said.

Mary chuckled. "Rumors begun, no doubt, by Agnes. Agnes is smart enough—and she's begged for the opportunity to show what she can do. When we met last summer, she begged us to make a decision. She wanted it in writing somewhere that if Pamela stepped down, she would be the top contender for the job. Some of my sexist cousins think a fashion magazine editor needs to be beautiful and sexy, not exactly Agnes' profile. Anyway, it was an odd conversation because everyone knew Pamela would never have relinquished her hold on that magazine. But to get Agnes to stop talking about it, we agreed to what she asked."

"She seemed to be confident of her position at the Danverses' party," Izzy said.

"Can you believe her? Two days after Pamela died? The family was upset about that. It didn't seem respectful, I suppose." Mary sighed. "Selfishly, I'm more interested in Ravenswood-by-the-Sea than the magazine discussions. I'm determined to finish this wonderful place and have a glorious opening that you will all come to." She looked up at a portrait of Enzo Pisano that hung above the fireplace. "I want to do it for him. And thanks to Nancy, it might actually happen."

"We'll get it done," Nancy said, her voice lifting and a smile lighting her face. "It will take more than a little red paint to stop us."

"Not a pretty sight to come home to," Birdie said.

"She's a little frightening in her zeal," Nancy said. "Why is she so adamant about this? You could have her arrested, Mary."

Mary shrugged. "At first I thought it was just the neighborhood thing, that she thought a bed-and-breakfast was too commercial for this elegant neighborhood, but now I don't know. She puts up signs; she's staging war at city council meetings. She seems determined to stop me. She's capitalizing on Pamela's murder, which is pretty awful. She's using it to paint the house as haunted or some other god-awful thing. But frankly, I don't think she believes a word of what she's saying. Something else is going on in her head, and I wish I knew what it was."

"Henrietta has always liked causes—but usually good ones," Nell said. "Remember her door-to-door campaign for Obama? Maybe she sees this as a cause."

Birdie laughed at the memory of Henrietta renting an old Cape Anne school van and a driver to transport voters. "She would have driven them herself except no one would get in the van with her. The woman is a terrible driver. But this is strange behavior, even for her. She's always been a good neighbor, welcoming new people with elaborate baskets of goodies—and she's the first one to bring soup when someone's sick. When Enzo had that spell a few years back, she was more dutiful than Meals on Wheels. She brought soup, lasagna, pot roast—a true Florence Nightingale."

Mary smiled. "I remember. She'd come in, lugging her wicker baskets filled with food—and drink, I might add. I think my grandfather gained ten pounds while he was sick. He loved it."

"So why would a nice person expend this kind of energy on something that won't affect her at all? She'll never even see the guests coming and going," Nancy said.

"Exactly," Mary said. "Why?"

So many "why's" rattling around in this big house, Nell thought, looking around the room as the others tried to make sense of Henrietta O'Neal. Her eyes traveled to the enormous fireplace with a hand-carved walnut mantel holding photos and pottery. The shelves beside it were filled with books and small paintings, and the recently reupholstered furniture was tasteful and comfortable. She remembered coming to parties in this room, parties Enzo proudly hosted, long after his wife had died. He was the consummate host, charming and with a contagious sense of humor. There was always laughter here. A happy house. Certainly not one filled with evil spirits as Henrietta would have the world believe.

The slamming of a back door pulled her from her memories.

"It's just Kevin," Mary said. "That back door sticks. Did I tell you he's going to stay on here? He'll work part-time at the Ocean's Edge, but once we're up and running, he'll handle breakfasts and a cocktail hour here for the guests."

"That's terrific," Izzy said. "I think I'll sign up for a weekend getaway myself. It would be worth it, just for those amazing little things Kevin makes with prosciutto and figs. He'll help put you on the map."

Mary laughed. "He's good; that's for sure. And it solves some problems for us. My Ed doesn't want to move here. He loves our little house. We see each other infrequently enough without having to search for each other like we'd have to do in this big place. But I'd feel better if someone were on the grounds during the night. So Kevin is going to take over the carriage house, keep an eye on things when the staff isn't here."

Nell listened and marveled at Mary's ability to wade through the tragedy that occurred on her back porch and think of some one else's needs at the same time. Clearly this wasn't just a business decision. This would help Kevin enormously. He was saving up for expensive classes at the culinary institute— and a rent-free apartment would be a great help.

"When does he move in?"

Nancy answered. "Probably not for a week or so. There's still some work to do in the carriage house. This week has set us back a little."

In many ways, Nell thought. Murder was more than a setback. It not only ended a life; it changed the lives of those left behind, and Nell suspected they had just begun to count the ways.

"We're all happy you're back writing 'About Town,'" Birdie said. "We missed your column."

"I thought people might think me uncaring to go back to it so soon, but the truth of the matter is that Pamela is dead, and we're not. Life goes on."

"Your column indicates that the murderer is someone who didn't live here?"

"Yes. Pamela didn't have the highest regard for people's lives. She fired people at the drop of a hat."

"But lots of people get fired and they don't . . . " Nell began.

Then she stopped. Mary Pisano was one of the strongest people Nell knew. But she was fragile right now. She had just buried her cousin, and for today, at least, she needed the murderer to be a blank face, someone removed from her life and her town—and most especially from her bed-and-breakfast. There were plenty of reasons to think it was someone right here in Sea Harbor. But for today at least, Mary needed to believe otherwise.

"I think I'll get more hot water for the tea," Nell said, picking up the teapot and changing the subject. "And maybe I can talk Kevin into giving us something from his oven."

Nell left the others discussing the bedrooms and especially Enzo Pisano's master suite—the highlight of which was a massive walnut bed, hand carved and brought over from Italy, piece by piece. "It's Mary's own presidential suite," Nancy declared proudly.

The wide hallway wound past a library with leaded double doors opening out to the back porch. Nell peeked in and vowed to come back to make friends with the wall of books that stretched from floor to ceiling.

Beyond it, the hallway curved to the right, past a small utility room, and the kitchen beyond.

The sound of low voices stopped Nell just before she reached the kitchen door.

"This isn't your house, DeLuca. If you have to smoke, there's the door." It was Kevin, his voice controlled.

"Testy, aren't we, now?" the deep, lazy voice of Troy DeLuca answered.

"I just have trouble with cheats, people who sneak away while on the job. Bill the crew for it."

"Do I detect a little jealousy, Cook?"

Kevin's laugh lacked humor. "Of what? You're a loser, De-Luca. *Over the hill*—wasn't that what she said?"

Nell could almost hear Troy DeLuca's sharp intake of breath. Then silence, broken finally by a spewing of words spit out in anger. "Look who's talking about a loser. We all know what's going on here, Kevey boy. We all know who's the one with nasty little secrets, now, don't we? Pamela told me all about it. . . . "

A heavy silence followed his words.

It was Kevin who finally spoke. "She's dead, gone," Kevin said. "So why are you still hanging around? There's nothing left for you here. You should have been fired long ago."

Nell turned and inched her way back toward the front of the house, anxious to get out of earshot.

She had almost reached the wide doorway to the living room when Troy's words filled the kitchen and the hallway, loud and mean.

"You bet she's dead, Kevey boy. There's justice in this mean world—and you wanted her dead as much as I did. Alleluia. The wicked witch is dead." The words bounced off the walls.

A stomping of feet and slamming of the back door brought stunned silence.

Nell walked into the living room. Mary stared at the floor, as if wishing it would open up and swallow her.

Nancy Hughes' face was as white as snow.

Minutes later, the sound of Troy DeLuca's motorcycle roared down the driveway and onto Ravenswood Road.

Chapter 14

$\mathcal{N}$ell knew Mary Pisano would be at Coffee's the next morning. On summer days, she commanded her own table beneath the giant maple tree in the corner of Coffee's patio, but winter and north winds brought customers inside to gather around the fireplace and settle into the well-worn chairs and couches scattered about the cozy shop.

It's where Mary wrote her column and where she salved her soul.

The day before, several workmen had descended on Ravenswood-by-the-Sea just minutes after Troy DeLuca made his dramatic exit. Mary and Nancy were called away to decide outlet locations and point out areas that still needed work. It clearly wasn't the time or place to dissect the encounter between the handsome blond painter and Mary's chef. They'd have to talk about that later.

Nell decided sooner was better than later.

She spotted Mary as soon as she walked into the coffee shop. She was alone as usual, dressed in jeans and a bright blue cable-knit sweater, her coat and bag piled on an empty chair next to her.

Nell recognized the wool sweater—Mary had spent all last

winter knitting it up. She'd even perfected knitting the cables without the cable needle, something Nell herself had yet to master.

Nell picked up her coffee at the counter and carried it over to Mary's chair. Georgia lay comfortably at her feet, her floppy tail welcoming Nell.

The strain in Mary's usually cheerful face was evident. Her eyes were lowered to the computer on her lap, its screen as black as her hair.

"I thought maybe I'd find you here," Nell said.

Mary looked up and smiled. "They called Kevin down to the station yesterday afternoon," she said.

Nell nodded. Ben had told her as much the night before.

It had been a blessed night at home, and over a glass of wine, a plate of mushroom-curado quesadillas, and Andrés Segovia's guitar soothing their tired bones, she and Ben had shared their day. It was an intimacy Nell cherished, a ritual begun in the early days of their marriage. Sharing their days, for better or for worse. It made everything else in life all right.

Ben told Nell that the police had found Pamela's wallet in the utility-room locker where Kevin kept his personal things. That, combined with the fact that he'd made his dislike of her known to the work crew, didn't help his cause.

The police had no motive, but they were checking.

"Ben mentioned the wallet," she said to Mary now.

"Kevin told me he didn't put it there. It's not locked—just a cubby for him to put his things in when he's working. Anyone could have done it. Someone wanted to divert attention from themselves to Kevin."

Nell pulled out a chair across from Mary and sat down.

A ham-and-cheese-stuffed breakfast croissant sat on a small table next to Mary's chair. She offered half of it to Nell, then glared at the pastry, as if chastising it. "A week ago I could eat two of you," she said. Her small laugh was tired. "Nancy is handling the workmen for me," she said. "I need time away. Time alone. It's good to have someone to take over, at least for a bit."

"Of course."

Mary drank her coffee and straightened her back, willing away the tiredness with a stretch. "Kevin Sullivan is a good guy. You know that, Nell. His mother is lovely. His father's a drunken lout, but that's not Kevin's fault. He does all he can to make life easier for his mother. A good son. Kevin wouldn't hurt a flea." Her hands waved in the air for emphasis, and Nell put out a hand to prevent the laptop from toppling onto the floor.

Mary went on. "Never in a million years could he have had anything to do with Pamela's murder, no matter what."

Nell waited. The "no matter what" seemed to be going somewhere.

"No matter that he didn't like my cousin," Mary said with finality. "Kevin was gentle, but he was a good judge of character, and he didn't especially like the way Pamela treated people. He . . . " She shook her head.

"Yes?"

Mary bit down on her bottom lip. Then the expression passed and the muscles in her face relaxed. "Nothing. It's simply that sometimes you know people well enough to know without a smidgen of a doubt what they could or could not be capable of. And no matter what Pamela might have done to Kevin, he'd never have retaliated in a violent way. He just wouldn't."

"So the question is, who did? Do you know what that conversation between Kevin and Troy was about, Mary?"

She slumped back in the chair. "Pamela had insisted on staying in the carriage house while she was here, even though there were enough bedrooms in the main house, and the carriage house still needed work. We thought maybe she had someone coming up from New York or Boston. That wouldn't have surprised anyone. I guess we didn't think that she'd find someone here in town so quickly. It usually took her longer."

"So she and Troy?"

"Yes. I'm sure they were fooling around. Kevin saw Troy headed toward the carriage house a few times when he was on the clock. And another time the crew needed Troy for something, and he was nowhere to be found—nor was Pamela. She missed a few conference calls with our lawyers." Mary shrugged. "I would have fired him, but frankly, Nancy urged me not to. 'It would be hard to find another painter,' she said. 'Let him finish the job and move on.'"

"Do you think the police need to know about this? Could he have . . . ?" *Murdered Pamela* went unspoken. Nell knew the thought had flitted in and out of Izzy's, Birdie's, and Cass' heads, too. But was it simply that they didn't like the man? Or did it have a more legitimate base? They knew that he had a temper— and that Pamela had squashed Troy's model ambitions . . . and his ego—quite soundly.

"I know Troy was here that day at some point. Kevin said he came by while we were meeting."

"What about Kevin?"

"I told him he could leave early because we weren't having a cocktail hour that day. Everyone was going to the Gull instead. Kevin said he'd be back later that night to do the breakfast preparations. And he did come back after he picked his mother up at the retirement home and dropped her off at home. But by then, the police had blocked off the drive and wouldn't let him in."

"Do you know what Troy meant about secrets?"

Mary's eyes locked into Nell's. "Everyone has secrets. You do. I do. Everyone. We keep them to ourselves, for better or worse—which is what makes them secrets. And revealing confidences won't help anything. It only hurts; trust me."

The subject was closed. Mary looked back at her laptop.

Nell didn't agree, but there wasn't any use in pursuing it, at least not right now. Sometimes revealing secrets was necessary, especially when it might reveal why a woman was found dead in a snowbank.

But for now, sleeping dogs would lie. And she would let them.

Nell looked down at the sleeping dog at Mary's feet. Loyalty and trust, she thought. And holding secrets. Just like her master. Sweet Georgia—the one creature who could solve this awful crime in a heartbeat, if only she could reveal what she'd witnessed on the porch that night. If only she could talk.

"I know you have things to do, Mary. I'll leave you in peace. But . . . you'll come to me if you need anything, all right?"

"Of course I will. You and Birdie, Nancy, Izzy, and Cass. All of you. I know you are there for me; I do."

"And I agree with you—Kevin is a good man. The police will realize that, too."

"Hopefully they will, yes. But in the meantime innuendo and gossip can so quickly ruin someone's life." Her eyes flashed and she straightened in the chair, her laptop sliding forward on her knees. "The future of Ravenswood-by-the-Sea is in jeopardy, too. And it will be until that person is found." She bit down on her bottom lip, her brows pulled tight, as if gathering all her strength to hold herself together.

As long as Nell had known Mary Pisano, she was always in control of her emotions. And she'd weathered some sizable storms, including her husband being lost at sea for three long weeks a few years ago. But in all those years, Nell had never seen Mary crumble.

Until today.

"I want my life back, Nell. I want it free of police and awful talk that's turning my grandfather's home into something ugly—and ruining the reputation of a fine young man in the process. Something needs to be done."

Nell leaned over and gave her a hug. When she stood back up, she felt the warmth of Mary's tears on her cheek. She walked slowly to the door.

"Now," Mary called out to her back. "It needs to be stopped. Now."

Chapter 15

*M*ary's words stayed with Nell as she moved through the morning. The repercussions of Pamela Pisano's murder were everywhere. Nell felt them while shopping at Shaw's, while attending the community center fund-raising meeting, and while walking beneath the canopy of crystal branches along Harbor Road.

She walked slowly, her eyes moving from one decorated window to the next. Windows sprayed with snowflakes, filled with pink and red poinsettias, garlands and green elves that looked out at her, oblivious of the lives unraveling around them.

Nell heard singing and looked down the street. A small circle of gray-haired ladies was gathered in the gazebo across from the historical museum, their voices lifting in holiday song and their breath white plumes against the cold blue sky. They were bundled in heavy coats with red and green knit caps pulled down on thinning hair. Nell recognized Moira Sullivan facing the group, directing the retirement-center chorus. She was smiling at the ladies, mouthing the words, her arms coaxing their voices—allegro, adagio. Crescendo.

It all looked so normal and lovely. She wondered whether Moira was aware of Kevin's problems. She hoped not—but suspected otherwise. She was probably worried sick about her son—in the agonizing way that mothers do. Praying away the nightmare of suspicion and rumor.

She turned away and pushed open the heavy glass door of McClucken's Hardware Store.

"Nell, my darlin', what can I do you for?" August Mc-Clucken, his thick arms lifting wide, stood behind the checkout counter.

The owner of the store looked like Santa Claus himself. His belly was full, his eyes twinkled, and his bushy white beard was carefully groomed in anticipation of playing the annual role he loved best—riding into the harbor on a lobster boat to hundreds of cheering children.

Santa Claus *would* come to town—Auggie McClucken would make sure of it.

"Printer paper and some cartridges, Auggie." Nell handed him the specifications and looked around the bustling store. "Hardware store" was definitely a misnomer, she thought. Space allotted for nails and screws vied with shelves crammed full of CD players, iPods, and GPS devices. On the opposite side of the store, shiny boat motors, paddles, and snowshoes were displayed in front of piles of rope and buoys.

Nell spotted Laura Danvers filling a shopping basket with Christmas ornaments. In the next aisle, Beatrice Scaglia examined two flat-screen televisions.

Nell walked over to Beatrice while Auggie filled her order.

"I think I know what Sal is getting for Christmas," she said, looking at the display of televisions.

Beatrice laughed. "We don't need a new television—who has time to watch those silly shows? But Troy insisted."

"Troy?"

"His farewell gift—along with a new laptop for me. It's for letting him stay with us, he said. The guy is full of surprises.

I didn't think he had two dimes to rub together, and here he's buying us TVs."

"Troy is leaving?"

Beatrice nodded. "He's making plans—'big' plans. But he agreed to finish up that painting at Mary's first, at my insistence. Mary has enough on her mind without her workers leaving her high and dry."

"Mary must be paying Troy well if he's buying computers and televisions."

"Seems so. We told him to hang on to his money, but he just laughed and said he had plenty of money, not to worry." She rummaged in her purse and pulled out a neatly clipped roll of bills. She held it up in the air. "Who knew? He gave this to me for the gifts and said he'd be insulted if I didn't take it. Do you think Auggie McClucken will take cash? Does *anyone* take cash?"

Nell stared at the roll of one-hundred-dollar bills.

Beatrice dropped the money back into her bag and looked up at the TVs, then lifted her palms in a "What's a woman to do?" gesture. She smiled at Nell. "So, which do you think Sal would like better, Nell—the forty-five-inch or the bigger one?"

Nell paid for her supplies and walked out into the sunshine, pulling her collar up against the wind.

For reasons that seemed as frozen as the tree branches, Nell found the tidbits of conversation in McClucken's uncomfortable. Mary Pisano was generous and was probably using some of her inheritance to pay the crew handsomely. But Troy had been on the job only a couple of weeks—certainly not long enough to afford such extravagant gifts.

And why would Mary pay him in cash? She'd be the last person on earth to try to shortchange the IRS.

It didn't make sense. Pamela had been a wealthy woman. Had she helped Troy out before she died? Nell frowned, her mind cluttered, filled with square puzzle pieces that should be round.

"Nell, you're going to get yourself killed if you don't look where you're going. One funeral this week is plenty."

Nell looked up and felt a pleasant rush erasing her troubling thoughts. "Father Northcutt, if you aren't a sight for sore eyes."

"Well, now, and I've heard worse said to me, Nellie. May I rescue you from this north wind?" Without waiting for an answer, the older man cupped her elbow in his wide glove and began walking her down the street, his gait slow and steady. "I find myself needing a cup of the Ocean Edge's French onion soup, the one with all that cheese covering the top. And there's nothing that goes better with it than a fine person like yourself." Father Larry brushed back a swatch of gray hair, ruffled by the wind, and quickened his pace.

Nell laughed as she mentally rearranged her afternoon schedule. It was a serious character flaw, she often told Ben—how quickly she could be lured away from a carefully planned schedule.

Ben said that on the contrary, it intrigued him. Charmed him, even—the fact that rarely was anyone allowed to impose on Nell Endicott's life. People were always welcomed into it and made to feel she'd been waiting just for them. No, Ben said firmly, it wasn't a flaw. It was simply Nell relishing the moment—something she did easily and graciously. That, and a firm belief that what needed to get done would certainly find its way to the surface in due time.

Either that, Ben said with a chuckle, or he'd end up doing it.

She hoped that was true, because if it wasn't, the Thursday night knitting group might be sorely disappointed at the dinner they got that evening.

.   .   .

All the tables at the Edge were filled, it seemed, until they saw a familiar hand waving at them from a booth at the back of the restaurant.

"I've been stood up," Ben said, slipping from the booth. "Jerry Thompson and I had just enough time for a beer before he was called away. Mind if I join you?"

"Join us at *your* table?" Father Jerry replied with a chuckle. "Getting two Endicotts for the price of one is a pleasure indeed."

They settled into the oversized booth, shielded from the others by tall padded seat backs. Along the wall, windows framed the harbor waters, providing a moving panorama as lobster boats moved in and out, weaving between the occasional sailboats.

Father Northcutt ordered soup for them, and Ben detailed his aborted meeting with the police chief. "Jerry mentioned the Pisano murder before being called away. The police are baffled. Pamela had her naysayers and folks who didn't like her, but real motive and connecting someone to the crime scene is still out of reach. With the holidays so close, he's anxious to wind it up, but he says it might be one of those cases that goes cold. It just doesn't make a lot of sense."

Father Northcutt was quiet, stirring several spoonfuls of sugar into his tea.

"You're unusually quiet, Father," Nell said.

His warm Irish smile did little to hide the worry in his eyes. "I think it'd be a shame if it went cold and left everyone pointing fingers at everyone else. And especially if, in the process, the Sullivan family was tainted in any way. Or Henrietta O'Neal for that matter. I hear people talking about her crazy antics as if they could point to murder. Ridiculous. There are fingers pointing all around, a sad way to approach this blessed season." Father Northcutt pulled his white bushy brows together.

"What do you think? Do you think it was someone local?"

The pastor paused before answering, creating a lull that

caused Ben and Nell to look at each other, wondering what thoughts were flitting across his priestly mind. Finally he spoke.

"I don't think a stranger killed Pamela Pisano. I think it was someone she knew, and someone we know. There's an urgency about this matter. I feel it when I meet people on the street, at the holiday parties, in restaurants. The longer this tainted energy pervades our town, the more chance of damage to those we care about." He took a drink of his tea. His eyes followed a tugboat chugging into the harbor. He looked back at Ben and Nell.

"I'm worried about what this burden is doing to Mary, that little sprite of a woman. Her column is lacking its usual charm and wit. And I'm concerned for dear Moira Sullivan and the long look on her face at daily Mass. And I could go on. The list of those affected by this is long—and you are both on it. We all are. And the longer the unknowns are allowed to absorb us, the nastier and uglier it all gets."

"That sounds like a rallying call, Father," Nell said.

"Perhaps it is, Nell. Perhaps it is."

Ben pushed his water glass aside as the waiter set down three soup crocks, steaming hot and smelling of sautéed onions, wine, and Gruyère cheese that melted down the outside of the bowls in finger-tempting rivulets.

"And may I offer you each a fine glass of Trollinger, compliments of one of our staff?" The waiter looked back over his shoulder, beyond the mahogany bar, to the kitchen doors in the distance.

Ben, Nell, and Father Larry followed his look.

Kevin Sullivan stood just outside the doors. He gave an acknowledging wave, a nod of his chef's toque, then disappeared back into the kitchen.

"I'd say you may," Ben said to the waiter and allowed a small amount to be poured into his glass for tasting.

"Well, sure as I'm sitting here, this proves my case," Father

Larry said after wine was poured all around. He swirled the liquid in his glass. "A common criminal would never recommend a Trollinger, now, would he?" He picked up his glass and examined the red wine, then looked at Nell and Ben across the rim, his eyes teasing. "Actually, a chap named Martin Luther was known to drink this particular variety, but I say we let bygones be bygones, all in the spirit of the season."

Nell and Ben laughed and held up their glasses.

"To friends."

"To bygones."

"And to reconciliation," Father Larry added solemnly.

Reconciliation.

Nell sipped her wine, playing with the priest's toast. A strange choice of words—but spoken with purpose. Was Father Northcutt trying to tell them something?

Reconciliation . . . The church's sacrament of forgiveness. Nell tucked the thought away and dipped her spoon into the sweetness of the Ocean Edge's winter specialty.

Father Northcutt and Ben had begun a heated discussion of the Pats' season and Super Bowl dreams, and Nell listened with half an ear, itemizing a grocery list for the knitters' Thursday night dinner in her mind.

She set her napkin down and looked around the crowded restaurant, nodding to several neighbors. She thought she glimpsed Kevin across the room and slipped out of the booth. The wine was a sweet gesture and deserved a personal thank-you.

Jeffrey, the Edge's bartender for at least thirty years, told her that Kevin had just left for the day. Headed to the bed-and-breakfast, he said. "He's the hardest-working guy around here, moving between two jobs as if the world would fall apart if he didn't." Jeffrey shook his thinning head of hair and leaned across the bar toward Nell. "And who knows? Maybe it would. But no matter what they're saying, Nell, he's a good boy."

There it was again, Nell thought. Even if people didn't believe it, it was like a fruit stain that you tried hard to erase, but a faint trace of it remained, even if just in the mind's eye.

A flash of bright yellow caught Nell's eye as she headed back to her table. A wall of towering poinsettias—red and white and a glorious pink—marked a more private section of the restaurant.

Agnes Pisano sat on the other side, alone at a table for two. She held a martini glass in one hand, and the other rested on the table. At least she thought it was Agnes. Nell slipped on her glasses. Her hair was different, cut shorter and highlighted with sweeps of blond woven through the dull brown. It hung loose about her shoulders. She wore a daffodil yellow dress, cut low with perfect stitching and fit. Nell recognized it as one she'd seen on the cover of *Fashion Monthly*. A designer dress, expensive and beautiful.

Nell had never seen Agnes' hair loose—it was always pulled back, snug and efficient, fastened tightly at the back of her head.

But it *was* Agnes, her cheeks flushed and her long face lifted in a smile. She was smiling at the air, it looked to Nell.

Nell lifted her hand in a wave, but Agnes didn't seem to notice, the wide red leaves of a holiday plant granting her privacy.

As Nell took a step closer, a shadow fell across the table, a chair pulled out. A tall man—dressed for the weather with a thick wool hat pulled down to his ears—sat down, his back to Nell. He leaned across the table in a familiar way and kissed Agnes lightly on the cheek. A chaste kiss, but one that seemed borne of familiarity—and one that sent a blush traveling up Agnes Pisano's neck. The man peeled off his gloves and set them on the table. A gold bracelet dangled from his wrist.

Nell hurried on to her own table, knowing instinctively that her presence would disturb Agnes' moment. She slid into the booth, her view of the table now blocked by waiters and plants and a large Christmas tree in the center of the restaurant.

It wasn't until Ben had paid the bill and Nell followed the two men through the restaurant that Nell had a chance to look over at Agnes once more.

The blush was still in place, the smile and daffodil dress stripping years off Agnes' life.

Across from her, his paint-stained hands flat on the table, Troy DeLuca smiled back.

Chapter 16

Sam was gone again.

"Boston, he said," Izzy explained.

"Well, that's not unusual. Everyone goes to Boston. There are a million things that would take Sam to Boston, including his job, Izzy."

Izzy scooped up a handful of stray knitting needles and dropped them into a basket on the table. Several skeins of red cashmere yarn were piled in another basket alongside a finished cashmere sweater, tiny and perfect, designed for a newborn. Izzy absently picked up the sweater, pressing its softness to her cheek.

Then she sat down and looked up at her aunt. "Sure, I know there are reasons for him to drive into Boston. I just don't know what they are, and I used to, because he used to tell me what he was doing. Sam doesn't say much these days, Aunt Nell. He's . . . he's like a swing, back and forth. He goes from being distant, to hugging me close as if I'm the only person in his world. Here one day, gone the next. I don't like it. I want my old Sam back."

Nell set her oval baking dish on a hot pad and sat down next to Izzy. She held her silence, not an easy task. Izzy was overreacting; at least that was what she hoped. But no matter; her sadness was real. Sam was quieter than usual these past days, true. But maybe both she and Izzy read too much into quiet spells. Quiet could be good.

"I don't know what's going on in his head. And he doesn't seem to want to tell me." Izzy traced the tiny roses crocheted onto the baby sweater, her eyes not meeting Nell's.

"Will he be back tonight?"

"No. Tomorrow. He's probably meeting with a gallery owner, someone who wants to exhibit his photographs; you're right. So why am I worried? Am I going crazy? We've always respected each other's need for space. But that space is widening. Some days I feel like I'm going to fall headfirst into the chasm. I'll reach out for him, and he won't be there. Or maybe it's me that won't be there."

Izzy's brown eyes begged Nell for an answer to the unspoken question.

Nell wrapped her in a hug. "Sometimes the closer you get to someone, the more difficult it is to understand their thoughts. But you and Sam have a foundation, Izzy. A history. It will carry you through this, whatever it is."

The jingling of bells on the front door announced Birdie's and Cass' arrival. Birdie held a bottle of Cabernet in her hands. Her cheeks were pink with cold. She unwound a wavy orange scarf from around her neck and slipped out of her coat. "I predict snow next week. I can feel it. We need a fresh dusting to cover up the gray."

"Yes," Izzy agreed. "Too much gray around here. Maybe it'll bring a little holiday spirit with it."

"I'm not sure it will do that, but it certainly will make things prettier." Birdie walked over and gave Izzy a quick hug. "That other thing will have to come from in here, dear Izzy," she said softly, patting her heart. "But it will. Mark my words."

Cass dropped a bag of sourdough rolls on the table. "Fresh

from Harry's oven. He added a small antipasto platter for good measure. Amazing what power a plaintive look has over that man."

"He's a teddy bear," Izzy said, shaking off her mood and getting up to help Birdie with her coat.

"How did he know we were having pasta tonight?"

"He's a mind reader." Cass slipped out of her jacket and hung it on a coat tree near the alley door, then headed toward Nell's casserole.

She lifted the glass top off the casserole dish, releasing the aroma of sautéed onions and garlic, butter and wine and sweet cream.

"Roasted veggies. Shrimp. Pine nuts. I'm in heaven," Cass said. She lifted a soup plate from the stack Izzy had set out and filled it with linguini, then ladled the vegetables, shrimp, and sauce on top and handed it to Birdie. Three more bowls followed, along with the still-warm sourdough rolls and sweet butter.

Nell carried Harry's antipasto platter over to the coffee table, and in minutes they were gathered around the fire, a ritual woven as tightly into their lives as their hats and sweaters and knit squares.

"To friends," Birdie said, lifting her wineglass.

"To the return of a peaceful season," Nell added.

Heads nodded—the small white cap that was Birdie's, Cass' mass of thick black hair, Izzy's multicolored tangle of waves.

Their nods held a promise.

The peace of the season would return, and quickly.

No matter what it took.

Izzy stoked the coals to life and put on a holiday CD, then sat down beside Birdie on the couch.

Once a few spoonfuls of linguini had taken the edge off appetites, Nell plunged in, the day's events weighing heavily on her mind. "We've all got a pile of things on our plates right now, but we need to help Mary out of this mess. It's suffocating her, and robbing the whole town of something that is uniquely ours. But especially Mary."

"And Kevin. And his mother. And the list goes on," Birdie said.

"That's what Father Larry said. It's like dominos. As awful as it is for her family, Pamela Pisano's murder is stealing something from all of us, and we won't get it back until her murderer is found."

"The merchants are trying to ignore it by playing their Christmas music louder, putting up more decorations, as if it will go away on its own if we just crowd it out of our lives," Izzy said.

"It's the elephant in the room." Birdie picked Purl up from the rug and put her on her lap. She scratched the cat's head thoughtfully. "So, ladies, that's the situation. What do we do about it?"

Cass coaxed a strand of linguini back into her mouth. In minutes, her heaping helping of linguini and shrimp had been reduced to a small puddle of wine sauce in the bottom of the bowl. "We talk about the painter for starters," she said. "There's something about that blond bomber that doesn't sit right. And he bothers you, too, Nell; I see it in your eyes."

Before Nell could reply, Cass went on. "Harry Garozzo isn't exactly a gossip, but when I picked up the rolls today, he managed to lean over the counter and whisper in my ear. He wanted me to check out the corner table. And sure enough, Troy DeLuca was sitting there, as big as life, showing off some fancy duds and making out—Harry's words—with the new weatherperson the station just hired. Harry said the guy pulled out a wad of bills that would choke a whale to impress his companion."

Birdie used a piece of roll to soak up the last bit of sauce. She chewed it thoughtfully. "Are the police looking at him? Is he a suspect?"

"Ben said the police have talked to Troy." Nell pulled her nearly finished blanket from her bag, settling it across her knees. Folds of blue, gold, and green circles fell to the floor in a brilliant puddle. "Troy is showy, so he's a natural suspect, I suppose. But according to Jerry Thompson . . . " Nell paused.

"'According to Jerry Thompson' . . . what?" Cass asked.

Nell held back. She was fine repeating things Ben told her that would make it into the paper in a day or so, but she wasn't sure this was one of them.

"You know we won't push you, Nell, if this is something Ben told you in confidence," Birdie said.

"But if it will help shed light on why they're talking to Kevin, I would like a chance to refute it," Cass said. "We're only trying to help, and you know this room is safe. Things stay here."

Nell nodded. Cass was right. It might not be public knowledge, but it might help bring them closer to figuring out the mess Mary was finding herself in. "Apparently the police have found no useful footprints, no fingerprints on the gun, nothing. The only thing the police have found so far that links anyone to Pamela's murder is her wallet, stuffed with money, found in Kevin's locker."

The room was silent.

Finally Cass set her wineglass down on the table, sloshing a few drops over the rim. "Well, that's ridiculous," she said.

"Okay, why?" Izzy said. "I'll play devil's advocate here."

"Why? Because Kevin couldn't have done it; that's why. What possible reason would he have? She came on to him; he pushed her away. Pamela may have had reasons to kill Kevin for rejecting her, but not the other way around."

Izzy picked up a skein of soft red cashmere and wound her

fingers through the soft loops of yarn. She folded her legs up beneath her and nibbled on her bottom lip. "Troy mentioned that Kevin knew something."

"Or had a secret," Nell said. "I think Kevin is wonderful, but regardless of how the wallet got in his locker, I think he's holding something back. Mary, too."

They nodded.

"Okay, so we don't think Kevin did it, but he's still a suspect until we have factual reasons for him not to be," Birdie said, emphasizing the word "factual" and attempting to apply order to their musings. She leaned forward and picked up the bottle of wine. "If we keep our eyes and ears open, we should be able to clear him quickly. His mother is suffering from all this, and that's not right."

"Kevin didn't deny it when Troy accused him of having a secret," Izzy said.

"A secret Troy knew about," Birdie mused.

"That's what it sounded like," Nell said, thinking back to the overheard conversation in Mary's kitchen. "Now, why would Troy know a secret of Kevin's—one Mary wouldn't tell us about?"

"I think we need to find that out," Birdie said.

"Do we know any more about Troy?" Izzy asked.

"He's ambitious—and a little full of himself. And he has motive." Nell repeated the story Rebecca Early had told them at the cookie exchange. Pamela's cold words were not taken lightly, according to Rebecca. "Troy was furious. And he has a temper—he smashed a photographer's camera when he lost a job in Boston. Pamela not only insulted what seems to be dearest to him—his looks—but she rejected him for her magazine, suggested others would do the same, and then laughed about it. He must have hated her for that."

"That must have been awful for him," Birdie said. "His profession jerked right out from underneath him."

"Not to mention his self-image. So Troy DeLuca is on the list," Izzy said. She wrinkled her forehead. "So why is it so clear to us, but not to the police?"

They all laughed.

"They deal with concrete facts, not feelings. And protocols. Their mistake, clearly." Cass pulled a bright green square for the KasCare project out of her bag and began working a row, her fingers moving quickly as her excitement grew. "That's one of the things that's so great about us." Her dark eyes flashed. "We don't have to follow the rules."

"Feelings and instinct matter," Izzy said, a tiny cherry-colored hat taking shape beneath her quick fingers. She smoothed out the yarn.

"Who is that for?" Nell asked, reaching over and touching the fluffy piece.

"Maybe Liz Santos' baby? I'm not sure," Izzy said. She looked at the hat again and smiled.

Nell watched a play of emotion flit across Izzy's face. She was imagining the sweet hat on a baby's head, the flaps covering pink ears and tied with the softest of yarns beneath a plump chin. Something moved inside Nell, a twinge, a memory of her own yearning. It hadn't worked out for Ben and her to have children, but it would for Izzy. Somehow she knew deep down inside her that Izzy would be an amazing mother someday.

"We're being too scattered about this," Birdie said, scolding everyone to attention. "Let's concentrate again on Troy DeLuca, just for a minute. He had motive, we've decided."

"And he has suddenly come into some money, it seems." Nell told them about the gifts Troy was buying for the Scaglias. "Beatrice was surprised at how quickly he'd managed to become solvent."

"That's odd," Birdie said. "Mary is paying him fairly, but not extravagantly."

"And there's another thing." Nell told them about seeing Troy in the Edge with Agnes Pisano. "They were friendly," she said.

"Agnes?" Cass' and Izzy's voices collided.

"Dining with two women in one day. Troy seems to be on a roll," Birdie said.

"What if Troy knew Agnes was next in line? He was working at the bed-and-breakfast during the family meeting days—he could have heard something to that effect," Izzy said.

"Agnes seemed comfortable with him," Nell said. "His chances of charming her into a modeling job are certainly better than they were with Pamela."

"Which brings us to Agnes. Shouldn't she be a suspect? She benefited—maybe more than anyone—from Pamela's death. Pamela's death gave her a job she'd wanted for years." Birdie took a sip of wine.

They fell silent, jarred by the thought of one cousin murdering another—for a job. But Agnes Pisano had changed almost overnight from a quiet, plain woman to an assertive, take-charge editor, and assumed the outer trappings to match the position. The caterpillar just waiting in the wings to fly into a glamorous new life.

"Agnes. Troy," Birdie said, as if scribbling them on an unseen dry-erase board.

"And Kevin," Izzy said reluctantly.

"Kevin," Birdie repeated.

"What about Henrietta O'Neal?" Izzy asked. "An unlikely suspect, true, but who knows?"

"She's causing a minor revolt over on Ravenswood Road, all intended to bring the bed-and-breakfast's opening to a dead end," Birdie said.

"And she's using Pamela's death as a reason that it be closed, insisting there is an evil spell around the house."

"Which is silly. Henrietta doesn't believe what she's saying." Nell thought about the woman, a generous, loving neighbor one minute, a destructive crusader the next. It didn't make sense.

"I suppose her name should be up there, as silly as it is," Birdie said.

"What else do we know?" Nell asked. "No fingerprints, for one. And Pamela must have known the person."

Cass smoothed out her finished eight-inch square, a bright green block with flecks of gold scattered throughout. Irish gold, Cass had called it, and decided she'd add more squares to make a boxy sweater for a teenager, a pattern she'd found on the Kas Web site. She was on a roll, she'd said. She set the square aside. "Why do you think she knew the person?"

"Because there was no sign of a struggle. Birdie and I could see that. The scene was almost gentle—like a child falling into the snow, looking up at the sky. Neat letters printed in the snow, no skirmish. Nothing."

"Except for Pamela's cigarette butts."

"I wonder if she was waiting for someone. There was a pile of them. Was the other person a smoker, too? Could they have been sharing a smoke, and then she was killed?"

The encounter between Troy DeLuca and Kevin in the kitchen replayed itself. Kevin, Mary's watchdog, sending Troy outside to smoke. "Troy DeLuca smokes," Nell said.

She thought again about the night Pamela was killed. Standing in the dark, seeing a curtain moving in the carriage house.

"I could have been seeing things," she said, describing what she thought she'd seen that night. "When we looked a second time, it was still. But could the murderer have gone to the carriage house, maybe looking for . . . "

Her words dropped off. Looking for what? The police hadn't noticed things missing. Except for her wallet. The one found in Kevin's locker.

Silence hung heavy in the room as needles clicked.

"What about the words in the snow?" Izzy said, looking up from the hat. " 'I'm sorry.' That's what the paper said. . . . "

Nell and Birdie nodded. The words printed in a bright crust of frozen snow, straight and neat.

"So what does that mean?" Cass pulled her hair back and pulled a band from her wrist around it.

"The murderer meant it to seem like a suicide note," Birdie said. "At least that's how it appears."

"But what an odd choice of words—'I'm sorry.' "

"I thought so, too," Nell said. "For Pamela, anyway. Mary said Pamela has never said she was sorry about anything her entire life. She certainly wouldn't do it before dying. If the murderer meant it to sound like Pamela, he—"

"Or she," Cass said quickly.

"Or she," Nell continued, "failed. I wonder if the words could be a clue. Could they mean something else? Could the murderer have *wanted* Pamela to be sorry for something?"

"Like sorry for calling him washed-up and basically ending his career?" Cass swallowed the last bit of wine and set her glass down.

"We're stacking the deck against Troy," Birdie said to Cass, waving a bamboo needle her way. "We need to step back, be objective."

Nell traced one of the squares in her throw, finding an odd comfort in the Persian blue yarn. It was flecked with gold, and a contrast to the more muted oatmeal squares and the rich emerald green and plum-colored blocks. Nell's blanket was to soften the end of Enzo Pisano's ancestral bed, Mary had told her. And Nancy had dictated the rich, bold colors. Manly colors, she'd suggested, and Mary had added, "But with a touch of romance."

Grandfather Enzo had loved to love.

A skein of warm gold yarn sat in her lap, a defining rope

around the squares, a touch of sunshine. Nancy hadn't suggested it—it had simply appeared, as those things sometimes did. A soft circle of sunlight.

She looked up to see Izzy carrying plates of warm apple cobbler to the table. A dollop of ice cream floated on top, dripping down the cinnamony sides of each dessert.

"You're right, Birdie," she said, setting them down on the table. "We need to be objective, but that doesn't eliminate Troy."

"No. But focusing too much on him could keep us from seeing something right in front of us."

"That old elephant in the room is back again," Cass said.

Nell chuckled. She attached a strand of golden yarn. "Talking to Mary and Nancy again might help us. Maybe some little thing they saw last week that didn't matter then might matter now."

"Mary's been so protective of Kevin," Izzy said. "I wonder why. I think he's slightly uncomfortable with it."

"Mary mothers. She's always been like that. I think with Ed gone so much of the time, she finds some comfort in it. Take Georgia, for example. And she follows a long line of strays that Mary has taken in."

Cass looked at Birdie, her brows lifted. "So Kevin Sullivan is a stray?"

"Of course not," Birdie said, glaring back. "You are twisting my meaning, Catherine Mary."

Cass laughed. She gave Birdie a peck on the cheek and helped herself to another scoop of apple cobbler.

"Mothering or not, Mary seems to think she has to shield Kevin from something. I wonder if we can delicately pull it out of her," Nell said. "Just like this knot in my yarn."

Izzy took Nell's needles away from her and expertly picked the knot apart. She handed it back. "Or him?" she suggested. "Why not talk to Kevin?"

"Good idea," Nell said. "It would be easier to get Kevin Sullivan to talk to us than to convince Mary to betray his confidence." It might be an awkward conversation, true, but a small price to play if it led to a murderer among them.

If it led the way to normalcy. To peace.

Pax. An image of the kindly Irish priest bending at the waist, his palms pressed together as he faced his parishioners. *Peace be with you.*

Yes, she thought with a curious certainty and a lightening of her heart. They would find it and bring it back in abundance, all those things buried in the muddle of murder. *Peace. Joy. Love.*

Chapter 17

$\mathcal{I}$t was late when the knitters finally put their plan in place, switched off the lights in the back room, turned on Izzy's alarm, and headed out the door. The shops along Harbor Road were closed, and all but the restaurants and bars were dark, save for small security lights and the dangling white lights of Christmas wound through the trees.

Izzy and Cass were off to a holiday party at Gracie Santos' Lazy Lobster and Soup Café—just old friends, Gracie had said— and urged them all to come. *Miniature lobster rolls . . . the best in town.*

Birdie looked tired, and Nell was her ride home. Her excuse, perhaps. As luring as the lobster rolls were, it had been a long day. Her mind felt fuzzy, filled with cotton candy. And buried in the folds of fluff were keys to a murder that she couldn't quite get her fingers on.

"My car is just down the street," Nell said, walking with Birdie passed the Brandleys' bookstore and Harry Garozzo's deli.

They waved to the delicatessen proprietor, his beefy form visible in the shadows of his darkening restaurant. He'd be back in the early hours of the morning, opening the kitchen to bake bread and breakfast pastries. Harry waved back, blowing them a kiss.

"Crazy man," Birdie said, shaking her head.

They looked into Harry's colorful window. It showcased his wife, Margaret's, talent for flowers and delectable surprises. Tonight it exploded with Christmas cactus, the tiny red buds ready to burst, and boughs of white pine, spruce, and variegated holly creating a holiday forest. Nestled among the branches were platters of imported cheeses, bottles of olives and mushrooms, and narrow vials of olive oil.

"I want one of each," Nell said. "Margaret is amazing." She nodded toward her car, parked across the street.

Birdie stepped from the curb, and Nell followed close behind.

Across the way, Tommy Porter, a young woman on his arm, emerged from the yellow door of the Gull tavern. He spotted Nell and Birdie and waved.

Before they could respond, a silvery Z spun around the corner, its wheels skirting the curve, heading directly toward the two women.

"Birdie!" Nell screamed, and pulled the older woman back against her body.

Birdie's boots slid out from under her, and she landed soundly at Nell's feet.

Tommy Porter was across the street in an instant, his jacket flapping in the breeze.

"I'm fine; I'm fine," Birdie said, dusting snow from her coat. "Don't fuss so."

"You could have been killed," Nell said, kneeling beside her and peering down the street.

The Nissan had pulled to a stop halfway down the block. The driver got out and looked down the street as the trio helped

Birdie to her feet and back up on the curb. A moment later, he drove on.

"Crazy fool," Tommy said, staring after the car.

"You sure you're okay, Miz Birdie?" A willowy woman, standing next to the young policeman, looked into Birdie's eyes. Enormous red earmuffs covered her ears.

"Fit as a fiddle," Birdie said, looking up and smiling brightly in recognition. "And you are looking mighty nice yourself, Janie Levin. Now, what are you doing here?"

Nell dusted off a concrete bench beneath a streetlight and insisted Birdie sit. "Just to catch your breath. You can catch up on Janie's life sitting down."

Tommy laughed. "Janie's with me. In fact, she's with me a lot, if you know what I mean."

Birdie looked from one to the other. "Well, now, that's lovely. Are you still working at Delaney Construction, Janie?"

"Nope. Tommy here convinced me that I should go to nursing school. What do you think of that?" She grinned. "And I almost had my first patient right here on Harbor Road, but I'm really glad I didn't."

"You'll be a fine nurse," Nell said.

"Yep, she'll be that," Tommy said proudly, and looped one arm around Janie's shoulders. He looked back down the street.

"Do you know who that was?" Janie asked, following his look. "I haven't seen a Z around here in, like, forever."

Tommy nodded. "It's a new one. Showed up yesterday. Troy DeLuca, showing off his manhood."

"That's Troy's car?" Nell asked.

"I saw him at city hall getting a temporary license plate. He's a character."

"And a terrible driver," Janie said.

"That, too."

"Tommy, did you happen to see Troy in Canary Cove that morning, the day that Pamela Pisano died? I was in the tea shop with her that day, and I noticed you through the window. . . . " *Staring at Pamela*, Nell thought, but she kept the words to herself.

"Yeah, I saw him. I was on duty, and we were patrolling around because Willow Adams noticed some weird papers plastered all over her gallery windows. Turns out Henrietta O'Neal had wallpapered Canary Cove with posters citing the evils of opening that bed-and-breakfast on Ravenswood Road. Troy was having a beer at the Palate—at nine in the morning. Flirting with Merry Jackson. Hubby Hank nearly killed him with dagger stares. So, yeah, I saw him."

"And you saw Pamela, too?" Nell wasn't sure why she was taking Tommy down this road. She could see that Birdie was beginning to shiver, but Tommy noticed, too, so he answered quickly and shifted his stance to protect Birdie from the wind.

"I thought I saw her through the tea-shop window, so I looked closer to be sure it was her; I'm not sure why. I didn't like the lady very much, though I suppose you shouldn't say that of the dead."

Nell noticed that Tommy's stuttering had all but disappeared. She wondered whether the young woman at his side had anything to do with it. "I suppose seeing her could open old wounds."

"You mean because she ditched my brother Eddie that summer?" Tommy laughed. "Yeah, that was a lame thing to do, leading him on while she had another guy on the side—but Eddie was okay about it. He was beginning to get the picture that Pamela would eventually dump him. I think she made it out like he was devastated—she liked to do things like that. She actually told people she was afraid he'd hurt himself. But that wasn't true. And he's sure better off. He's married to a real nice girl over in Gloucester. Even gave me my first nephew a month ago."

"That's great, Tommy. Congratulations."

"So Pamela was seeing another man that summer?" Birdie asked.

"An affair," Janie blurted out. "A torrid affair. At the same time that Eddie was spending his hard-earned money on her. Awful woman." She shook her head, and her ponytail slapped one shoulder, then the other. "Eddie's wife, Susie, is my cousin, and she told me all about it. The other guy really fell for Pamela—hard. Like, granite hard."

"What happened?"

Janie's cheeks blushed with the excitement of her story. "At first it was glamour plus. He gave her expensive presents. Flew her to fancy places. Susie's mom used to take care of Mrs. Pisano at the nursing home, and she heard stuff. The guy was totally in love with Pamela. He wanted her to run away with him." She rubbed her freezing hands together, and her skinny boot heels tapped on the sidewalk as she talked.

"Run away? That's dramatic."

"The guy was obsessed with her, I guess."

"Obsessed," Nell repeated the word, wondering exactly what Janie meant by it. Obsession could be an awful thing. A disease. Or it could be an exaggeration. "Was Pamela in love with him?"

Tommy shook his head. "Who knows? But she wasn't the kind that loves, I don't think. Eddie says Pamela got her kicks by playing with people, like little kids do with dolls. Getting them to do what you want. Then throwing them away when they no longer entertain. That's harsh, but Eddie says it was pretty accurate."

"It's a wonder the whole town wasn't talking about this."

"They were sneaky. Never knew who the guy was, but knew the sordid details," Janie went on, caught up in the drama. "The guy was rich, and that helps hide things, if you know what I mean." Jane's brows lifted straight up into her wispy bangs.

"She was here that whole summer, helping her mother. I guess it's how she handled boredom," Tommy said.

"What happened to the relationship?" Birdie pushed herself up from the bench and picked up her knitting bag.

Tommy shrugged, but Janie seemed to have an inside track. "When the guy started getting so possessive and demanding, Pamela cut her summer here short and headed back to New York to one of the magazine's offices to get away from him. Susie's mom says her leaving so suddenly upset her mom a lot."

"And the man?"

"He, well . . . " Tommy started.

"He went berserk," Janie blurted out. "Susie heard it on good authority. He was so nuts about her. He'd do anything to get her back. Anything. You know, like *Fatal Attraction*?"

Tommy frowned at Janie. He opened his mouth to speak, then closed it again.

"Could this man be a suspect, Tommy?" Nell asked. "He certainly had motive."

"No," Tommy said quickly. "Absolutely not."

His words were blunt and definitive.

At the surprised look on Nell's face, he quickly closed the subject, directing his concern to Birdie. "Miz Birdie, I think you need a hot toddy or something to warm those bones. It's wicked cold out here."

Janie immediately followed his example and turned her full attention to the small woman standing beside her. "Tommy's right—you need to get inside where it's warm." She touched Birdie's hand gently, as if to take her pulse, but instead looked into her eyes intently. "Do you know that if your tissue temperature drops below freezing, your sweet little blood vessels could be severely, even permanently, damaged?"

As he stood next to his girlfriend, Tommy Porter's chest puffed with pride.

Birdie held back a smile. "I didn't know that. Thank you, dear," she said.

They said their good-byes, and Birdie and Nell hurried across the street to Nell's car.

Tommy and Janie held vigil on the curb, making sure the two women reached the car safely—and without any veins freezing.

Nell and Birdie slipped out of the wind and into the comfort of the car. Nell coaxed the engine to life and turned the heat up high.

They sat in quiet for a minute, watching the young couple walk slowly down Harbor Road, arms looped around bulky jackets, Tommy's head inclined toward Janie's. Unaware of the cold or the world around them.

Nell and Birdie chuckled, their warm breath fogging the windshield.

Yes, Janie Levin would make a fine nurse, they agreed.

Birdie's sweet unfrozen veins were most certainly a harbinger of that.

Chapter 18

*N*ell sat across the kitchen island from Ben, watching him slather a thick slice of toast with raspberry jam. Her elbows rested on the butcher-block surface, her chin cupped in her hands. She resisted catching the dollop of jam that dripped onto the countertop.

Thick. Sticky.

It was how she felt. Even a long shower hadn't washed away the uncomfortable debris of her dreams. Instead, her thoughts glommed together, an amorphous mass that she couldn't pry apart into discernable thoughts. Thoughts with meaning attached—if only she could figure out what the meaning was.

"Snow's in the forecast for the weekend. Maybe tonight or tomorrow, they're saying." Ben looked over his reading glasses at Nell.

"Good. We need a fresh coat to pretty things up. It's awfully gray out there."

"I think it will take more than snow." Ben took a drink of coffee, his eyes lingering on Nell's face. "You moved a lot in your sleep. Like you were trying to get away from something."

"I suppose I could have been. I don't remember."

It took two more cups of coffee, but slowly and deliberately, Nell repeated the knitting night conversation, throwing in the episode with Tommy Porter at the end.

"Maybe you were running from the runaway Z. Crazy guy, to drive like that on a snowy road."

"We were fine. Tommy and Janie were very helpful."

"This Troy guy bothers me," Ben said when Nell finished talking.

"He bothers me, too." She got up and poured fresh granola into a bowl. Sharing the rough puzzle pieces with Ben was comforting. As if in the simple telling, the edges would become smooth.

"I think Troy and Pamela were having an affair. I keep thinking back to the night of the murder and the moving curtain in the carriage house. I think it was him."

"Why?"

Nell sighed. "I wish I knew why. I just think it."

Ben walked around the island and ran a finger up and down her back. "I don't discount your intuition, Nell. Never have."

Nell rubbed her head against his shoulder. "I know. That's why I married you."

"But if it was Troy behind the curtain, that means he knew Pamela was dead."

"Maybe. Although it was dark and one of the lights on the porch was burned out. He might not have seen her body from that window. Maybe he just saw us." But she didn't believe that, and she knew Ben didn't, either. If he was there, he saw.

"Or maybe he was the one who killed her, and then went up to the carriage house for whatever reason—maybe to get rid of evidence linking them together? And then saw you and Birdie out there."

"Lots of people knew those two were spending time together. Mary suspected it. Kevin knew. Lord knows who else—

probably the whole work crew. So I'm not sure why he'd care about getting rid of evidence that linked them together."

"And there's always the last 'maybe.' Maybe Troy was somewhere far away, like he told the police. He was at a movie out at the mall. Alone. Just wanted to get out of the Scaglias' house. Maybe the curtain never moved at all."

A perfectly reasonable thing to say. But the curtain did move. In hindsight, and for no good reason, Nell was sure of it.

Nell walked across Harbor Road, headed for the historical museum and a board meeting she had almost forgotten about. She walked quickly along the path and looked up just in time to see a small bustling figure with an armload of white paper tucked under her arm heading toward her.

A walking stick clicked along the shoveled sidewalk as she walked.

Tap. Tap. Tap.

Nell stared at it.

"Nell, sweetheart, what are you looking at?" Henrietta O'Neal stopped, cocked her round head, and stared at Nell. "You look like you've seen the ghost of Christmas past."

Nell shook away her thoughts and looked at the woman standing directly in front of her, shadowing the sidewalk with her stocky figure. "Henrietta, I'm sorry. That was rude of me. I was looking at your walking stick."

Henrietta lifted the stick into the icy air and smiled at the hand-carved piece of walnut. Her face glowed. "It was a gift. It's very lovely, isn't it?"

Nell nodded. It *was* lovely. Absolutely. Henrietta's gnarled fingers wrapped around the carved handle as if it had been molded just for them. Tiny lines of gold were pressed into the carved handle, spreading out like the wings of a butterfly, graceful and delicate. The cane itself was rubbed to a high sheen, the walnut velvety smooth, all the way down to the narrow bottom and the rubber tip adhered to the end. A work of art.

It was a perfect walking stick for helping someone remain steady on forested pathways and slippery, snowy sidewalks.

A suitable stick for tracing straight, neat letters in a snow-bank.

"Someday I might tell you the story of my walking stick, Nell. It's a wonderful story. But not today. Today I am busy."

Nell took a deep breath. "Busy?"

"I am taking the mayor to lunch to see if the yacht club's fa-mous chowder and a martini might coax some sense into him."

Nell glanced at the posters under Henrietta's arm. She knew what they said. She could easily guess, too, what favor Henrietta was going to force upon Mayor Hanson.

It was a difficult position to put Stan Hanson in, since Henri-etta's family foundation contributed to nearly every major civic cause. And it was very uncharacteristic of Henrietta to use her wealth to garner favors.

"Henrietta, Mary has enough on her plate, don't you think?"

"And I am trying to relieve her of some of that. A bed-and-breakfast, to be specific. Someday she will thank me."

With that, Henrietta made her way around Nell and pro-ceeded down the pathway to Harbor Road, her stick tapping out a defiant rhythm that startled Nell with its intensity.

She watched her for a minute, then crossed the street and walked up the museum steps.

"We're about ready to start," Laura Danvers said, meeting Nell at the door and nodding toward the small conference room. "It will be a quick meeting. Everyone's busy."

That was music to Nell's ears. She had plenty on her plate, not the least of which was to check on Izzy. She'd never call it that, of course. Izzy would cringe at the thought of someone checking up on her. She would remind Nell she had once been a part of a thriving law practice in Boston, had worked with her share of unsavory characters, had walked home alone at night. Why would she need someone checking up on her?

And she would hide matters of the heart behind her enormous brown eyes. *Off-limits*, her smile would say.

But in that silent language that she and her niece shared, it would be clear to Nell that Izzy was grateful to have her there, even at arm's length.

Nell was greeted by a festive table. At each place Laura had placed a tiny Christmas cactus and small wrapped package. Platters of Christmas cookies lined the table, and hot mulled cider simmered on a gas burner, filling the air with the scent of cinnamon and cloves.

"The present is to thank you for your hard work this year," the board chair said.

Oohs and aahs greeted the unwrapping of small silver replicas of a schooner, which celebrated its birthplace on Cape Ann.

Laura rapped on the table for attention and announced that the sterling-silver charms were Nancy Hughes' thoughtful and generous contribution.

Of course, Nell thought. Nancy, more than anyone, understood the hours volunteers put in to keep the museum operating. And Nancy would think to express thanks with an appropriate memento.

Cups of cider were passed around as people thanked Nancy for the gift, sampled Laura's wonderful cookies, and chatted about tree lightings and parties.

There was hope, Nell thought, listening to the chatter. Perhaps they'd find a way around Pamela Pisano's tragic death, even with the threads dangling loose and threatening. But as she watched people's faces and listened to the ebb and flow of the conversation, she heard it. Beneath the gaiety ran the tense underpinnings of fear. Sometimes what wasn't said screamed louder than actual words.

Sitting next to her, Harriet Brandley leaned over and touched her sleeve. "Nell, I was wondering, well, how is our dear Sam doing?" she asked.

"Sam?" Nell asked, surprised at the question. "Sam Perry?"

Harriet nodded, a look of concern on her face. Spending most of her waking hours in the Sea Harbor bookshop right next door to Izzy's knitting studio, Harriet kept up on everyone's lives—and her caring about them was always genuine.

"Sam's just fine, Harriet. Why do you ask?"

"Well, I just thought . . . well, no reason. Of course he's fine. Silly of me."

Nell tried to read the expression on her friend's face. Harriet wasn't a gossip. A breast cancer survivor, she knew the importance of others' concern. "Do you think there's something wrong?"

"No, of course not. Archie took me into Boston yesterday—to the hospital—for my checkup. And I saw Sam. He was probably visiting someone, that's all. It's the mother in me." She laughed lightly. "We sometimes find worry in places it doesn't belong."

Laura tapped her glass with a spoon, voices hushed, and heads turned in her direction.

Nell pushed Harriet's words to a corner of her mind. Harriet was right—it was easy to fabricate useless concern. She knew Sam had spent the night in Boston. And that was his business, not hers. Not even Izzy's, as Ben had so astutely pointed out. We all needed space.

Laura announced the agenda. "First, a little housekeeping. We need a painter to do some touch-ups here at the museum before the harsh weather destroys the wood. Someone very good, not too expensive, and willing to get up on a ladder in this weather. Any suggestions?"

"Beatrice Scaglia's houseguest is a painter," Nell said. "He's done a good job at the bed-and-breakfast—right, Nancy?" No matter what her feelings about Troy, there was no reason to keep him from working. "I think he's leaving soon—but he might be able to do it before he leaves."

Nancy Hughes' smile fell away. "No, I don't think we should use him here, Laura."

"But I thought . . . " Nell began.

Nancy continued, her head shaking with emphasis. "He wouldn't be the best choice. He can be sloppy—and we can't have that at the museum. We'll find someone better, Laura. I'll take care of it."

Nell frowned. Hadn't Mary said Troy was a good painter, and that's why they kept him on—in spite of his rudeness?

She wondered briefly whether Nancy was holding something back. Did she know more about Troy DeLuca than she was letting on? The museum was very special to her. Perhaps she wanted to protect it from Troy's antics.

She glanced at Nancy.

She was sitting still, listening to Laura as she moved on to the next item on the agenda, avoiding Nell's eyes.

But when the meeting came to a close, Nancy grabbed her coat and hurried after Nell, catching up with her at the door.

"He's not a good painter, Nell," she said in hushed tones, as if sharing a secret. "And I'm sure he's leaving soon. I don't think we'd want him here. You can understand that. I don't know what it is, but there are bad vibes around that fellow."

The next minute, Nancy was gone, down the steps and across the street to her car, leaving Nell standing alone at the door.

Nell had a list of things to do. It was Friday, and though Ben would be the one bundling up to grill the trout on the snowy deck—she had promised to stop by the market to pick up odds and ends. They never knew exactly who would show up for Friday night dinner—but Nell suspected there'd be a demand for Ben's martinis this week—it had been a rough one.

She also wanted to stop by the bed-and-breakfast. Although Nell had toured the first two floors, she had never seen the master bedroom suite on the third floor. Mary said the wooden bed was a masterpiece, and since that's where Nell's knit afghan, with its bold design and soft chunky yarn, would lay, she wanted to make sure it was perfect before finishing it up.

"Come see," Mary had urged.

Birdie called as Nell was walking toward her car.

Nell explained her errand, and that she wanted to check the room's colors.

"That's nonsense," Birdie had replied. "You simply want to snoop around that gorgeous house."

Birdie was right. She wanted to snoop.

In the next breath, Birdie volunteered to go along, just as Nell expected her to.

They passed Henrietta O'Neal as they drove into the driveway of Ravenswood-by-the-Sea. She was offering snacks to Georgia, who had come out to the edge of the property to meet her. She waved gaily at them as they drove by.

"I hope those kibbles aren't poison," Birdie said, frowning. "For the life of me, I don't know what's gotten into that woman. Some of the neighbors think she's a bit daft, but I think she's sharp as a tack. She knows exactly what she's doing."

"The problem is the rest of us don't know what she's doing." Nell told Birdie about her encounter with Henrietta earlier that day. "I've gotten used to the posters—I don't even see them anymore. It was Henrietta's walking stick that bothered me."

Birdie listened carefully.

"I've watched Henrietta walk along Ravenswood Road

with that walking stick in hand for so many years, I don't even see it anymore. You're thinking a walking stick could possibly print letters in snow? An interesting thought." She looked back out the window at the dog sitting happily at Henrietta's feet, the walking stick wedged beneath her arm as she tossed treats to her.

Nell nodded, reading her thoughts. "Yes, and Georgia likes Henrietta."

"And might easily have followed Henrietta out on the porch that night. She would have been comfortable being outside with her."

"Yes. But Henrietta O'Neal couldn't have killed Pamela Pisano. . . . " Nell struggled with the image. It refused to find a comfortable place in her head, regardless of the walking stick and Georgia's affection. "She'd have no real reason, for starters. If she thought murdering someone might prevent the B and B from opening, she would have killed Mary, not Pamela."

They looked back at the dog and the woman. Friends. Happily communicating at the end of the snowy drive. A woman determined to close down Mary's bed-and-breakfast, no matter what it took.

"It makes no sense," Nell said as they parked and walked up the steps.

The front door was unlocked, and Nell and Birdie walked into the soft crooning of Bing Crosby, still dreaming about a white Christmas. A tall secretary stood in the spacious front hall. It was new since their last visit, perhaps pulled from one of the bedrooms upstairs. A tiny bell sat on the top, next to a white poinsettia. All looked ready for the first guest to come in, tired and hungry and in need of a comfortable room and a hot toddy. Just across the hall, a fire danced in the fireplace and tiny lights blinked on the tall Frasier fir—the perfect place to rest after a journey.

"How absolutely lovely," Nell said. She tapped the bell.

Mary appeared as if by magic. "I suppose I need a better system to announce people's arrival—something that rings as they walk in the door. But for now, that old bell I found in the attic works just fine."

"It looks like you're expecting your first guest."

She sighed. "Not quite. It's my practice run—wishful thinking, maybe. If I put everything on hold until this mess is cleared up, I'll feel like I've given in. And that's something I refuse to do. So I'm moving ahead, getting things ready, making beds, plumping pillows."

She pointed to a small computer sitting on the secretary. "I even had the computer hooked up today. It's my concession to modernity. Nancy thought I should have a gold-edged book with a ribbon marking the page for guests to sign, but I thought, enough is enough, and bought the computer."

"Do you have any idea when you'll actually open?"

Mary shrugged. "I still don't know. We still have some paint touch-ups to do. Nancy is making sure that gets done before this storm hits. But that's not the big thing. The main thing is shaking free of the bad vibes about this house, squelching the rumors. And I don't think that will happen until Pamela's murderer is found."

"And if they don't find him?" Nell asked. Ben had told her that there'd been talk of that. The police had only feeble circumstantial evidence, such as Pamela's wallet among Kevin's things and an argument someone heard Pamela having with her cousin Agnes. The police didn't take Henrietta seriously, Ben had said, and even though the knitting group was coming up with its own list of possible suspects, a list based on intuition and feelings wouldn't carry much weight with the force. "Frankly," Ben had said, "there's a push to close the case. They feel sure it was a directed murder, not a random, drive-by killing. So it isn't as if other people are in danger. People don't want the intrusion of an investigation interfering in their holidays. They want it over."

"If they don't find the murderer, I don't know what will happen," Mary said. "That's not an option for me. This heavy black shroud has to disappear. Did I tell you my manager—that nice Halley Stanley—resigned before she even started? She was here for a week, learning how I wanted things handled, and then, all of a sudden, she up and left. I think Henrietta scared her off. In addition to everything else, I'm about to strangle that woman."

"Georgia seems to like her," Birdie offered.

"Yes, she loves Henrietta. I don't get it, but Henrietta is very kind to Georgia. She'd beat me with her walking stick if she had half a chance, but she couldn't be nicer to Georgia. But enough about my little neighborhood nemesis; let me show you the upstairs. It will keep me from feeling sorry for myself."

Mary led the way up the wide, winding staircase. Halfway up, an upholstered window seat invited guests to sit and look out the round window at the snowy pathways crisscrossing the back of the estate. Or to snuggle up with a book. On the second floor, Mary had turned several small sitting rooms into bathrooms so that each bedroom suite was complete in itself with a modern bath, wide beds, Egyptian cotton linens, and comfortable seating and balcony areas.

Birdie and Nell followed her from room to room, admiring familiar art, pottery, and paintings from Ham and Jane Brewster's studio, carved wooden fishermen and fiber art from Willow Adams' Fishtail Gallery. And imagining the Seaside Knitters' soft throws gracing each bed.

"You need to invite the whole town to your grand opening. Once people see what you've done, you'll be booked for years. I can't wait to put Izzy's parents up here the next time they come. Caroline will fall in love with the place."

"I hope so," Mary said, but her words were flat, without that split second of joy they'd seen in her eyes when they had walked through the front door earlier, just as her first guests would do.

They followed her back to the center staircase that continued up to the third level. "This is where Grandfather Enzo stayed, even after Grandmother died. Can you believe that he stayed on the third floor? He put in that chair lift"—she pointed to an electric chair fastened to the wall on one side of the stairs—"but never used it, as far as I know."

On the third floor, at the top of the stairs, love seats and a desk filled a cozy sitting area. On either side a carved double door opened into a bedroom.

"That room was Grandmother Helen's," Mary said, pointing to one side. "It's dainty and feminine, just like she was. They each liked privacy, but my grandfather was quick to tell me they'd meet on each other's turf when it pleased them—which was often, he'd say. Then I'd change the subject fast, not sure how far he'd go in detailing his love life."

She led them into the other room, an area as spacious as a small apartment. "And here's the royal boudoir."

Casement windows filled the far wall, a fireplace, leather chair, and bookcase another. But gracing the third wall was the pièce de résistance, the massive bed, carved from thick, dark walnut with fleur-de-lis gold plume finials. It was the largest bed Nell had ever seen.

"Amazing." She walked over to the elaborate headboard and ran her fingers over the carved swirls, loops, and intricate ropes.

"It makes you want to meet the artist."

"We know one of them," Mary said. She walked over and guided Nell's fingers to a spot just at the edge of the headboard, moving her fingers around a less polished carving.

"It's a heart," Nell said. She put on her glasses and looked more closely. Then she laughed. "Enzo Pisano was a romantic."

"An understatement," Mary said.

Birdie leaned in. She chuckled. In the center of the roughly carved heart, her fingers traced the letters. "E.P." and "H." "Enzo and Helen. And Helen's period is a tiny 'O.' Or maybe it's another heart, a heart within a heart. Fancy."

"As was she—fancy, I mean," Mary said. "Grandmother Helen knew antiques, and when I found this carving after Grandfather died, I was amazed that she'd let him carve in this gorgeous wood. She wouldn't let him sign Christmas cards—he was too sloppy."

"Love," Birdie said. "It allows many things."

"Grandfather brought this bed over from Italy for her. It's priceless. Nancy researched it for me—Italian Renaissance style, she said. We think the craftsman put it together right here in this room."

"This explains why Enzo didn't move down a flight or two as he got older," Birdie said. "How could you leave this amazing bed?"

"And you'd never get it down the stairs without dismantling it," Mary said.

Nell looked around at the rest of the room. A watercolor of the harbor hung over the fireplace, and framed photos of Enzo deep-sea fishing hung along a narrow stretch of wall.

She walked over to the window and looked out, then backed up quickly. "Oh, my." Nell took a deep breath.

"Are you all right?"

"A touch of vertigo. I forgot how high up we were. "

"It's the tall ceilings and the deep slope in the back. It's probably more like a fourth or fifth story." Mary pointed to a door near the windows. It opened to a balcony, just big enough for two chairs and a table. "It didn't bother Grandfather. He loved sitting out there."

"A martini deck," Birdie said. "Sonny insisted we have one off our bedroom."

"Did you ever have a martini on it?" Nell asked.

Birdie's white brows lifted playfully. "We had lots of things on it."

A loud noise from below the windows brought them all to the window. Kevin Sullivan, wearing heavy gloves, was dragging a ladder into the backyard.

"We need to paint the eaves before it snows again," Mary explained. "The paint has peeled away, and Nancy is afraid the wood will rot." She pointed toward the roof overhang along the back of the house.

"Someone's going to climb all the way up here?" Nell asked.

"Clearly not you, Nell," Mary teased.

"I'm a sensible sissy—who prefers keeping her feet on the ground."

Birdie watched Kevin lay the ladder alongside the back porch. "He's a hardworking fellow, isn't he?"

"The best," Mary said. "I need to catch him before he leaves. Are we through here?"

Reluctantly they left the grandeur of the Enzo Pisano suite, as it would be called, and followed Mary down a flight of back stairs that went all the way down to the kitchen. "There's coffee brewing," she said over her shoulder.

Kevin stood at the kitchen door on a black rubber mat, stomping the snow off his boots. "Coffee's still hot," he said.

Beneath the smile he looked older than he had just days ago. Or weary, perhaps. "You're not getting up there, are you, Kevin?" Nell asked.

Kevin shook his head. "I'm not much of a painter, I'm afraid." He looked over at Mary. "Nancy was having a fit about the painting. She was in a stew today but said Troy'll be here to finish the painting midafternoon. Who knows if he'll show? Rumor has it he had a wild night last night, but Nancy said he'd show or else."

"Which reminds me—where's that metal ladder the construction crew used?"

"The construction guys took it away. Too bad; this damn thing weighs a ton. But it should work."

She frowned. "Are you and Nancy getting along all right?"

Kevin laughed. "Don't you have enough on your mind without worrying if your staff gets along? Yah, we're fine. She's a hard worker. Sometimes a tough taskmaster and kinda rigid and bossy for my taste. That's okay, though. But DeLuca? Not so much."

Mary began pouring coffee while Kevin grabbed his car keys from the desk and pulled his hat back on.

"How's your mother?" Nell asked him. "I saw her group singing in the square the other day."

"She's fine, thanks. She loves all that, the Altar Society. Helping Father Northcutt with his projects. Directing those old ladies in song. It's pretty much her life. And keeps her away from my pa. Not a bad thing."

"She's a good woman."

They all understood the meaning behind Birdie's words. Stories of Kevin's rough, hard-drinking father had circulated for years. A nice man in the morning, a mean one when he hit the taverns at night. The contrast with his sweet wife and fine son was startling.

"So I'm outta here. Going to Boston for the night. But DeLuca has a key if he needs anything. The fire's out in the fireplace, and I checked all the doors. I'm working at the Edge Saturday night, but Nancy says the carriage house is move-in ready if you say it's okay—maybe Sunday?"

"Absolutely," Mary waved him out the door. "Go. Have fun."

His tall shadow moved passed the kitchen windows as he headed down the steps to the parking area. A familiar path. The snow was entirely cleared away now, the porch so clean it didn't seem to belong to the rest of the snowy landscape. No snow. No blood. No reminders, except the images imprinted in their memories.

Nell shivered, wrapping her fingers tight around the coffee mug. "Mary, the person who did this—do you think they walked around the house to get to the porch or came through the backyard? The garage?"

"None of the above. The police said unless the person had wings, there was no way he or she came from the far backyard without leaving prints. The only steps around the side of the house since it was shoveled earlier that day were yours. Pamela would have gone out the den door—that's the one guests use. But I think the person who killed her went right out this door. The kitchen door. And that's how Georgia got outside."

"Couldn't Georgia have gone out with Pamela?"

"No. Pamela didn't like Georgia, and the feeling was quite mutual. I think that's one of the reasons my grandfather couldn't quite warm up to Pamela. Georgia was his love. Pamela would have had to offer the sweet thing a steak to lure her outside, and I'm not sure even that would have done it."

They looked through the windows, challenging the porch to tell them something, to relinquish its secrets. At that moment, Georgia bounded up the steps and to the kitchen door, her large paw knocking to get in.

Mary let her in, and she made the rounds, insisting on head scratches from each of them before settling down in her bed beneath Kevin's desk.

"I've gone over that day a million times," Mary said. "The police think it happened about six thirty that evening. Usually at that time of day there would still have been people milling around, my family, the workmen, deliveries. But the family had agreed to meet at the Gull to unwind. The construction guys finished early that day. And I left to pick up some candles Nancy wanted for the dining room, and then on to meet her for a dinner meeting. I left Georgia here because I knew I was coming back that night to meet the two of you."

"And Pamela?"

"She never intended to go to the Gull. Her excuse was vague, but we all figured she was meeting someone, probably in the carriage house. Troy, maybe? He came around looking for her, and they talked during a break, maybe making plans."

"For that night?"

"Apparently. Troy told the police she had blown him off. Who knows if that's true or not."

"Was there anyone else she was seeing while she was here?"

"You mean a man?"

Nell nodded. "Tommy Porter said she was involved with some man a few summers ago—in addition to his brother Eddie."

Mary nodded. "It was a few years ago, the summer she moved Aunt Dolores into the nursing home. I remember because she was here most of the summer, taking care of the house and Aunt Dolores' things. The thing with Eddie Porter was unfortunate—the way they were all over town together. Agnes and I knew it was doomed, that Pamela was just bored. But you don't tell a guy that."

"What about this other man?"

"I had forgotten about that until you mentioned it. But yes, there *was* someone else. Pamela wasn't usually secretive, but she was this time, never mentioning who the guy was. I think he was the reason she tossed Eddie aside. She talked about jewelry, clothes—kind of expensive gifts, so the guy had money. One weekend she asked Agnes and me to check on Aunt Dolores because she was flying off to Maine or somewhere. And then he started calling her. It was intense, almost scary. One night we were having dinner with Grandfather, and Pamela was in the hall, screaming over the phone, telling him to leave her alone or she'd call the police. She seemed genuinely worried. And she went back to New York a couple weeks earlier than planned just to get away from him."

"Who was he?"

"She never said. She showed off the expensive gifts—but that was it."

"Do you think that whoever it was carried a grudge?"

"And killed her?" Mary said, her brows lifting.

"It's possible."

Mary thought for a minute, giving the idea time to percolate. "I don't think she got any strange phone calls these past days, at least none I knew about. And she's been in Sea Harbor often the past couple years, so it seems odd that whoever this guy is would pop up all of a sudden. Nancy or I would have known if anyone strange had been hanging around here, and Pamela stayed here the whole time. But back then, she was spooked; I remember that. He wouldn't let go of her. Frankly, the way she treated men, we were a little surprised it hadn't happened sooner."

"Tommy Porter seemed sure this guy didn't do it, but he didn't explain why."

"If Pamela threatened to call the police, maybe Tommy had an inside track," Birdie said. "He's a policeman—he wouldn't rule out a suspect in a murder case lightly."

Nell nodded. Birdie was right. But right or wrong, it didn't take away the niggling feeling that refused to budge. Tommy might be right. But it was like an out-of-place stitch in a perfectly worked cashmere sweater—one that refused to give up its hold until it was fixed.

Birdie looked outside again. "So Pamela was the only one left here that night?"

"I think so. She was out there smoking when I left."

"There was a pile of cigarette butts on the porch," Birdie said.

Mary nodded. "They were wet from the snow, so the lab couldn't get other prints, if there were any."

"The silence of snow," Nell murmured.

"Mary," Birdie said, her brow pulled tight. "This thing between Kevin and Troy—what was that about? Did it have anything to do with Pamela?"

"They just didn't like each other, that's all. Two very different personalities with next to nothing in common. Pamela had come on to both of them; I suppose they had *that* in common. And both of them ended up disliking her. But that was it. No story there."

The ringing of Mary's phone ended the conversation.

Birdie thought Mary seemed relieved.

"If the phone hadn't rung," Birdie said to Nell on the way home, "she would have figured out another way to end the conversation. Once we started talking about Kevin, she was ready to move on."

Nell agreed. There was definitely something about Troy DeLuca and Kevin Sullivan that Mary didn't want to talk about.

It hadn't been the time to convince Mary it might be useful information, but the weary look in her eyes told Nell that the right time might be just around the corner.

Chapter 19

*P*eople wandered over to the Endicotts' home earlier than usual Friday night, bringing in the cold, damp air with them. Izzy—with Sam on her arm—was the first to arrive.

Izzy seemed happy, but guardedly so.

Nell hugged them both.

"How's Boston, Sam?"

"Sin city, Nell," he said. "Stay away."

He had good color, Nell thought. A smile. And he hadn't lost any weight that she could tell. Sam Perry was healthy.

She looked around Sam's broad shoulders to Ben, standing over a tray of trout at the kitchen island, watching his wife.

He looked over the rim of his reading glasses. His eyes said, *See, Nellie?*

Earlier, when she'd told him about Harriet Brandley seeing Sam in Boston, Ben had bristled slightly, an unusual reaction from her calm, even-tempered mate. "His business," he'd said. "Not ours. Not even Izzy's, unless Sam makes it so."

Those were Nell's thoughts, too, of course. But seeing them together was the real salve she needed to soothe her mind.

Danny Brandley came in next, carrying a platter of miniature lobster rolls.

"Did you make those?" Izzy asked, her brows lifting. "I know Cass didn't."

"You're right, she didn't, and yes, I did. Ben inspires me. But I'm a failure at catching lobsters. So Cass catches, I cook 'em."

"A match made in lobster heaven," Nell said, putting the platter on the island.

Danny laughed. "Or hell, depending on your take."

Cass followed close behind, her cheeks wind chapped and her strong arms and body nearly buried in a thick green fisherman's sweater Izzy had made for her. She carried two bottles of wine. "I don't think I will ever be warm again," she said. "It was so cold on the water this morning."

She walked over and pulled one of Danny's arms around her shoulders.

"Brazen hussy," he said, and pulled her close. "Is that all I'm good for?"

Cass lifted her dark brows and shrugged. "You tell me, mystery man."

Danny Brandley had moved back to Sea Harbor to write a mystery novel. But rather than turn into a writing recluse, he'd succumbed nicely to Cass' advances and had effortlessly become a part of all their lives. Mary Halloran was thrilled with her daughter's interest in Danny and had exchanged her pleading prayer novenas at Our Lady of the Seas to ones of thanksgiving.

Cass pulled free to give Nell a hug. "Where's Birdie?"

"Harold is driving her over. He doesn't have enough work to keep him busy, and driving Birdie's monstrous Lincoln around town seems to fill a need." Nell wasn't quite sure what Birdie's gardener did these days, even in the summer, but he and his Ella had lived in the cozy carriage house over the Favazza garage for so long, they were a part of the family. They would have a home there forever—Birdie made that abundantly clear.

Jane and Ham Brewster came in, followed closely by the

Wootens. Don Wooten carried two cherry pies and a container of rum ice cream.

Rachel and Jane headed for the fireplace, rubbing the life back into their hands. Nell followed with a tray of martinis. "Ben's cold remedy," she said, handing one to each of them.

Jane fingered a hand-carved angel tucked into the pine branches on top of the mantel. She breathed in the smell of Christmas. "Any news on the Pisano case?"

Rachel sighed. "Poor Mary. Not only is she dealing with the police and a murder, she has Henrietta O'Neal on her hands. She just won't give up. She's at my office door nearly every day." As a lawyer for the city, Rachel was in the middle of everything from property squabbles to new development.

"She plastered our galleries with posters a few days ago before we got to work. She's on a mission," Jane said.

"In an odd way, she's a welcome distraction," Rachel said. "Her antics are far more benign than searching for a murderer."

Cass wedged her way into the group with a small plate of lobster rolls. "Speaking of murderers, tell me what you make of this: Danny and I went to the Ocean's Edge last night for a late drink in a quiet place. But it was not to be. There sat Troy De-Luca, holding court and peeling dollar bills off a huge wad. He was treating everyone, even us. He said it was his swan song, that he was leaving Sea Harbor—tomorrow, I think he said."

Nell felt it again—that mixture of relief and dismay at Troy's leaving. Relief that the unpleasant man wouldn't be around. But were they letting a murderer get away?

"Apparently Troy has plans," Jane said. "Agnes Pisano came in the gallery yesterday to buy some art for an apartment she's leased in New York while she gets the magazine under control. She mentioned that she was having Troy do a photo shoot in *Fashion Monthly*."

"So she's really going to hire Troy?" Cass grimaced.

"I think she's sorry for the way Pamela treated him."

"Which might have been reason to kill her," Rachel said quietly. "I'm surprised Agnes isn't more tuned in to that. Pamela was her cousin, after all. If there was any indication at all that Troy'd been there that night, I think he'd be sitting in jail, not entertaining people in a bar."

There. Rachel had put it out there. A thought they were all toying with.

"And if he didn't do it," Nell said, "I can't shake the feeling that he's somehow connected to it." And if Troy disappeared, would they ever find out the truth?

"Agnes has benefited from her cousin's death," Jane said. "She probably doesn't want to rock the boat. I think she's keeping herself as far away from the investigation as possible."

They all stood sipping their drinks in silence, pondering the unimaginable—that anyone they knew, anyone they saw every day, an acquaintance, a relative, could possibly have put a gun to Pamela Pisano's head.

"Where do you suppose Troy got the cash?" Cass asked, breaking the silence. "Could he have taken it from Pamela?"

"He couldn't have stolen enough to make a down payment on that silver Z he's been riding around town. Unless—"

Unless what?

No one had an answer. Troy had gotten money from somewhere, and they all knew it wasn't from painting Mary Pisano's bed-and-breakfast.

Ben's booming voice from the kitchen announced that grilled trout was waiting.

"Food!" Cass said with an exuberance that broke the group into laughter, shifting the mood in an instant. They filed into the dining room and gathered around the old oak table, its thick surface rough with nicks and carvings that spoke of the lives lived around it.

A cold breeze from the front door was followed by Birdie, breathless as she hung up her coat, slipped out of her boots, and rushed into the room.

"Now the party can truly begin," Ben greeted her as Sam pulled out a chair between himself and Ham Brewster.

"Thank heavens I didn't miss the food. And you better have saved me a martini, Ben Endicott." She shook her finger for emphasis.

The group shuffled around while Ben did her bidding, returning as Birdie finished explaining her late arrival.

"We're late because I insisted Harold drive up and around the bed-and-breakfast, just to be sure Henrietta wasn't lurking out in the cold somewhere. This campaign of hers will be the death of her."

"Was she?" Nell said, worried. The temperature had dipped and the wind was picking up. Henrietta seemed to be oblivious to weather.

"No, thank heavens. Mary hasn't been staying there, so I thought it was worth checking. After all the racket over the weeks, it seems ominous when it's quiet over there."

She smiled and took the martini Ben handed her. "Bless you, sweet Ben."

"So all was quiet. That's good."

Birdie nodded. "Troy's fancy car was in the drive, so he may have been finishing up some work for Mary."

"Were there other cars around?" Kevin said Troy had a key. A sudden image of a wild farewell party in Mary's beautiful estate flashed across Nell's mind.

"No. It was peaceful. Troy wasn't burning the house down or anything."

Ben tapped his glass, and the room fell silent. His eyes found Nell's. He lifted his glass and his eyes locked into hers, the way he began all toasts.

"Peace," he said. "To friends and to family."

"Hear, hear."

Glasses chimed as they sipped their wine and unfolded napkins across laps.

"And to the beginning of a lovely holiday season," Birdie added.

The beginning . . .

Nell looked around the table at the faces of people she loved, lit softly by flickering candlelight. They all hoped for that beginning—the lifting of suspicion and ugliness that mingled right alongside the festive trees and carolers and bells. She looked over at Birdie, at Izzy and Cass. She could read their expressions nearly as well as Ben's, as her own mind. Their hope as bright as the stars all over town.

Ben carried in a platter of Colorado trout, brushed with lemon juice, soy sauce, and ginger. He had grilled it outside, and the fragrance of sizzling coals wafted in behind him.

"Perfection, dear Ben," Birdie said. "Absolute perfection."

Bowls of jasmine rice followed, its nutty flavor enhanced with roasted red peppers, capers, and bits of bright green arugula.

Izzy brought in loaves of crisp French bread and a platter of roasted asparagus in a buttery dill sauce, then turned up a CD of Nat King Cole's, his warm voice filling the room with "O Tannenbaum." The next CD, Nell knew, would be livelier. Izzy gave in to Nell's sentimental holiday music but liked it best when followed by something with more beat and rhythm.

The evening went by in a flash, far too quickly, Jane Brewster observed as they sorted through coats and boots in Ben's den and prepared to go into the dark, cold night. "This is what we need more of—friends, Ben's martinis, good food, Christmas cheer."

They all agreed, and Nell and Ben stood at the door waving

them off, watching until their taillights disappeared down the hill.

It was late. Most Christmas lights were out, save for the ones in the Endicotts' own yard. Moonlight filtered through the bare tree branches, turning the snowy yard into a blue landscape.

Ben wrapped one arm around her waist and locked the door with the other.

"Izzy and Sam seemed okay," he said, whispering into her neck.

Nell nodded, her head moving against his chest. "A little quiet, perhaps."

They walked into the dim light of the kitchen, bodies still close. "He wants to meet me for coffee next week."

"Sam? Why?"

"I don't know. To talk to me about something."

Harriet Brandley's words, as if waiting for an excuse, tumbled back into Nell's head. "He isn't sick," she said softly. She was sure of it.

But something wasn't right. They didn't have the old Sam back yet. But he was going to talk to Ben, a good thing. At least, if there was something on his mind, he'd be sharing it with the wisest person she knew.

Ben switched off the overhead lights and started up the stairs. "Coming?"

"In a minute." Nell stood at the kitchen window, looking out into the profound darkness of night, to places beyond her vision.

Her thoughts were pulled to Ravenswood-by-the-Sea, imagining the beautiful estate, peaceful. Quiet. A sudden chill ran up and down her arms, and she turned toward the stairs and the comfort of Ben's strong arms and warm body.

Peaceful. Quiet. Just the way it had been the night they'd found Pamela Pisano's body in the snow.

Chapter 20

$\mathcal{N}$ell walked into the Seaside Knitting Studio carrying a thermos of coffee, her knitting bag slung over one shoulder.

Mae Anderson laughed when she spotted the thermos. "As talented as our missy is, her coffee is god-awful." She pushed her glasses up the bridge of her nose. "Hope you have enough in there for me."

"As always, Mae." Nell chuckled and glanced toward the back room. "It's noisy for this early hour."

"Packed. It's not even an official class. Just folks stuck in the middle of making Christmas gifts. They need Izzy's surgical expertise. And yours, I presume. Izzy said she was calling in reinforcements."

"The text message just said, 'S.O.S. Come quick.'"

Nell looked into the room. Mae wasn't exaggerating. It was crowded, with coffee mugs littering tables, a box of Dunkin' Donuts on the sideboard, and balls of brightly colored yarn everywhere. Needles clicked; knit sleeves and toes and thumbs were held up in the air to get Izzy's attention; voices filled the air.

Nell spotted Mary Pisano sitting near the fireplace, her laptop on her knees. Next to her, Birdie was admiring Nancy Hughes' cowl-necked sweater. It was nearly finished, knit in a luxurious beige and deep pink cashmere. Birdie was touching it lightly with her fingertips the way knitters did, resisting the urge to press it to her cheek.

Even Agnes Pisano was there, tucked away in the corner behind her cousin Mary, working on a lacy purple shawl. Nancy Hughes was beside her. Therapy, Nell thought. Everyone needs a touch of normal. The sweetness of living in the present.

Someone had brought a platter of Santa-shaped cookies, which were being handed from one group to the next and quickly disappearing. Nell waved at Izzy, grabbed a few paper cups from the bookcase, and headed over to the fireplace.

"It's good to see you doing something other than worrying, Mary," she said.

"Nancy's idea. She insisted we needed a break."

Hearing her name, Nancy leaned into the conversation. "Not *we. You*, Mary." Nancy pointed to the laptop and looked up at Nell. "But look at her idea of a break. Writing her column."

"Which I love to do. So it is a break. It's hard these days, though. I keep wanting to write an open letter to the person responsible for Pamela's death, begging them to own up to it, to clear their conscience. To give us back what's been taken away."

Nancy just shook her head and got up to refill her coffee cup and offer Beatrice Scaglia a hand with a lazy scarf that had just fallen off her needle.

"Have you heard anything new?" Agnes asked Nell. "Ben sometimes has an inside track—"

Nell shook her head. "I think it's confusing to the police. Maybe we need to broaden our thinking. Back away from the trees."

"What do you mean?" Agnes stopped counting stitches, and her hands went still.

"Pamela came to Sea Harbor often, not just that trip a couple weeks ago. But we're only looking at her activities during that short period of time. What about the bigger circle of Pamela's Sea Harbor life?"

"Her childhood?" Mary asked.

"I was thinking more of relationships she might have had here the last few years. Relationships with men who lived here, perhaps."

Agnes scooted her chair forward to hear better. "That's interesting. Pamela didn't confide much in me, probably not you, either, Mary. But when she was stuck in Sea Harbor, as she used to think about it, she survived by finding men to entertain her—we knew that. Even our grandfather worried about it. Sometimes it turned messy. Sometimes it was just casual."

"Like with Troy DeLuca—a good-looking body that was handy," Mary said.

Agnes nodded. "Troy was just a toy to her. She used him, and then she insulted him. There would have been a better way to handle not hiring him."

"Which you are doing?" Birdie asked.

"I know people think I'm simply flattered by his attention. That's ridiculous. I'm not a fool. *Fashion Monthly* has a shoot planned for men's fashion, and there's no reason not to throw him this small carrot. It might make up a little for Pamela's insults. I have no intention of making him a fixture at the magazine. Frankly, I don't totally trust him. He has loose lips, if you know what I mean, and I don't like that in a person."

"Loose lips?" Birdie frowned.

"Spreading tales. He told me last night that the police had found Pamela's wallet in Kevin Sullivan's belongings. Now, I've known Kevin since he was a kid delivering my newspapers. And he was honest to a fault. So Troy is stirring things up, telling tales; that's what I mean."

Birdie and Nell looked at each other. Mary's face was expressionless. Agnes wasn't asking them to confirm or deny Troy's assertion, which was a good thing. She clearly didn't believe it, and there was no reason to tell her otherwise. But how did Troy know about the wallet?

Agnes went on. "I also know it seems I moved very quickly into taking over this magazine, that I was just waiting for my chance, that I benefited from my own cousin's murder, a very suspicious and horrible thing to do. A motive for murder, for sure."

"That is how it looked," Birdie admitted. She followed up her bluntness with a laugh. "It was unlike you, Agnes, dear."

"Thank you, but it wasn't entirely unlike me. There's some truth to it. I was ready. I've wanted this position ever since Pamela sweet-talked Grandfather into giving it to her instead of me because I wasn't pretty enough. So I waited; I bided my time. I knew someday Pamela would get tired of it or move on to greener pastures, and when she did, I'd be ready. I got better at writing and editing. I took courses on magazine production and design. If I had wanted to oust Pamela sooner, I could have."

"How?" Mary asked.

"I could have told Grandfather that she was the one who crashed his prized Austin-Healey that summer we were all together for their anniversary. He'd have yanked the magazine from her in a New York minute if he'd known. But I had promised her I wouldn't tell, so I didn't. If I didn't get rid of her in that surefire bloodless way, I certainly wouldn't have killed her to get the job."

"Pamela smashed that car?" Mary said, her eyes filling her face. "Good grief."

"A couple too many beers at the club, a wild drive along a bumpy dirt road, and a tree that got in her way."

Mary held back a laugh.

Agnes' honesty was refreshing. Maybe they had all misjudged her. The tone in her voice was firm and intelligent.

Matter-of-fact. Nell smiled. "Something tells me you'll bring new, exciting ideas to the magazine."

"I second that," Birdie said. "Put me on your subscription list."

Agnes shrugged, and a sly smile tugged at her lips. "All this proves one thing, I suppose. You can't judge a book by its cover."

They laughed, and Birdie patted her knee. "You look every bit the editor, my dear. Even without wearing Prada."

"Maybe giving Troy this opportunity will help him get his act together," Mary said.

"Speaking of Troy, did he know before Pamela died that you were in line to take over *Fashion Monthly*?" Nell asked. It might not have been a murder motive for Agnes, but Troy was another matter.

Agnes and Mary looked at each other, considering the question. Then Agnes' frown lifted. "No, he couldn't have. The only real discussion about that occurred last summer—though I'm sure he eavesdropped every chance he got on our meetings. That's the kind of guy he is, in my opinion." She paused, then added in a softer voice, "But he's not to be tossed out like dirty bathwater, either. No one deserves that."

A sudden noise from the front of the store broke into the conversation. A loud tapping on the hardwood floor followed. Seconds later Henrietta O'Neal appeared in the arch, filling it with her square body. Her face was bright red, contrasting vividly with her white snow pants, a puffy white jacket, and a knit hat.

A fleeting image of a snowman flashed across Nell's mind, and then someone walked up behind Henrietta, changing the image entirely. She glanced over at Birdie.

Towering over Henrietta—tall, thin, and his face as white as Henrietta's jacket—stood Harold Sampson, Birdie's driver and groundskeeper.

The room hushed. People stopped knitting. Mary pushed her laptop aside.

"What in heaven's name are you doing here, Harold?" Birdie was up in a flash, her knitting falling to the floor. "Is Ella all right?"

Before he could answer, Henrietta spotted Izzy and waved her walking stick in the air. "I'm sorry to interrupt your little session, sweetheart, but it's important."

Izzy motioned that it was fine, then waited, puzzled.

"Are you all right?" Mary stood and stared at Henrietta.

Henrietta seemed confused at Mary's question but happy to have found her.

Behind the short woman, Harold shook his head. *Henrietta is not all right*, the movement said.

Nell moved next to Mary, feeling the need to steady the small woman. The incongruity of the scene in front of her portended something comical—or something terribly tragic. She looked into Harold's eyes.

They weren't laughing.

"Henrietta?" Mary said again.

Henrietta grew serious, focusing her full attention on Mary. Her voice was earnest, her message matter-of-fact.

"It's you I'm looking for, Mary Pisano. It's about that painter you hired," she said simply. "He's dead. Plumb dead."

Chapter 21

$\mathcal{I}$t was a sorry-looking group that crowded into Birdie's Lincoln Town Car and traveled along Harbor Road, up to the Ravenswood neighborhood.

Henrietta explained Harold's involvement right away. She had seen him coming out of Birdie's drive and flagged him down.

"I was going to the post office, Miz Birdie," Harold said.

She told him she needed a ride immediately. It was a matter of life and death, she said, though she supposed now that wasn't entirely true, since the painter was already dead.

But it was an emergency, nevertheless.

When she had called 911 to report the accident and get an ambulance, Esther, the dispatcher, told her exactly where Mary would be.

"Bless Esther for taking such care of us," Birdie murmured, sitting next to Harold in the front seat. Nell and Mary sat in the back on either side of Henrietta, listening intently as she related the morning's events.

"I was out for my morning constitutional when I saw a car in the Pisano driveway. I thought Mary and sweet Georgia were there," Henrietta said. "I wanted to take Georgia for a walk. She needs more exercise than Mary is giving her, poor thing." Henrietta reached over and patted Mary's hand. "It isn't your fault, sweetheart. It's all this trouble you're having."

Mary, her face as pale as snow, said nothing.

Nell held her silence, too, but with difficulty. It wasn't the time to remind Henrietta that she was the source of many of Mary's problems, at least the accumulating small ones.

"When no one answered the front door, I went around to the kitchen door," Henrietta continued.

"It was locked, Henrietta," Mary said quietly.

"Yes. I had a key." Henrietta pulled a key from the pocket of her jacket.

Mary stared at it.

"But when I went around back, I saw him right away, clear as day. He'd fallen off the ladder onto those granite rocks. There was paint everywhere, on the ground, the snow, his jacket." Henrietta's voice broke slightly as she remembered the scene. She paused for a minute and then continued. "His body was twisted like a pretzel, and he wasn't moving, but I walked over and checked his pulse. He was cold. I knew he was dead. I knew it. One just knows. . . . " Her voice trailed off.

"How awful for you." Nell thought back to finding Pamela in the snow, her body still and lifeless. The image was difficult to erase. Henrietta would now have a similar burden, and Nell wished there was a way she could relieve her of it.

Henrietta rested her head back against the seat as if telling the story had robbed her of that day's energy.

Harold made a right turn and drove slowly up the drive to Ravenswood-by-the-Sea. The ambulance was already gone, but two police cars were parked in the brick parking area. Chief Jerry Thompson stood at the edge of the drive. Tommy Porter was there, and Father Northcutt stood between the two men. Their heads were lowered, their shoulders hunched, hands stuffed in pockets.

At the sound of the car, they stopped talking and squinted against the sunlight. Harold pulled up next to the police car, and spotting Mary, Father Northcutt walked over and opened the door.

"Mary, Mary," he said, the thickness in his voice giving away his feelings. "You didn't need this now, did you, my dear."

Mary's small body was swallowed up in the older priest's embrace.

She pulled away and looked at the police chief. "He was painting the eaves, Jerry." And then she added, almost as if it had just occurred to her. "Yesterday."

They nodded. Body temperature had told them as much. Troy had died more than sixteen hours ago.

"And no one was at the place since yesterday afternoon?"

Mary shook her head. "It's probably the first day in weeks that there hasn't been traffic at one time or another. I left early yesterday. Ed's boat was in—and Nancy had invited us to dinner. On Fridays the workers always leave early. Kevin went into Boston."

"I walk by here every single day," Henrietta chimed in. "That's what I was doing this morning. I walk early, Jerry; you know that." Henrietta tapped her walking stick on the driveway with a rhythm that escalated with excitement.

Birdie spoke up. "I came by last night. Harold and I drove in to check on things because I knew Mary wasn't here." Birdie apparently felt no need to explain that she was checking up on Henrietta to be sure she didn't deface the place. "That fancy Q or Z or whatever it is—the silver car—was here." She looked over at the car that had almost knocked her over just a few nights before. "It was about seven or seven thirty," she added.

"Did you look around the grounds?" Tommy asked.

They hadn't gotten out of the car, Birdie said. It was cold and she was late for dinner at Nell's. "The security lights were on, and Mary's lovely Christmas lights lit the yard and twinkled around the porch. I knew Troy was finishing up some painting and was probably cleaning up. Nothing seemed unusual."

Nell stood a few steps behind the others, looking up at the beautiful old house. It was Christmas perfect. Magnificent. A Norman Rockwell painting.

And the scene of two tragic deaths.

"Well, we've got to check the grounds, Mary; you understand," Chief Thompson was saying.

"Do you think the wind pushed the ladder over?" Nell asked. She could see the ladder in her mind's eye, propped up against the house's overhang, reaching nearly to the sky.

Mary must be feeling the awful truth. She and Nancy had insisted Troy do this, climb the ladder and paint the eaves. It wasn't an unusual request, of course. It was what painters did. But this time the consequences were awful enough to nurture unforgettable regrets.

"The ladder didn't fall," Jerry Thompson said.

"Troy just fell off?" Nancy said.

"Had he been drinking?" Mary asked. "I told Nancy that was a worry—"

"There was a bottle of whiskey in the storage shed. He'd had a few drinks but wasn't drunk." A look passed between Chief Thompson and Father Northcutt. Then the chief looked back at the women. "The two rungs near the top—the ones Troy would have had to stand on to reach the eaves—were broken."

"Broken? What do you mean? The ladder was fine. We used it just days ago to fix some Christmas lights. It was fine." Mary's voice was high, unnatural.

"I mean that the top rungs were weakened so that if anyone weighing more than fifty pounds or so stepped on them, they'd split in half instantly. Fall apart, essentially. The sides of the ladder were greasy, so grabbing on would be futile—and the eaves happened to be directly over that pile of landscape rocks—exactly where the body would land."

"Someone wanted him to fall off that ladder," Tommy added.

The only sound was the flapping of gulls overhead and the tapping of Henrietta's walking stick on the brick drive.

Faster and faster.

Nell looked over at Mary. Her face was pale, her body seeming to shrink with the news.

Birdie moved closer to her and put one arm around her shoulders.

"It's cold," she said simply. "I'm taking Mary inside," and everyone began to move.

Henrietta insisted on walking home, but Harold drove Nell back to her own car, parked across the street from Izzy's shop.

She turned the key in the ignition and then sat there, unmoving, her hands on the wheel. Up and down the street shoppers moved quickly, their heads tucked low, their arms filled with packages. Across the way, a steady stream of customers moved in and out of Izzy's store. She'd called Izzy from Mary's to fill her in, but Mae said she was busy with a baby-sweater class. The earlier group had dispersed soon after Henrietta's news was assimilated, and by now, Mae supposed, the whole town knew that another tragedy had occurred in Mary's backyard.

"And Nancy?" Nell asked Mae. "Is she there?" She realized they'd nearly forgotten her in the rush to get Mary back to the bed-and-breakfast earlier. Yet she was the one other person who would be feeling this tragedy terribly. They'd insisted the painting be done this week. Next week, Troy would have been gone. Perhaps the outcome would have been different.

Cass had offered to take her home, Mae said, but she'd said no. She needed to walk, to process what had happened. It was how she handled things, she told them. Walking kept her sane.

Nell slowly pulled into traffic and headed east. The walk home would have given Nancy time alone, Nell reasoned. Now she well may need a shoulder to lean on.

She drove toward Canary Cove, then turned left just before the art colony began. The road wound up behind the artists' galleries to a neighborhood that looked out over the sea— comfortable old homes that now anchored some of the most desirable real estate on Cape Ann.

A million-dollar view, the Realtors advertised, and Nell agreed.

She pulled into a driveway at the end of the winding street, driving beneath a canopy of snow-covered trees. Set in the middle of the wedge-shaped property was Dean and Nancy Hughes' spacious gray-shingled home. And beyond it, the endless sea.

Nell loved the Hughes home. When Nancy was director of the historical museum, she entertained the board lavishly once a year, a luncheon Nell marked early on her calendar so she wouldn't miss it. Nancy Hughes knew how to entertain. Her husband often said that's what earned him his partnership in a prestigious law firm—Nancy's spiced rum and memorable dinner parties. Not only that, Dean boasted; she could carry on conversations about art, politics, and Cape Ann history with the stodgiest Boston client that he'd bring into their home.

She parked in the circle drive and walked up the steps.

Nancy answered on the second knock, a teabag in one hand and her cell phone in the other. She accepted the hug Nell offered her and ushered her in out of the cold, surprised at the visit.

"I wanted to be sure you were all right. This is all so awful," Nell began.

Nancy stopped her. "It's Mary we need to think about. I talked to her," she said, leading Nell into the family room. "But please tell me how she really is—she isn't always honest with me, and I know this is hard for her." She looked down at the tea bag dangling from her fingers. "I'll get us some tea; then we'll talk."

Nell watched Nancy disappear down the hall. It was typical of her to assume that Nell had come to report on Mary—not to be sure Nancy herself was doing all right. It was Nancy's way.

Nell wandered around the familiar room, waiting for Nancy's return. Beautiful pine beams traversed the ceiling, and floor-to-ceiling windows pulled the sea directly into the room. It was soothing and breathtaking at once. Nell walked over to a collection of framed photos on the mantel.

There were shots of Nancy and Dean on trips, at museum and gallery events, drinking martinis on the deck of a yacht and at their cottage in Maine. A picture of Dean and Nancy in front of a plane. In the center was a photo of Nancy and Dean on the elaborate altar of Our Lady of the Seas. Nancy's wedding dress was elegant, her face bright with promise.

It was a promise dashed ten years later when Dean's life ended so abruptly, unnecessarily. It was the worst kind of abandonment, in Nell's mind, and she wondered how Nancy dealt with it. How anyone would deal with it. Anger, guilt, loss. Such a mixture of emotions. One way Nancy handled it was clear— she plunged in headfirst when anyone needed her skills, her expertise, or simply a friend. She filled her days with great purpose. And she carried the love of her deceased husband like an Olympic flame.

"You've found my rogues' gallery," Nancy said, coming into the room. She set a tray of crackers and cheese and two cups of tea on a glass-topped coffee table.

"I remember good times in this room. Dean was a fine man."

"It's a quieter house now, without him." She pointed to French doors that opened into the den. "That was his favorite room."

Nell glanced into the small paneled room where she and Nancy had often discussed museum business. But it was clearly Dean's room. Trophies spoke of his love for the outdoors— biking, sailing, skiing. Another wall was devoted to his passion for hunting.

"I've kept everything exactly the way he loved it. But it doesn't bring him back."

Nell felt the absence of Dean, too. The house was somber, in spite of the wintry sunshine flooding the room and warming the pine floors.

"You've had your share of things to deal with, Nancy."

"Everyone has things." Nancy sat on the love seat and poured them each a cup of tea. "Look at what Mary is dealing with."

Nell sat across from her. "Of course. But you've been drawn into it, too, and it's not your mess. It doesn't seem fair."

Nancy sipped her tea, her gaze wandering to the den, then to the sea beyond the windows. Her face was sad. She turned back to Nell. "If Mary and I hadn't insisted Troy paint those eaves, this might not have happened."

"We all do things like that, at times—make decisions we regret, take a wrong turn, say something—things that inadvertently have a bad outcome. It's not intentional. It's life."

"Or death." Nancy bit down on her bottom lip. "But you're right. It wasn't anyone's fault. Bad things happen."

"And if someone truly wanted to get Troy, it would have happened anywhere."

"Yes," Nancy said. She played with a napkin, her fingers folding back each corner neatly. "There's no need to worry, Nell. I'm resilient. I'll make it through this all right. You know that. And I'll help Mary through it. She's a good person."

Her words were decisive, the way she was when the museum had faced a crisis or the board wavered on something

Nancy thought important. She was a strong woman. Ben had said as much when Nell had called him earlier to tell him what was happening. Nancy would be fine, he said—she would not let guilt eat away at her. And Mary would be fine, too.

"Nancy, how many people knew Troy was going to be painting yesterday?"

"Probably dozens. The work crew. Anyone who was in and out of the bed-and-breakfast. Kevin, of course. Mary. Me. The Scaglias. Maybe Agnes? She had drinks with Troy at the Gull the other night. And I'm sure he had complained loudly about it in the bar the night before. Even Henrietta O'Neal probably knew. She was here so often, she knew as much as anyone what was going on. So many people knew."

That was probably true. Beatrice had even mentioned it in McClucken's the other day. It was one of those trivial comments tossed out and forgotten because it carried no real consequence. Something few would be interested in.

Except someone who might want Troy dead.

"Did Troy mention having enemies? Could he have been in some kind of trouble?"

Nancy hesitated, and Nell worried about putting her on the spot. But finally she spoke. "People didn't like him much. I wasn't crazy about him, and Mary wasn't either. Kevin hated him. He and Troy were at each other a lot. But I can't imagine anyone wanting him dead."

"He seemed to have come into some money lately."

"Maybe the Scaglias were helping him out. They were generous to take him in."

Nell shook her head. "No. They thought the money was from Mary, that she was paying him too much."

"He'd done some modeling. He probably had savings. I think that business is lucrative."

Nell knew that wasn't true, but it didn't seem appropriate to get into his financial troubles with Nancy. Beatrice and Sal had taken Troy in because he couldn't pay rent. Savings seemed a long shot.

Yet suddenly he had fistfuls of cash. Not a gold card. Not money in the bank. Cash.

"I think these deaths have to be connected," Nell said, thinking out loud.

Nancy frowned. "What would the link possibly be?"

"I don't know. But there are so many loose threads. Just like in knitting. Sometimes if you follow those strands to the other end, you find they're attached at the same place somehow."

"Is that what people think?" Nancy folded the edge of her napkin back, then smoothed it out on her knee.

Nell regretted talking about Troy with Nancy. It clearly made her uncomfortable, and she could understand why. The whole mess was just too close for comfort. Aloud she said, "I don't know what the police think, but I know they're thorough. They will find out who did this. You and Mary need to concern yourselves with getting Ravenswood-by-the-Sea ready to open its doors the instant this case is solved. And I am sure it will be soon."

Nancy nodded, then glanced at her watch. "Speaking of the bed-and-breakfast, I should go over there and make sure Mary is all right. I told her I'd come by." She stood and began filling the tray with napkins and cups.

Nell nodded absently. Her thoughts were following a maze of soft yarn. She pictured Purl, crawling into her knitting bag and pulling all the yarn into a soft puddle on Izzy's floor. She'd been knitting a sweater for Izzy's mother, a cashmere hoodie that Caroline could wear on crisp Kansas City days. To football games and walks on the Plaza. It had taken Nell hours to straighten out the mess, but little by little she'd tugged the purples from the blues, following the loops and tangles diligently, slipping one through another until the source was right there in front of her. The connection.

She stood and slipped on her coat. "Nancy, I don't mean to dwell on this—I know you're uncomfortable about it—but do you know if there was something going on between Kevin and Troy, other than a dislike for each other? An argument, maybe? Mary is so protective of Kevin. But I think whatever it is might be important. It might help us get to the bottom of Pamela's murder."

Nancy started walking toward the kitchen.

For a minute, Nell thought she was going to ignore her question, pretend that she hadn't heard her. Then she stopped and turned around.

"You're right. Mary is very protective of Kevin. It's her motherly instinct, I think. She's taken Kevin under her wing. But he and Troy . . . well, it was all tied up with Pamela. But I don't think I'm the one to talk to you about it. I think you should talk to Kevin. Kevin has no one to protect but Kevin. He'll tell you what you need to know."

Chapter 22

$\mathcal{N}$ell found Cass and Izzy sitting in the back of the Seaside Knitting Studio, contemplating opening Birdie's last bottle of wine.

"Finally," Izzy said, jumping up. "Where've you been?" Without waiting for an answer, she launched into a description of the turmoil that had followed Henrietta O'Neal's announcement in the knitting studio that morning. "It made me wonder what life before cell phones was like. There was a whole symphony of ring tones after all of you left. Dozens. And calls going out just as fast."

"People knew who Troy was, but not too many had a chance to get to know him," Cass said. "It takes the edge off the fact that someone fell off a ladder and actually died." She uncorked the bottle of wine.

"I suppose that's true," Nell said. "When it's impersonal it becomes exciting."

"Like reading *People* magazine," Izzy said. "It's not real."

"Except it is. Whether we knew him well or not, Troy De-Luca was killed in our friend's backyard."

Izzy wrapped her arms around herself and shivered.

"Cass, that's the last bottle of wine," Birdie scolded, her boots connecting to the hardwood steps with a sharp click. "Mae is out there locking up. And here you three are, drinking my wine. It's going to snow, you know. You should all be going home."

"Birdie, you sound like the weather guys trying to scare us into stocking up for three months, like bears." Cass poured a glass of wine and handed it to her. "Here. Calm down."

"Another person is dead." Birdie slipped off her gloves and took the wine. "And in poor Mary Pisano's backyard. If I didn't know better, I'd subscribe to Henrietta's theory that evil spirits are attacking the old Pisano place. How much more can we expect that poor woman to take?" She stopped long enough to take a sip of the wine and sink into the nearest chair. Her coat bunched up around her until she was nearly invisible. "It has to end."

Nell poked life into the dying coals in the fireplace, put another log on the fire, and sat down beside her. "I realized today that I was nearly convinced Troy murdered Pamela. There were still some loose ends, but I thought—or maybe wanted to think—that he did it."

"Maybe he did kill her, Aunt Nell," Izzy said. She placed a hunk of Vermont cheddar and baked pita bread on the table. "He's dead now, but he was alive when Pamela was murdered—and we know he had a temper."

"That's true. He had a terrible temper. Beatrice said he smashed a photographer's camera. . . . "

"No," Birdie said, sitting up straight and flagging her finger in the air. "I don't think so. His motive wasn't strong enough, even for an ornery critter. We know he didn't know Agnes was going to take over the magazine before Pamela was killed. That motive may have carried a little more weight than the fact that Pamela insulted him. Besides, I don't think Troy was the brightest crayon in the box, and somehow, if he'd done something like that, he would have left something incriminating. We'd know it." She took a sip of wine, and then went on. "But here's something to think about—what if he *knew* who killed her?"

The fire crackled, and flames shot up, throwing shadows against the walls. Outside, the sky darkened and the wind whistled down the alleyway.

Finally, Nell spoke. "I think Birdie's right that he didn't kill her. That reasoning makes sense."

She thought again about the moving curtain in the carriage house. She had finally dismissed it as a figment of her imagination. Now it came back, more vivid, flapping wildly in the window. "But he might have been there. He might have seen the murderer from the carriage house."

"So whoever killed Pamela might have killed Troy—"

"Because he knew."

"Maybe."

"But who knew that Troy was painting yesterday?"

"Lots of people." Nell repeated her conversation with Nancy. "Anyone could have gone into that garage to cut the ladder rung. The garage was full of tools."

It could have been anyone. But the one they wanted to block out was Kevin. The nice, handsome man who made great coffee and cinnamon rolls in Mary's kitchen.

Kevin . . . dragging the heavy wooden ladder out to the backyard, getting it ready for Troy to climb to his death.

"We need to talk to Kevin," Nell said. "I tried to get some information out of Nancy, but she clammed up. She encouraged me to talk directly to Kevin, not put Mary in the middle." And she had expressed it oddly, Nell remembered. *Kevin has no one to protect but Kevin.*

They all agreed someone should talk to him. It might be nothing, as Mary insinuated. It might be something.

Birdie nodded and repeated it, as if making a list: "Talk to Kevin."

"And there's someone else we need to talk to." Nell couldn't shake free of the old affair that Tommy had told her about. There was someone out there, someone that they possibly knew, someone who had been obsessed with Pamela. "We need to find out who that was. If for no other reason, so I can get rid of this ghost that's following me around. Someone whose relationship with Pamela was volatile enough that even Pamela worried about it and left town to get away from him."

A growling sound caused Purl to leap to the window seat, her tail in the air and her back arched.

Cass laughed, a robust laugh that lifted the heavy air in the room, scattering it. "That was me, Purl. There's no lion ready to pounce. But if someone doesn't put food into me very, very soon, I may be out hunting for one."

Their plans came together in minutes—Birdie would use her magic to get them a table at the Ocean's Edge for dinner—just the four of them. Time to talk and piece things together. The men would be on their own to enjoy one another's company and a rerun of some football game they'd already seen several times, feasting on the Italian deli's fried clams and chicken spiedini. Sinful . . . and delicious.

They piled into Nell's car, excitement fogging the windows. There was something in the air, not the least of which was the expectation that they were finally beginning to melt the abominable snowman thundering his way through their tiny town.

As expected, the Harbor Road restaurant was crowded and noisy when the four women walked in, but a word from Birdie had the hostess leading them through the maze of tables to one saved just for Mrs. Favazza and her friends, the young woman said happily.

Nell looked over the sea of people, hoping to catch sight of Kevin, but the bar area between the tables and the kitchen was packed with moving bodies.

She spotted Father Northcutt settled in the same booth he had shared with her and Ben earlier in the week. He found it difficult to say no to his many invitations, especially if they centered around food. Father Larry loved to eat.

Catching her look, the priest lifted a glass in the air and nodded, all the while continuing his conversation with Sal and Beatrice Scaglia.

Nell's smile fell away. What a sad day for the Scaglias. This certainly wasn't the way they wanted to send Troy on his way. But they were in good company. Father Larry would say the right thing, make it as right as such a wrong could be made.

"Coming, Nell?" Birdie tapped her on the arm and pointed toward the table. Izzy and Cass had already ordered baskets of calamari and Thai egg rolls.

"Sit, you two," Cass called out. "We ordered your fave—the spicy ginger plum sauce for the egg rolls."

Nell shook away the uncomfortable thought about Sal and followed Birdie to the table. Handsome married men. She had to stop seeing them all as potential murderers.

The waitress brought the appetizers and warm hunks of sourdough bread, fresh from the oven, and Birdie ordered a bottle of wine.

Cass swallowed a bite of egg roll and beamed. "Now I can think again," she said.

Izzy polished off several pieces of calamari and cleaned her hands with a hand wipe. She pulled out a half-finished square in the softest of pinks. "These squares for the knit-a-square blankets are the best take-along projects we've ever done. Laura Danvers says she takes hers everywhere—pediatrician's office, board meetings, even to her husband's fancy law dinners. And it keeps me from devouring the entire basket of calamari."

Nell pulled out her own square. She'd nearly forgotten it was in her bag. Somehow they all thought more clearly with needles and yarn in their laps, fine food on the table, and wine at their fingertips. And needing clean hands to knit slowed down the evening and gave them plenty of time to think.

"So where were we before my stomach so rudely interrupted?" Cass took a long drink of wine. "We're operating on the assumption that whoever killed Pamela killed Troy. Right?"

"It makes the most sense," Nell said.

The others agreed.

"It will help move us along until something proves the theory wrong," Izzy said.

The waitress appeared, and the women fell silent, quickly perusing the tall menu and ordering a mix of seafood with drawn lemon butter, monkfish, corn and lime salsa, Asian salad, and lobster ravioli. Once the waitress was out of earshot, they continued.

"Troy saw the murder and the murderer knew it."

"But wouldn't he have killed Troy right away? Why days later?"

They fell silent.

"Because maybe he kept it from the murderer at first. And he found out only afterward? Or maybe there was a reason the murderer didn't think Troy would say anything."

"Like money?" Nell said. Like the sudden windfall that brightened Troy's life.

The restaurant crowd began to thin out as the knitters divided their time among eating, thinking, and tossing ideas into the air to be mixed and seasoned like the spicy sun-dried tomato linguini disappearing from Cass' plate.

Over key lime pie they talked about Henrietta. "That's a mystery in itself," Birdie said. "We need to find out what has changed that lovely lady into a troublemaker."

"If I ever run for office, she'd be my first pick for a campaign manager," Izzy said. "She'll do anything to meet her goal."

"Let's hope not—her current goal is to shut Mary down. And that would be awful."

Nell looked around the restaurant while Birdie talked, watching the waiters efficiently wiping tables, turning the music down a notch as the evening grew late. At the bar, Jeffrey wiped water spots off glasses, listening with one ear to stragglers sitting on the high stools, unburdening their woes.

She spotted Kevin coming through the kitchen door, car keys in hand. Her eyes followed him as he made his way to the bar. He talked with Jeffrey briefly, one elbow leaning on the polished surface. It was when Jeffrey walked away that Kevin spotted Nell in the mirror, watching him.

He turned, nodded a hello. He paused a minute, looking down at the floor as if seeking an answer. Then, perhaps finding it, he took the beer Jeffrey held out and walked in their direction.

They welcomed him warmly and invited him to sit.

Kevin squeezed in between Nell and Izzy. "I heard about DeLuca. It's been hotly discussed in here tonight. Jeffrey has five versions. Said I could pick my favorite."

"I don't know if I want to know what they are," Birdie said.

Kevin's head dropped, weary from hours in the kitchen—or maybe the burden of yet another murder occurring far too close to home. "I don't suppose you've heard any legitimate news? Do the police know anything?"

"It's so soon," Nell said. "They know the ladder was tampered with."

"The ladder I nicely carried out for him." He grimaced. "The crew had taken the metal ladder away. But this one looked okay to me. Nancy thought it'd be fine to use it for that little bit of touch-up work. She'd used it herself to fix some Christmas decorations on the carriage house."

He took a swig of his beer and continued talking.

"I thought for a while DeLuca killed Pamela. Then maybe stuffed the wallet in my locker to get the spotlight off him. But I don't know—maybe it was just because I didn't like the guy."

Nell listened and knew they were all thinking the same thing. Troy probably *did* put the wallet in Kevin's locker to shift attention from himself so he could more easily go about his business of blackmailing. He knew he'd be a suspect. And if he'd been in the carriage house that night, he could easily have taken it from Pamela's purse. How else could Troy have known about the wallet? Ben had confirmed to Nell that it wasn't public knowledge.

"Was Troy around the night Pamela was killed?" Izzy asked.

"Yeah. He was there in the afternoon. He told me he'd seen Pamela that morning. I'd already heard about it—rumors fly around this town. She'd teased him publicly in a nasty way, I heard. I couldn't stand DeLuca, but I don't like cruelty much, either."

"So he came back to Mary's after that?"

"Yeah—rode in on his bike. The Pisanos were in the library, finishing up the meeting."

"Was he there to work?"

"Nope. He wanted to see Pamela. To make things right, 'to talk some sense into her' is what he told me. He asked when they'd be through with the meeting."

"Which was?" Cass asked.

"You never knew with that group, which is what I told him."

"So he left?"

Kevin shrugged. "He went out on the porch for a smoke

first—I could see him through the window. I thought he left after that, but now that you ask me, I'm not sure. I had to move some things around in the garage for Nancy, then left to pick up my mom. I planned to come back later to get things ready for breakfast. He wasn't on the porch when I left, so I assumed he'd gone." Kevin paused, trying to remember. He shook his head. "I can't say for sure. His bike might have been there when I left."

Kevin shifted on the chair and looked around at all of them. He took a long swallow of beer. Then he stared at the bottle, rolling the neck between his fingers. "I didn't mean to interrupt. I saw you all here—and I was feeling so lousy for Mary. She doesn't need this."

"We're glad you came over, and no, she doesn't," Nell said. She paused for just a moment, not sure of her timing. She looked around at the others, a safe group. And then she plunged in. "Kevin, I don't want to barge in where I shouldn't, but there's something I've been meaning to ask you, something I think might help us understand Troy and Pamela. Maybe it won't, but Mary is reluctant to talk about it. Nancy suggested we talk to you."

Kevin frowned. "About what?"

"I'm not sure. But there was something going on between you and Troy. A disagreement? Maybe over Pamela?" She paused. Eavesdropping was awkward to admit, but she went on. "I was standing in the hallway that day you and Troy argued. Troy said that you were both glad she was dead. He talked about secrets."

Kevin clenched his jaw. He stared at the beer bottle, then picked it up and took a long swallow.

"We know that Pamela made your life a little difficult, hanging out in the kitchen every chance she had—"

Kevin put the bottle down. "She could be mean. She knew how to pull my strings. But it bothered Mary more than me.

Pamela'd throw her arms around me, that kind of thing. But then she finally moved on to Troy and everyone was happy, for a day or two, at least."

"So nothing more happened?"

Kevin drummed his fingers on the table. Finally, he looked up, his expression hard. "Yeah, something else happened. Pamela was a real pain in the you-know-what. She embarrassed me in front of the Pisanos right and left, even after she and Troy started fooling around. She'd put her hands on me, kissing me. I tried like hell to get rid of her, but she expected me to like it, to be flattered, you know? She told me I was playing hard to get and that excited her. One day she came in the kitchen, doing her usual act. I'd worked late the night before here, and my defenses were squat. So I told her to get away or she'd be sorry. She wouldn't. I was so mad, I wasn't thinking. I knew there was one thing about me that would make her leave me alone. Something she'd be the last person I should tell. But I was exhausted and mad as hell."

He took another drink, then continued.

"So I told her what I hadn't even told my own mother. I told her the truth. I told her I was gay. She wasn't my type, I said."

Kevin looked up, as if waiting for a reaction.

Izzy and Cass looked at each other as if waiting for the end of the story.

"So, what does that have to do with Troy?" Izzy asked. "Or anyone, for that matter. At the least, you probably should have told Pamela a lot sooner. It might have saved you a lot of grief."

Kevin frowned. "Don't you get it, Izzy? I've never . . . I've never talked about it before, never told anyone."

Cass drew her dark brows together until they nearly touched each other. "Kev, I'm not getting you, here. So what?"

Kevin stared at her. "So what? So this will be really hard on my folks. My mother spends as much time at church as she does at home. And my pa? Can you imagine him when his buddies in the bar find out about this? Joke about it? It won't be pretty for anyone; you know what I mean? He'll blame my mother and make her pay for it. He could hurt her badly.

"But Pamela? She thought it was a huge joke. Her mother is at the nursing home where my mother works. She was going to tell her she'd met her gay son, as she put it. And then she told Troy—who started in with the jokes and ridicule. I don't know which was worse. I hated them both for it." He sat back in the chair and welcomed the beer Cass had flagged from the waitress.

"So that's it," he said. "Mary overheard the whole thing. She knew I was desperate that my pa would find out and do something stupid—or worse. I was trying to find the right time to tell my mother before Pamela did. And then Pamela was murdered—and it wasn't as urgent anymore."

Birdie sighed, loud enough to draw smiles and lighten the mood. "First of all, I know your mother, Kevin Sullivan, and shame on you for not giving her more credit." Birdie shook one finger in the air. "She loves you, for heaven's sake.

"And secondly, Pamela was being cruel. You had rejected her and she was using the only thing she could think of to get back at you. A double shame on her."

Nell looked at Cass and Izzy. Kevin's confession meant nothing to them. Maybe they knew it already, probably so, but the fact was that it didn't matter. Just like it didn't matter to Jeffrey at the bar, and the multitude of others who knew Kevin. It was his business, not anyone else's, just like Izzy's relationship with Sam was definitely off-limits for public discussion.

The lightbulb went on in Nell's head as Birdie was ordering Irish coffee for everyone. Of course. She should have realized this right away.

Mary wasn't trying to protect Kevin because he was gay. She wasn't trying to hide his secret from the world.

She was trying to hide him from the police—and with good cause.

His reaction to Pamela's threats to talk to his mother and Troy's cruel teasing gave him a nice, neat, pat motive for murder. Perhaps even two murders.

Chapter 23

$\mathcal{T}$hat night, the much-predicted snow finally fell—lovely flakes that hushed the town. Nell cradled a mug of coffee in her hands and looked out the kitchen window the next morning. Snow mesmerized her. She felt like a child again, safe and protected in a white world. It was always new, always a miracle.

Ben watched her from across the room. "Bus drivers, cab drivers, pilots, commuters—I don't think any of them share your awe, Nell. They're only thankful that it's Sunday and not the beginning of a messy workweek."

"The kids love it. Look—" She pointed out the back window to a few neighborhood kids traipsing through their wooded backyard to a short hill beyond. They were bundled up in bright red scarves and puffy jackets, carrying snow saucers, sheets of plastic, a wooden sled. Anything to get them down the hill faster than the sled next to them.

"Remember when Izzy and her college friends would come up here on weekends and do that very thing? Only they'd head for the bigger hill—over near Sam's house."

Nell turned and leaned against the counter. "And speaking of Sam—I was so busy telling you about my day yesterday that I didn't ask."

"I noticed that. Sam's fine."

"That's it? Fine?"

Ben pulled the Week in Review section from the *Times* and smoothed it out on the table. "Fine."

Nell looked at him closely. "Fine. All right." She wouldn't get any further, but Ben's worry lines were absent, his face calm. He was holding something back, but it was something neutral, not good or bad. Years of holding tight to client confidences made Ben Endicott as safe and immovable as a bank vault. She walked around the table and kissed him lightly on the ear. "So be it."

"I think it'll be all right, Nell," he said simply, and continued to scan the column headlines.

"I wish I felt as confident about everything going on up on Ravenswood Road. Talking with Kevin only worried me more."

"You don't think he's guilty, do you?"

"No. But I only think that because I like him. He was *there*, Ben; he didn't like Pamela, and she could have hurt his mother terribly. And Troy knew all about it. That fellow had about as much integrity as a slug. What will people think who don't know Kevin or don't care about him?" She thought again about the hardness in Kevin's voice and eyes when he talked about the ridicule and the cruel way both Pamela and Troy approached people. It was a look that gave her chills and made her wonder, not for the first time, what would push a person—even a good person—to murder.

Aloud she said, "Mary feels responsible for putting Kevin in the middle of all this. She's the one who lured him to Ravenswood-by-the-Sea in the first place."

"I saw the chief at the club last night. We talked briefly at the bar, and he says Troy DeLuca's death has confused the investigation. They were looking into some gambling debts, a rather wild lifestyle, then the money he was throwing around. He was definitely a person of interest. And then suddenly he's dead."

"Beatrice said he was broke when he came to Sea Harbor. Looking into his sudden windfall made sense. Maybe it's still important. Jerry thinks the two murders are connected, doesn't he?"

Ben laughed at the tone in her voice. "It's clear you've all decided they are. Jerry would be silly not to agree, now, wouldn't he?"

"They're connected, Ben."

Ben slipped off his glasses and reached for the coffeepot. "You're probably right. It makes sense. It's just your methods of deduction that I wonder about." He refilled Nell's mug.

"Don't knock our methods until they fail. Then I'll listen."

"That's fair, I suppose."

Ben paused.

Nell watched the worry lines appear, the frowns so deep across his forehead that she could trace them easily with her finger. And she knew what would come next. It was a thought that certainly hadn't escaped any of them, but saying it out loud would make Ben feel better, just like it made her feel better when Ben drove into Boston with her words trailing after him, *Drive carefully, Ben. . . .*

"This is heavy-duty stuff, Nell," Ben said. His elbows pressed into the butcher block. He held her gaze, his intelligent blue eyes locking into hers. "Two murders, probably by the same person. There's someone out there who doesn't hesitate to kill people—for whatever reason. This is nasty, dangerous stuff."

Later that day, Izzy and Nell snowshoed out Nell's backyard and down the path behind the Endicott home. The trail fanned out and widened beyond the trees, looping lazily alongside the beach access road, heading north, with smaller, veinlike pathways breaking off and moving up into neighborhoods bordering the water. In summer, it was a well-trafficked path, with neighbors and friends, kids and teenagers and summer people, all headed to the long stretch of beach, the yacht club, or the breakwater beyond. In winter it boasted an easy snowshoeing trail, not much elevation, winding through stands of pine and oak.

The quiet surrounding them was so thick and lovely that Nell felt sure that if she stumbled, the quiet would be like an airbag, holding her up.

Their backpacks were light, holding shoes and water, dry socks and energy bars, a place to fold up parkas if they needed to strip down a layer.

"We don't get that much time together these days," Izzy said, "just the two of us. It's nice."

An understatement, in Nell's opinion. Exercise with Izzy always did wonders for her body and soul. It was exactly what the doctor ordered for a bright, snowy Sunday.

"I thought we'd head toward Sam's house. My mother sent me some Arthur Bryant's Barbecue Sauce from Kansas City and asked me to give some to Sam. 'His favorite,' she said." They came to a slight incline and skied down on their shoes, the breeze tossing Izzy's hair about her head. "She thinks she's fooling me, but I know exactly why she does things like that."

"Why is that?" Nell leaned into her poles as they moved through a stretch of powder.

"It's the connection. She brings Sam up all the time. And sending him things through me adds strength to that connection. I can't explain it. But I know my mom."

"She loves Sam."

"That's part of it. Why did I hook up with someone my entire family knows and likes? It makes it more complicated." Izzy moved her poles to skirt a small boulder in the path. "Speaking of Sam, did he and Ben have a nice dinner last night?"

"They always do. Ben didn't say much."

Izzy pointed with the tip of her pole to a trail that meandered off through the trees. "This is the turn to Sam's. We can take it slow."

"Are things better with Sam? Normal? Okay?"

"Still a roller-coaster ride. But I have new resolve. I'm not going to let it get to me. If I know anything about Sam Perry, it's that he'd never, not in a million years, intentionally hurt me. So whatever's going on in that thick head of his, it's well-intentioned." Her breath plumed up in front of her. "At least that's my story today, Aunt Nell. Ask me again tomorrow—it may be different. A couple days ago, his moods nearly sent me packing. Or him packing. But today's a new day. End of story."

The low-rise path took them up through a scattering of white pine and mountain laurel, which gave way to a yard and wide deck that spanned the back of the house. It was an ideal spot for whale watching and martinis after a day at the beach. From the elevation, they could even see the yacht club pier, sailboat races, and winter fishing.

Izzy had found the house for Sam, and it was next to perfect. Part beach house, part cozy family home, in a friendly neighborhood. Clean and simple with plenty of glass and wood. When Nell saw it for the first time, she knew Izzy had found her own dream house. But Sam was writing the check. Her niece was a clever girl.

"Is Sam home?"

"I don't know. But home or not, I'm not lugging these heavy jars back home. He also has some photos for the studio that he keeps forgetting to drop off." She stomped clumsily up the three steps to the snowy deck, her snowshoes creating webs in the powder, and peered through the windows. "Let's try the front."

The other side of the cedar-shingled house faced Magnolia Street. There was no car in the gravel drive. Izzy looked through the windows on either side of the door, then fished a key from her pocket. "Breaking and entering," she said.

They sat on the small bench outside the door and unclipped their snowshoes, then walked into the small entry hall. The house was open and airy, with views of the deck, the trees, and the endless sea from almost every spot.

Nell wandered into the family room at the back of the house while Izzy fished through a stack of envelopes on the hallway table.

A simple fireplace with a cherry mantel and soapstone surround anchored one end of the room. Although Sam had lived here almost three years, the house hadn't changed much. The built-in bookcases and cabinets held a few more books, perhaps, and Izzy had hung one of Willow Adams' magnificent yarn sculptures above the fireplace, but it was clean and simple. Too clean and simple.

It needed a woman's touch. Izzy had made inroads where she could, but the stark beauty of the lovely home lacked the warmth her niece could bring to it, given a chance.

Nell shook off her meanderings and looked back down the hallway, where Izzy stared down at a Federal Express envelope. Nell couldn't read the look on her face, but it definitely didn't reflect the sunny conversation they'd had on the way over.

"Izzy?"

Izzy's head flew up, as if she'd been caught with her hands in the cookie jar.

"What?"

Nell frowned. "Ready to go?"

"Oh, sure." She stared down at the envelope again. "It's Sam's mail. I shouldn't be looking at it."

"No. You shouldn't."

"But look." She held the envelope out for Nell to see.

The letter was addressed to Samuel Perry.

"It's from Boston General Hospital."

Nell had seen the return address immediately. Harold Adams, PhD, MD. Boston General.

"Sam had a physical?"

"No. He goes to Doc Hamilton, just like the rest of us."

"Maybe the medical practice is buying some photographs from him?"

"An overnight letter to buy photographs?" Izzy flapped it in the air.

"Izzy," she said gently, "it's Sam's mail."

"What is he keeping from me?" Izzy's face fell, and a look of anguish filled her eyes. She stared at her aunt, begging her to explain away the fear.

Her voice was thick, tears pushing hard against her words. "Aunt Nell, what's wrong with Sam?"

"It's unfortunate that Izzy looked at Sam's mail."

"It wasn't exactly like that." Nell sat at the kitchen island, nursing a glass of wine, her eyes following Ben as he whisked together a green chili paste, a little wine, a cup of coconut milk. "I don't think it was intentional. She was looking for some photos, and there it was."

Ben placed the liquid over a low flame, tossed in a handful of chopped scallions, and stirred it with one hand, holding his wineglass with the other. Sunday night dinner at home—alone—was uncommon during holiday season, and Ben was determined to make the most of it. A roaring fire. Music. Nell.

And a home-cooked meal.

"Try Thai," Nell had urged. "It's easy; I'll prompt from the wings."

"Does Sam know she saw his mail?" On another burner, Ben heated olive oil in a skillet and tossed in chopped scallions and garlic, grated fresh ginger.

"I suppose she'll say something to him."

"Then that's the end of it, isn't it? For us, anyway."

"She's worried, Ben; that's all. It was from a hospital. And he's not been himself these past few weeks. You've noticed it."

"I understand. It's a tough thing—sharing. And it's new to Sam. He's—what—almost forty? Never been married. He's a very private guy. What couples choose to hand over to one another is so individual. It's not a right or wrong thing, it's . . . it's personal. Sam's proud."

"Izzy wants to know she can trust him."

"Maybe it isn't about trust." Ben lifted the lid and checked the jasmine rice. Its nutty aroma brought a calmness into the air. Soothing. He took it off the burner and fluffed it with a fork. "Maybe it's a matter of who Sam is."

Who Sam is.

"So it ends up being a choice they both have to make," Ben went on. "What they are comfortable with. What trust means to each of them."

Nell watched Ben while he talked, his strong chin resolute. His eyes moving from the rice to the sauce to Nell's face.

He smiled at her. His eyes suggested she let it go. The expression on his face spoke of many things.

In the end, it was the sweet guitar music and scallops swimming in Ben's spicy coconut sauce that convinced Nell to let it go—at least for tonight.

And over a nightcap several hours later, Ben convinced her they had their own sharing to attend to.

Chapter 24

$\mathcal{C}$offee's was thinning out, the early-morning drinkers already gone and the lunch crowd not yet lining up. Nell searched over the tops of heads for Cass' black hair. She held a jumbo-sized cup of Coffee's special brew in her hand.

Monday was always a holiday for Cass, even during the thick of lobster fishing. She liked the tenor of a day that found most people heading back to work. She could own her own leisure, she said, rather than succumb to weekend special events dictated by the newspaper.

Summers found her parked on the patio, a sixteen-ounce triple cappuccino with real whipped cream sitting in front of her, her feet up on a bench, looking at the sky or a magazine or a book.

In winter she sat in front of the fire, her feet on the stone hearth, windows behind her. It was her chair, she declared to Clarence Lanigan, and the owner dutifully tried to shoo others away if he knew Cass was coming.

"Saved for you," Cass said as Nell approached. She lifted a stack of magazines from a chair and put her feet on the floor.

"I don't imagine you endear yourself to people waiting for a place to sit," Nell said, looking around.

Cass laughed, unbothered. "Izzy's joining us for our private tour."

Birdie's dramatic description of Enzo Pisano's bedroom had intrigued Izzy and Cass. They begged for a tour, and Mary would love the distraction.

Cass' brows lifted, and her eyes focused on a spot behind Nell. She waved.

Nell turned and looked up at Tommy Porter.

"Hey, Tommy," Cass said. "Looks like you're off today?" She eyed his jeans and heavy suede jacket. "Join us."

"Just off for the morning," he said. "It's crazy around the station. The chief has us all giving up some off time."

"You've got a mess on your hands."

Tommy nodded. He pulled up a chair and straddled it. "A royal mess. But I don't mind. It's my job."

Tommy Porter had never left Sea Harbor except for two years at Northern Essex Community College. The first policeman in a family of fishermen, he loved his work passionately, was proud of his degree in law enforcement, and according to Chief Thompson, was doing a crackerjack job. Nell smiled at him. "Any new developments?"

"Still trying to pull apart this DeLuca mess. No fingerprints, nuthin'. People here weren't crazy about the guy, but no one knew him well enough to kill him, far as we can tell."

"Could it have been an accident?"

"Not likely. The rungs were cut. An easy thing to do, and no one would notice. Cut on a slant, they fit back together just like normal. I suppose it could have been intended for someone else. But Mary says that ladder isn't used much. The workmen brought their own."

"Any motives?"

Tommy shook his head. "I wanted him to be the guy that killed—"

Footsteps interrupted his words. He looked up. "Hey, Izzy."

Izzy pulled up a chair. "Tommy, you look like you could use some sleep."

"Yeah, I guess. It's nuts. If we could keep Mrs. O'Neal away from that place, it'd be a little easier maybe."

"What's she done now?"

"Just the usual. Today she put up new posters. There's one over there on Coffee's bulletin board. It has photos of the spot where Pamela Pisano died and one where DeLuca fell. It says, "Would you want a friend or relative to sleep in this house?""

Nell sighed. "That's got to stop."

"Free speech," Tommy muttered. "She sure has somethin' stuck in her craw."

"It seems that way," Nell said.

"Did any of you know Pamela very well?" Tommy asked.

"Kind of like everyone else. Not well. But since she dated Eddie—you probably knew her better," Izzy said.

"Not so much. That was a while ago. What I remember from that summer is the other guy, like I said. The guy who was nuts about her."

"What do you remember?" Nell asked.

"It was brought up again at the station when she was murdered. Some of the guys talked about how the guy was obsessed, but it's not relevant to this case. . . . " He paused, as if to say more, then thought better of it and took a drink of his coffee.

"Why do you suppose everyone in town knew Pamela was hanging out with your brother, but the other affair was kept secret?" Izzy asked.

"Easy, Iz. As my mom says, money can cover all kinds of sin."

"Money?"

"They said the guy had money. He arranged it so things were kept under the radar. All quiet. Maybe his business might have been hurt if people knew? I dunno. Had a fancy vacation house somewhere up north, too, I heard, so he could get away from here with her."

Tommy checked his watch, then stood and slung a backpack over one shoulder. "I'm taking my girl to lunch at Harry's Deli. Good to see you guys."

"Tommy." Nell stopped him with a touch to his sleeve. "There's one thing that mystifies me."

"What's that?" Tommy lifted his brows.

"Why would someone who was obsessed with Pamela Pisano, had an affair with her, and who lives right here in Sea Harbor not be singled out as a prime suspect in her murder?"

"Oh, that's easy," Tommy said. He looked around at the three women and started to walk away as his words traveled back over his shoulder. "The guy's dead."

A short while later, Izzy, Cass, and Nell piled into Nell's car for the short ride to Ravenswood-by-the-Sea. They turned Tommy's comments inside out, but the facts were clear, even Nell had to admit. A dead man could not have murdered Pamela.

"But there's still something fishy there," she said as she pulled into the drive. "We can't give up on this."

"I agree," Izzy said. "At first I couldn't figure out how something from her past figured in. But a man obsessed. That gives me the creeps. Remember *Fatal Attraction*? So scary. I think there's more to the story."

"Like, why did the guy want the affair kept secret?" Cass said. "Pamela Pisano was a catch. Eddie Porter had no trouble being seen with her."

"And why was an affair a hot topic at the police station?" Izzy added. "It's not exactly a crime. You'd think they had better things to do."

The renewed energy in the car was electric, and Nell felt a

surge of adrenaline shoot through her. Her heartbeat quickened. The light at the tunnel's end beamed brighter. She wasn't sure how they'd get to it. But it was there, luring them on.

Nell pulled up beside Mary's parked car, and they got out, each lost in her own thoughts, playing with strands of yarn and trying to make them fit.

It might take some head scratching, but they'd figure it out.

And Nell had a good idea where they could start.

Birdie was in the kitchen with Mary, keeping her company. They'd put on a pot of coffee and heated up a plate of Kevin's cinnamon rolls. "No tour is worth its salt without a touch of cinnamon," Birdie said cheerfully.

"Is Kevin here?" Nell asked.

"He's at the restaurant today," Mary told her. "He's been on edge. It's good he's busy. But he's moved into the carriage house. It's a relief to have someone spending nights here until this is all resolved."

Nell wondered if Kevin had shared his conversation with them with Mary. She guessed not, and wondered briefly if that's why he was on edge. But she'd ask Birdie later. "Resolved?"

"I met with the lawyer and the insurance company this morning. The consensus is that we find the murderer before we officially open the doors to guests. Start fresh, was how they put it."

Mary's voice was resigned.

"So you'll let the masses in as soon as we wind this up," Cass said, licking sugar off her fingertips. "It's not going to take long. My mother's huge family will be here for Christmas. She always insists on putting Uncle Clancy and his crazy wife, Sheila, in my apartment. This year they are staying at Ravenswood-by-the-Sea. Or, better yet, maybe I'll stay here. So, friends, let's move it."

Cass left no room for argument, and all around the kitchen silent resolutions were made. The lights of Ravenswood-by-the-Sea would be shining brightly, welcoming guests, before Father Northcutt's joyful bells beckoned his flock to Midnight Mass.

They laughed their way up the winding staircase, Cass insisting on trying out the electric seat fastened to the wall.

"I'm glad someone is using it." Mary laughed. "I never saw Grandfather use it. He managed these stairs like a teenager."

Nell walked behind Mary. The lightness in her step was refreshing. This was the tonic she needed today. Something that required no thought, just good friends and a dose of laughter.

Izzy and Cass swooned when the doors to the suite opened.

"Wow. Talk about a bed," Cass murmured, running her hands across the top of the walnut headboard. "This is a whole tree house. An entire family could sleep here."

"He had this little stool built to help him up."

The small walnut stool stood at the side of the bed. Nell had missed it last time she was here. Swirling carved lines ran down its sides, fanning out like birds' wings and outlined in gold. She looked closely at the stool. The craftsmanship was remarkable—and familiar. She'd seen it somewhere. . . .

"Here's the famous heart," Izzy said. "Cass, come see."

The two leaned close to the headboard, fingers tracing along the carving.

"Oh, Enzo, you fox, you," Cass whispered, her fingers dancing along the surface.

Behind her, Mary laughed. "He'd love this attention."

Nell examined the heart again. "E.P." and "H" with a large round period. Held together forever in the crudely carved heart. She looked back at Mary. "What was your grandmother Helen's middle name? Odelia, maybe?"

Mary shook her head. "It was *Mary*. The family was big on Mary. Everyone had one somewhere in her name. Pamela Mary

Elizabeth. Agnes Elizabeth Mary. Grandmother was Helen Mary Elizabeth Jane."

Izzy traced the letters with the tip of one finger. "I guess his knife slipped and made the period big. But it doesn't change the message. Imagine someone loving you enough to mar a valuable antique."

"That was Grandfather, the great lover," Mary said wistfully. "I wish he were here right now to help me with this mess. He gave me the idea, you know. It was shortly before he died. He said he could just imagine the pleasure people would have spending nights here. And I think he meant pleasure in every sense of the word."

"He'd be proud of you."

"I think he would. He'd like the updating, the freshness. Mostly he'd love life and laughter filling this house."

"It won't be empty," Birdie told Mary. She said it with certainty. "It will open to great fanfare—and soon."

Each of them knew better than to doubt Birdie.

Later, when they piled back into Nell's car, they felt the good vibes of Enzo Pisano's sweet carved heart. A hopeful heart.

Nell turned the key in the ignition. She waited, ramping up the heat and tapping her fingers on the wheel. Thinking about the house, the man who lived there. The carved bed and the lovely stool. A romantic to the core.

Next to her, Birdie's brows were pulled together, searching for something in her head that she was having trouble finding. "That stool was lovely," she said out loud. "It looked so familiar."

Nell nodded. "Carved walnut," she whispered.

Cass leaned forward, her fingers tracing an imaginary line on the back of the front seat. "Are you all thinking we're missing something here?"

"The carving," Izzy said softly. "Of course."

"The initials. I *knew* that darn period was an 'O,'" Cass said.

Slowly, Nell stepped on the gas and began driving down the drive, the air heavy with their thoughts and the enormous satisfaction of puzzle pieces slipping smoothly together. "It fits," she said.

"Perfectly," Izzy added gleefully. "Who would have thought?"

It was like a wonderful complicated cable sweater that looked so confusing, and suddenly, with one stitch, it all fit together and completed the twist in an amazing way.

"Nell, stop the car. Look over there." Birdie pointed toward the Ravenswood-by-the-Sea sign, refinished and free of Henrietta's red paint. The gold letters popped bright in the sunlight.

Nell pulled to the side of the drive.

A few feet in front of the Ravenswood sign stood Henrietta O'Neal, her unbuttoned coat flapping in the cold breeze. A sharp wind whipped blue curls about her head.

She seemed not to notice the car. She stared straight ahead at the house, her gaze frozen in place. In her hand, gripped tightly, was her walnut walking stick.

But it was the expression on Henrietta's face that mesmerized the four women watching her from the car and confirmed what they now knew to be true.

It wasn't the look of someone about to spray-paint a sign or mount inflammatory posters or destroy a neighbor's property.

It was a look of excruciating longing.

A look of someone who had loved deeply and fully—and couldn't bear the thought of it completely disappearing.

Birdie pressed one hand against the dash. "Of course," she said, her voice a whisper. "It's love, not hate, that rules Henrietta's crazy Irish heart."

Henrietta seemed not to mind when they packed her in Nell's car for the short ride to her own home down the street. She seemed to be in another world, a lovely world that she didn't want to leave.

"A cup of tea?" she said when they pulled up in her circle drive.

They all went in, and Izzy rummaged around in the kitchen of the stately old home, finding tea bags and cups, a match to light the six-burner stove, while Cass built a rousing fire in the living room.

They settled Henrietta in front of the fire, a blanket covering her knees. She was chilled to the bone. Nell rubbed her hands between her own, bringing color back into her gnarled fingers.

"This is lovely," Henrietta said. "I should have worn my hat, shouldn't I?"

She didn't ask where they'd come from or why they were there. But her eyes were clear and bright.

Birdie settled in next to her. "You loved Enzo, my dear," Birdie said. "That's lovely."

Henrietta nodded. "He was the greatest love of my life."

"We saw the heart he carved for you on that lovely old bed. *E.P. loves H.O.* Henrietta O'Neal."

Henrietta rubbed away the tears that sprang to her eyes. She looked at the women who hovered around her, and the old Henrietta rose from the ashes.

She sat up straight.

"We loved each other," she said simply and firmly.

"Mary never knew," Birdie said. "Why didn't you tell her, Henrietta?"

"Tell his granddaughter? His flesh and blood? Sweetheart, how could I do that? We were—how would you say it, Cass? Shacking up? Oh, my. I couldn't tell anyone. What would my parents think?"

"Dear heart," Birdie said gently, "your parents have been dead for thirty years."

"And rolling over in their graves for some of them, don't you know." Henrietta shook her curls again. "The respectful thing to do was to keep it private. And don't forget—Enzo was Italian. Italian! I can hear my father bellowing in shame, 'An Italian, Henrietta? Italian!' And what would the others say—my grandchildren? My great-grandchildren? Great-Nana Henny is . . . oh, for the sake of the good lord."

A noise from the hallway stopped Henrietta's lamenting short. She looked at the doorway.

"Henrietta, I had no idea." Mary stood still. She nodded her head toward the door. "It was open. I came over to see if you were all right. I saw you out there, and it was so cold. . . . "

A deep red blush worked its way into Henrietta's cheeks.

"What a lovely gift you gave each other," Mary said, her eyes moist. "Thank you, Henrietta."

Henrietta slowly released the air held tightly in her ample chest.

"Your grandfather was a lovely man, romantic and charming."

Mary smiled. "I knew something special was happening to him those last years. I could hear it in his voice, but I didn't imagine that he was in love. I should have known."

Henrietta seemed to puff up before their eyes. Her eyes sparkled. "One day the mailman told me he had the flu. That's how it all started. So I brought him chicken soup. Who wouldn't?"

She looked around at all of them for confirmation, her head nodding.

"One thing led to another; well, you know how that can be." She paused, collecting her memories, sorting through them in her mind, and then went on.

"When you haven't been touched by someone for a while, it's quite a lovely thing. A hug, a touch, your skin warmed by another. It brings fire into your soul. You come alive.

"And then one night Enzo asked me to spend the whole night with him, to be with him. But I couldn't, you see. I couldn't make it up those foolhardy stairs. Not in a million years. So slick and steep. And so very many of them."

"So he installed the electric chair for you," Mary said.

Henrietta nodded. "It was at Christmastime. A perfect gift to give one another, he said. And that darling man would walk up next to me, making sure I didn't fall off, humming little tunes, all the way to the top. All the way to that magnificent bed."

"With the stepping stool that matches your walking stick," Nell said.

She beamed. "He had them both made for me. Georgia liked the stepstool, too. She'd climb up and sleep there in the bed, keeping our feet as warm as toast. Sweet pup. She still sneaks over to see me now and then."

Henrietta sighed and settled back in the chair. "It's all I have left; don't you see? Those memories. I couldn't bear the thought of strangers in *our* bed. Strangers who aren't even family. Enzo would have hated that. I had to stop you from doing that, Mary. You understand, sweetheart."

"Of course," Mary murmured, more to herself than to the others. She stepped from the room for a moment, rummaging in her pocket for a tissue.

When she returned, the others were gathering coats and boots, and Henrietta was ambling off to the kitchen to slip a frozen pizza in the oven and fix herself a Scotch and soda.

"Now, shoo, all of you," she said. "It's been a long, long day, and this is our cocktail hour. I have some things I need to discuss with Enzo."

Mary gave her a kiss on her wrinkled cheek and whispered, "Me, too, Henrietta."

Chapter 25

"One mystery solved. It gives me hope that the solution to the next one is just around the corner." Birdie slipped out of the car, then looked back at Nell. "I can't help but think it's similar to this—it's right there in front of us."

Nell nodded. So close they could touch it. Maybe Henrietta and Enzo's sweet story would spur them on.

The drive back to Izzy's shop was quiet, Henrietta's story replaying in their heads. Each of them absorbing it in a personal way.

Enzo loves Henrietta.

And so he had.

Nell idled in front of the shop, and Izzy got out with a promise to call later.

"Where are you headed, Cass?" Nell asked her remaining passenger.

"A stop at the bank. Then home. And I'd love a ride if you're offering one."

"Of course I am." Nell drove the short two blocks down Harbor Road, pulling up in front of the bank while Cass ran inside. She kept the engine running, the heater blowing warm air around her legs and feet.

Up and down Harbor Road people went about their Monday business, bustling to keep the cold at bay. Shoppers were out in full force. College students home for the holidays, hugging old friends on the street. On the outside, so normal.

Nell wanted to hold on to the magic of Henrietta's lovely story. But it kept slipping away, blurred by the cold reality that in that same home—a home in which two people had loved so deeply—another two people had been coldly murdered.

A tap on the window pulled her free of her thoughts, and she looked up into the face of Tommy Porter. He leaned close, straddling the seat of his motorcycle, his gloved hands gripping the bars. He had changed into his uniform, a heavy blue jacket and hat with thick earflaps keeping him warm.

Nell rolled down the window.

"You going to be here long, Nell? It's a loading zone." He pointed to the sign.

"Just for a minute, Tommy. I'm waiting for Cass."

"Well, that's a kind of loading, I guess." He grinned and revved the engine.

Nell started to roll up the window, then stopped halfway and motioned Tommy closer. "Tommy, I know I've been asking you a lot of questions lately, but there's something you said to me the other day that doesn't make sense."

"Not the first time that's happened." Tommy laughed.

"Why was the police department so interested in Pamela's affair that summer? Not with Eddie, with the other man. Was it just gossip in the break room? Why did they even care?"

Tommy thought back over the years. His eyebrows came together intently. "I was brand-new on the force back then. Not really in on things. But I kept my ears open like you do when you're the new kid on the block." His frown disappeared as his memory cleared. "Oh, yeah. I remember now. It was police business; that's why they talked about it."

"How so?"

"Pamela Pisano had filed a restraining order to keep the guy away from her—it was all very hush-hush."

Nell frowned. "So you know who the man was?"

Tommy rubbed his cheek with a gloved finger. "Dunno. It seems the record of it disappeared. Weird, huh?"

He looked over at a group of youngsters walking by, their eyes bright as they passed the Village Toy Store, then turned back to Nell. "But why dredge up all that old stuff? We gotta think about the present, about the holidays coming. Right? And that means that Santa Claus comes in Wednesday on the boat. See you there?"

With that he gave a nod of his furry hat, revved his engine, and drove on down the street.

Izzy had texted everyone Monday night.

She didn't have any morning classes and the knitting room was free, so how about they meet for coffee and something from the new bakery over on Central?

No one had to ask why. The loose yarns were tangling up their lives. And knitters didn't suffer loose yarns gladly. Sleep was interrupted, parties had been canceled, and the beds in Ravenswood-by-the-Sea needed warm bodies sleeping in them.

Nell picked up Birdie at nine on the dot. "What's the racket over at Mary's bed-and-breakfast?" she asked as Birdie climbed in the car.

"Racket? It can't be Henrietta. . . . "

"No, she's basking in the pleasure of coming clean and having her memories shared. It looks like Mary's work crew."

"Mary said there were still some things that needed attention."

"A drive-through can't hurt," Nell said, heading back out Birdie's driveway to the street. "Be sure Mary's okay."

But they both knew it was more than that. Too much was still unresolved at Ravenswood-by-the-Sea to let even ordinary sounds go unchecked.

Nell turned into the drive and drove toward the house. Several men stood near the garage, dragging equipment out of the storage area. A truck was parked beside Mary's small car.

Birdie opened her window. "You young men have done a tremendous job over here."

One of the men doffed his hat, and Nell recognized the crew's foreman, Tom Asner, a broad, muscular man with a boxer's nose and a gentle smile.

Just then Mary came down the back porch steps. She wrapped her wool sweater around her and walked toward them, calling to the men. "Guys, Kevin just took some rolls from the oven and there's plenty of hot coffee. Help yourself."

"Final repairs?" Nell said.

Foreman Tom answered. "Oh, there're some of them, too, but today's more for takin' things apart, right, Mary?"

"It's the bed," Mary said to Nell and Izzy, as if that explained everything. Her eyes sparkled like they did after publishing an especially heartwarming "About Town" column.

"The bed?" Nell looked at Birdie, and in the next second it dawned on them both what was being dismantled.

Enzo Pisano's walnut bed.

"It's going to Henrietta's," Birdie guessed.

"Yes. Where it belongs. And these fine gentlemen are going to carefully take it apart, piece by piece. . . . "

"Just like Humpty-Dumpty," Tom said. "Only this time it'll be put back together just fine. Best-made piece of furniture I've ever seen. A privilege to work on it. We're bringing in a guy from Boston—restoration expert—who'll give us a hand over at the other house. Some Christmas present, wouldn't you say?"

Nell smiled. An amazing Christmas present. "Does Henrietta know?"

Mary nodded. "Kevin made Irish breakfast scones and picked up some Italian pastries at Harry's. We had a nice blending of cultures this morning, pastries, a few mimosas, and a pre–house warming for her new furniture."

Birdie pressed a hand to her chest. Good news was delicious. The men gathered up the toolboxes.

"Do the workmen keep their equipment here?" Nell asked.

"Usually, until they're done."

Tom called Mary over with a question, and Birdie and Nell watched as the men piled up large felt mats that would protect the pieces. Some of the long pieces wouldn't make it around the circular staircase, one of the men explained, so they'd wrap them and lower them through the windows.

Two men walked back to the truck and began unstrapping a ladder.

"There's the metal ladder," Birdie said, looking at Nell. She called out through the open window. "Why do you drag that monster back and forth? Wouldn't it be easier to leave it here until you're done?"

The man shrugged, chewed on his tobacco. "Sure, easier. We left it here for a while, but last week they said to take it away. Needed the room. Something about kitchen equipment—a new table, appliances being delivered."

"Kitchen equipment?"

"Yeah—they're getting some new stuff. Heavy-duty. So Kevin said to take our big things away, including the ladder."

Nell saw Mary look over, listening to the conversation.

"Coffee'll get cold, guys," she called out. "Kitchen door is open."

The men lumbered off, and Mary waved to Birdie and Nell

from the steps. "Close your window. It's cold out," she yelled, then disappeared around the corner of the house.

"If the ladder had stayed . . ." The thought caused Nell and Birdie both to take a deep breath. *Kevin sent the ladder back. Why?*

"Well, the ladder didn't stay. For whatever reason. And let's only hope that no one feels guilty about it. Living with those deadly 'if only's' is destructive," Birdie said.

But when they arrived at Izzy's shop, a box of *koloches* in hand, the feeling lingered. Nell felt she was drowning in "if only's." And what did it matter in the long run? If someone was going to murder a person, would any of that matter? Would they simply find another way, another time, another circumstance?

Mae was just opening the shop, turning the computer on and checking the cash drawer. She wore a cluster of holly in her salt-and-pepper hair, and the nose of her snowman lapel pin blinked every few seconds.

"Be prepared," she greeted Birdie and Nell.

"Like a Boy Scout?"

"It couldn't hurt." Mae gave them an unreadable look and went back to her cash box.

They spotted Cass' boots at the steps near the curved opening to the back room, and they heard the familiar voices of NPR anchors, pulling them into the day with news and radio interviews.

What they weren't prepared for was the square body sitting in the big leather chair by the fireplace. Henrietta O'Neal sat with Purl curled up in her ample lap, her face glowing. She looked twenty years younger than she had a scant twenty-four hours before.

"What's going on?" Nell asked, looking around for Izzy.

As if on cue, Izzy appeared through the alley door, carrying a brown cardboard container of Coffee's strong brew. She looked at Nell and Birdie, lifted her shoulders in a slight shrug. Her eyes told them she had no idea why Henrietta was sitting in her knitting room like a queen holding court.

"I'm here to help find the murderer," Henrietta said, without preamble. "Mary Pisano needs to open that beautiful home to guests; she needs to get on with her life and with writing that sweet column of hers. I may have . . . slowed it down some. Now I need to help."

"You're sweet to offer," Nell began. She gathered up the mugs and held each one while Izzy pressed the spigot. "But you've plenty going on at your own house, with that beautiful bed coming your way."

"I certainly do." Her eyes teared up, but she blinked the tears away and continued. "But I want to help with this. I'm fond of our fine police force, but sometimes they're held back by their own fussy rules. We don't have to put up with that rubbish."

Nell held back a smile. That certainly described the way Henrietta operated. She handed her a coffee mug and set the platter of filled pastries on the table.

"Who do you think did it?" Cass asked. She sat cross-legged on the couch, a pile of colorful knit squares at her side. She bit into a poppy-seed *koloche*.

"Well, I'll tell you what I think, and then I'll be off. It was someone who hated Pamela Pisano." She poked her finger in the air. "Troy DeLuca simply got in the way. He made the mistake of attaching himself to Pamela. He was sneaky. He wanted something."

But not what he got, Nell thought. No matter how sneaky he was, he didn't deserve that.

"Sometimes when I couldn't sleep, I'd walk down Ravenswood Road, just like Enzo and I used to do. And I'd see him sneaking up those steps to the carriage house. Sometimes he'd be doing it in the middle of the day while the other workmen were pounding away."

"And after Pamela died?"

"I'd see him then, too. I would have fired him, but Nancy said they'd paid him to paint. And he had to finish it."

Henrietta scootched to the edge of the chair. "I'm a good snoop. And I'm even better when I'm motivated. I'll be back. But one thing—Enzo worried about Pamela. About the way she played with men. He said it would get her killed one day."

She was gone before they had a chance to comment. Her stocky figure moving from side to side, the walking stick tapping its way through the knitting store.

"Confirmation," Birdie said.

"Trouble with men. But who could have hated her enough to kill her?

"Troy must have seen something, just as Nell suspected from the beginning. We know they were having an affair and he knew his way to the carriage house. He was there, waiting for her, probably to try to convince her of his worth as a model."

"He saw the murder," Izzy said. She wiped bits of fruit filling from the corner of her mouth.

"And he was blackmailing the murderer, not a wise thing to do, but it fits what we know of Troy," Birdie said. "He was broke and not very smart."

"The murderer had money." Nell thought of the fancy car that nearly ran them down. And the show of cash at the Edge. Troy got plenty of money from someone. "Or at least a way to get it easily."

"Maybe he asked for more and more, and pushed the person too hard."

"The murderer needed a way to get in the house and into the

kitchen to wait for her that night. All the Pisanos had keys, and it probably wouldn't have been hard to get one, especially with all the deliveries, the equipment, the workmen in and out." Cass grabbed another pastry.

"Someone who knew Pamela was going to be there alone that night," Nell said.

They were silent for a moment, devouring the *koloches*. Drinking coffee. Following strands of yarn and thinking back to that night. Thinking of the people who knew schedules and traffic patterns.

Thinking of someone who actually worked there? But no one would say Kevin's name out loud.

Nice people didn't kill.

"The murderer had to have had access to the ladder to fiddle with it," Cass said.

"And it seems too coincidental that the steel ladder that had been there all along was missing that night." Izzy rolled a needle between her hands, her brows pulled together tightly.

"They needed the room in the garage," Nell said, with more conviction than she felt. It was logical, she tried to convince herself.

Birdie began casting on stitches. Another soft square in a lavender wool. A soothing color. But her thoughts—lined up alongside Nell's—were anything but soothing.

"I suppose that makes sense," Izzy said.

"Maybe we need to revisit that night," Nell said, anxious to move away from the ladder. Maybe there was something else they'd heard but hadn't tended to. Perhaps in the repetition something would magically appear.

"Mary and Nancy both left early the night of the murder. And Mary was late getting back." *And if she hadn't been late . . .* The thought stuck there, uncomfortable. *Why was Mary late getting back?* Nell tried to remember. Dinner at the Gull. A bottle of wine. The restaurant was probably busy that night, with all the college kids home. Thursdays were party nights.

There it was again, the uncomfortable feeling of looking at something right in front of you and not seeing it.

"Troy was alone here when the ladder broke," Cass said. "Convenient. In case he didn't die from the fall, there'd be no one there to get him emergency help."

"We have all the threads," Izzy said, "but we're not working them right. They're still tangled. We need to know more about the man who died, the one who was obsessed with Pamela. Think outside the box. Think outside the bed-and-breakfast."

But the man was dead—a dead-end road. And yet it didn't feel that way. Nell thought back to the night Pamela was killed, the "I'm sorry" written in the snow. Someone wrote that message for her. They wanted Pamela to be sorry. For what . . . ?

"Pamela had a restraining order issued against the man. But it disappeared from the records, Tommy said. In a small town like this, you wouldn't want people to think someone had taken out a restraining order on you. The guy had friends protecting him, maybe? So perhaps that's the path we follow. Someone who is holding a grudge."

"But why kill her?"

"Why, indeed. It sounds flimsy, doesn't it? But maybe it's not."

"It doesn't *feel* flimsy," Izzy said. "We need to find out who this man was. His family. Siblings."

"And why did the restraining order disappear?" Nell was uncomfortable. She sensed the others were, too. She suspected they were all protesting the direction in which they were going, examining friends and neighbors, people they worked with. And the uncertainty of what they'd find, whom they might hurt.

The clicking of knitting needles echoed loudly in the room.

"We're an inch away," Izzy said.

"Sometimes those inches are the most difficult."

Especially when it meant a life.

"I wonder if Esther Gibson remembers any of this," Nell said. The longtime police dispatcher had enough Sea Harbor happenings stored away in her memory to fill a dozen movies. Some probably X-rated. "I'll talk to her."

A short while later, Birdie left to teach her tap-dancing class at the retirement home. Maybe a visit to Dolores Pisano in the adjoining nursing home was in order. "She has some lucid moments," she said.

"Good idea. But I need a sleuthing hiatus for a couple days," Cass said. "Pete and I have the honor of bringing Santa into the harbor tomorrow on the *Lady Lobster*. You'll all be there to greet us, I hope?"

Nell put her knitting away. "We all need a bit of Santa. We'll be there—right in the middle of those sweet happy little folks."

And maybe Santa would read the big folks' thoughts and bring them a wish. An end to this turmoil. Even if that meant hurting people in her life. Even then.

Nell gathered her things and walked over to the back windows, looking out at the harbor. Sailboats bobbed in the cold sea, tiny Christmas lights outlining the sails. Fishermen lumbered along the wharf, dragging nets and hauling traps with practiced ease. Across the harbor, up on the bluff, the children's park was filled with Santas big enough to climb on. A sleigh and reindeer alongside the snow-covered swings and monkey bars.

Familiar and comfortable. Carefree.

Izzy came up behind her. "It looks like a dozen other holiday seasons," she said. "It just doesn't feel that way."

Nell nodded.

"We haven't had time to talk much the last couple days. Alone, I mean."

"No."

"I'm proud of you, Aunt Nell. I know it's killing you not to ask about Sam."

Nell smiled. "You mean since committing your first felony in his home?"

"You're presuming that mail tampering was my first?"

Nell chuckled. "I suppose I can't be sure."

Izzy moved closer, her arm brushing Nell's. "Sam and I haven't had much time to talk, either—he was gone yesterday—Boston again. But I told him about being at the house. I apologized for looking through his mail. Told him I'd seen something from a hospital."

"And?"

"He asked if I had opened anything, and I said no—that I wanted to but didn't. He laughed, and then he hugged me and told me he wouldn't have me arrested if I'd make him those burritos he loves."

"That was it?"

"Yes. He said that things would work out, and that instead of worrying about imaginary things, I should concentrate on what I'm getting him for Christmas. So I've backed off. I want to get through Christmas. Then I can deal with this better. His secrecy—his personal life. I hate it, and I will have to deal with it. Just not right now."

Secrecy. A looming presence in their lives these days. Nell slipped an arm around her niece's waist and they stood together for a long time, wanting to think about nothing more complicated than the noses of harbor seals poking through the icy waters and watching the harbor life play out before them.

A calm and ordinary day.

Chapter 26

*E*ach town did it in its own unique way, but Sea Harbor was sure its way was the best. As soon as new calendars appeared in kitchens, the Wednesday before Christmas was circled in red, right along with birthdays and anniversaries.

It was a special day—the day Santa Claus came to town.

The festivities began at twilight, when Fire Chief Alex Arcado arrived in his truck and together with his stalwart team prepared the fire pit on the harbor green. They lit the first log to great cheering from a crowd of children, bundled up like Eskimos and waiting patiently with sticks and marshmallows. Families stood at the ready, their eyes peeled for the first sighting of the jolly man in red.

Pete Halloran's Fractured Fish band entertained with numerous rounds of "Frosty the Snowman" and "Rudolph the Red-Nosed Reindeer," the kids and grown-ups joining in, stomping boots and clapping mittened hands. Vendors passed out hot dogs and cups of chowder, lobster rolls, hot chocolate, and fish sandwiches on warm buttered hoagies.

Ben and Nell walked through the crowd toward the bonfire. They spotted Mary Pisano with Henrietta on her arm and waved them over. Agnes, dressed in a brilliant blue puffy coat, was on Henrietta's other side. Her hair hung loose and full to her shoulders.

She looked ten years younger, Nell told her.

Agnes brushed away Nell's compliments. "The magazine staff in New York isn't shy about commenting on clothes or hairstyles. This is my one concession to keep them quiet and force them back to real work. And I told them as much. I'm not in this to look beautiful. I'm in it to publish a beautiful magazine."

"Well, for whatever reason, you look like you're enjoying yourself, Agnes," Ben said. "And that's as it should be." He waved at a vendor and walked off to collect a tray of hot chocolate.

"Thank you. I've been back and forth this week, and I am enjoying the work. But frankly, there's too much unfinished business here with my family to completely enjoy anything. These murders are sucking the life out of us." Worry shadowed her face. "Pamela was family—and for better or worse, we were connected to Troy, too." She looked up at the sky as if trying to put words to her emotions. "I was supposed to meet with him Saturday down in New York to talk about his fashion shoot. He was thrilled about it, and then he never showed up. At first I was angry, that I'd gone out on a limb for him and he blew us off. Then Mary called with the awful news that he was dead. Murdered. And in Grandfather's backyard. It leaves you wondering why this is all happening to us . . . or who's next."

"No one is next," Birdie said with authority. "This is the end of it."

Nell agreed. "It's too close to all of us."

"And there are too many coincidences, things that, looking back, must have been planned carefully," Birdie said.

Agnes frowned. "Like what?"

Nell picked up the conversation. "The bed-and-breakfast had people in and out all the time. Yet those two times, the house was empty. Was it chance? How would the murderer have known that it'd be empty?"

Mary nodded. "I've thought about that, too. Whoever did this planned it carefully—but it wouldn't have been difficult to find out that information. You keep your eyes and ears open, you find things out."

You keep your eyes and ears open . . .

An innocent comment, but both Mary and Nell were acutely aware that too many innocent comments were pointing the wrong way.

They were pointing to the kitchen at Ravenswood-by-the-Sea. Pointing to Kevin Sullivan.

"Everyone is so focused on Ravenswood-by-the-Sea," Mary said. "The murders may have happened there, but I think we need to look beyond the Pisano family meeting and the kitchen help to find this murderer," Mary said with conviction.

But Nell didn't need convincing. She believed that to be true. It had to be true, or a very nice man was guilty of a horrible crime.

Clapping and laughter and hundreds of small cheering voices drew their attention to a sturdy white and maroon lobster boat, slowly making its way toward the pier. Bells jingled on the sides of the boat, and a group of playful elves atop the boat's cabin were kicking their red-tipped shoes and shaking tambourines in the air.

At the site of the boat, Pete and the Fractured Fish broke out into their own raucous rendition of "Here Comes Santa Claus."

And standing up on the bow of Cass' beautiful *Lady Lobster* was the man they'd been waiting for—Santa Claus in full dress, his thick white beard blowing in the breeze, his wide black belt circling his middle. August McClucken outdid himself, his "ho ho's" rolling all the way from ship to shore. Standing beside him was a new and welcome addition. Waving her heart out, her round cheeks as red as her stocking hat, was Mrs. Claus.

Ben lifted his binoculars. He lowered them and smiled broadly. "It's our own Esther Gibson."

Esther was grinning, her white hair billowing about her. Round rimless glasses defined her clear eyes, and a red velvet cape trimmed in white was pulled tight across her ample breasts.

Cass guided the boat in, then killed the engine as they neared the dock and looped ropes over the post. The elves—some of Esther's grandchildren—paraded off first, and next came Mr. and Mrs. Claus, patting children on the head as they made their way to a giant throne set up near the Fractured Fish band.

For the next hour, Santa listened and smiled, lifting little bodies on and off his wide knee. Esther sat dutifully at his side, handing out small bags of candy and toys.

As the fire died down and the firemen covered the glowing embers with sand, the temperature dropped sharply and parents scooped up happy children and hurried them off to bed.

A small group of friends stood around the fire rim, their attention focused on Izzy, her arms filled by a baby.

"Do you want to keep her for the next few days until all my shopping is done?" Laura Danvers teased. "She's much quieter in your arms."

Izzy grinned down at the chubby baby girl. "I'd keep her in a heartbeat."

Laura laughed and took the baby, settling her in a carrier while her husband gathered up the older children. "You need at least six of these, Izzy," she said.

Izzy smiled.

A year ago she would have had a comeback, some quick, clever retort. Tonight, at least in her aunt's eyes, she was hiding something that looked suspiciously like yearning.

"There you are, dearies; how did I do?"

Esther Gibson walked over to the group, swinging her red cape dramatically. A knit stocking cap was pulled over her gray hair.

"The real McCoy," Ben said.

"The kids loved you, Esther."

"And I didn't even need a costume, though I don't know if that's such a good thing." She patted her middle.

"I'll bring the car around," Ben called out as he and Sam made their way across the harbor grounds.

Izzy and Nell walked slowly on either side of Esther, helping her over the snow-packed ground.

"Is there anything new on the Ravenswood Road murders?" Nell asked.

Esther shook her head. "My poor men are working like Trojan horses, but I think it might become one of those cold cases like on TV. Nothing leads very far. Poor Kevin Sullivan's name is tossed about like a ship on an angry sea, but I tell them exactly what I think of that. I don't mince words with the men. That's how you have to treat them."

"Esther, do you remember a few summers ago—just before Jerry became chief—when Pamela Pisano was here helping her mother move into the nursing home?"

Esther thought back. "Poor Dolores," she said, her memory clearing. "She just couldn't handle it in that big house any longer. She was forgetting things, wandering off."

"Pamela had a problem with a man that summer, I understand."

"Yes," Esther said. "One she brought on herself, but a problem nevertheless."

"Mary remembers a restraining order."

"Yes."

"It was kept quiet."

Esther nodded.

"Why?" Izzy asked. "When I got my first speeding ticket over on Eastern Avenue, the entire town knew it before I got back to Aunt Nell's."

"I remember that," Esther said with a wise nod of her head. "Forty-five miles when you should have been going under thirty, dearie. But this other situation, well, sometimes things need to remain private. Pamela had put a spell on this man—or whatever it was she did that made men follow her around like puppy dogs. The chief told us he was a respectable and generous man who simply went crazy over her, head over heels. He was obsessed with Pamela Pisano; that was the word the chief used."

There was that word again. But Nell could tell from Esther's tone that she had far more sympathy for the obsessed man than for Pamela Pisano.

"That still doesn't explain the need to keep it so quiet."

"It was old Chief Roberts, God rest his soul. He was a kind old man, too old for the job but a good family man. His heart was in the right place."

They had reached the curb on Harbor Road, and Esther's husband, Richard, sat behind the wheel of his truck, tapping the horn.

"So the chief kept it secret? Got rid of the records?"

"Yes."

"Why?" Izzy asked.

Esther frowned at Izzy and Nell as if they had missed part of the conversation. She turned and told her husband to hold his horses. Then she looked back, shaking her head sadly.

"He did it because he was a gentleman. The man asked him to do it. He wanted to protect his innocent wife."

Chapter 27

"*T*he man's *wife*," Izzy repeated the next afternoon as the knitters carved out time for a late lunch at Harry's Deli.

"The guy was goofy over Pamela, but he wanted to protect his *wife*. The dude should have thought of that before having an affair. But I suppose news of a restraining order would have been really awful for her," Cass said, piecing it together. "He saved her that, at least."

"Exactly. The affair would have been spread all over town."

That was the conclusion Nell, Ben, Sam, and Izzy had come to the night before, as well. After talking with Esther, they'd stopped for a drink and a sandwich before heading home. The small bar and grill over in Essex offered a little privacy along with great olive and fennel tuna melts.

Sam and Ben had listened while Izzy and Nell talked. They replayed Esther's comments and tried to fill in the gaps about the man who had fallen in love with Pamela Pisano, and a wife behind the scenes.

Ben was going to meet with Jerry Thompson in the morning. Even records that disappeared sometimes might not *really* disappear. Besides, he said with clear intent, the chief needed to know about this new direction in which they were heading. He might have a logical explanation for all their suspicions and be able to shred them to pieces in an instant.

Nell fervently hoped so.

She looked around the deli table at Izzy, Birdie, and Cass now. For days they had struggled with Pamela's murder, not finding a thread that would tie the clues together. Perhaps they were about to find it.

Thursday afternoons were normally quiet in the restaurant, but today there was a constant buzz as people ordered pastries and deli trays for the holidays, or took a break from holiday shopping for a cup of soup or grilled pastrami on rye.

"I saw Pamela's mother yesterday," Birdie said without preamble. She pulled a pad of paper from her backpack and set it on the table. It was filled with scribbled notes in Birdie's small scrawl. "Dolores Pisano is a lovely lady, even now."

"Did she know you?"

Birdie shook her head no. "She said she did, but then she called me Angela. She seemed to have a difficult time dealing with the present. But when I asked her about the past, like the summer she moved into the nursing home, she remembered things in excruciating detail."

They leaned in closer.

"Did she talk about Pamela? About her problems that summer with a man?"

"Not directly. I think Pamela protected her mother from the sordid details of her life. But Dolores did remember a few things that were odd. She remembered the day Pamela came to tell her she was going back to New York. Pamela told her it was important, that it was crucial she leave, even though she had promised her mother she'd stay another few weeks."

"Did she tell her why?" Izzy asked.

"I couldn't tell. I talked to one of the nurses who's been there as long as Dolores. She said Dolores was very upset when

Pamela left early. She was just becoming comfortable in the nursing home, and Pamela's abandoning her was difficult. She took a turn for the worse. Wouldn't eat. Didn't want to be there. But then a strange thing happened, and she rallied."

"What was that?"

"Dolores told me about this herself. She started receiving beautiful bouquets of flowers, every single day. Enormous arrangements, roses and orchids, lilies and birds of paradise. Each day they were different, one arrangement more beautiful than the next. Dolores described them in amazing detail, like a photographer might. She remembered the kinds of flowers, how tight the buds were, the brilliant colors. It was amazing."

"Were the flowers from Pamela?"

"The nurse said no. Pamela was edgy when she heard about it, nervous that someone was sending her mother flowers, and she asked the nurses to check them carefully. They thought that was an odd request—but did as she asked. The flowers meant so much to Dolores, though, that they always gave them to her. The nurse said she'd never seen such beautiful blooms."

Birdie sat back in her chair as Margaret Garozzo set four bowls of steaming clam chowder on the table.

"Then another odd thing happened. One day, about a month later, the flowers stopped coming. Just like that. No notice. Dolores remembered the exact day. September 15. The nurse couldn't verify the date, but she said Dolores sometimes remembered obscure things from her past—like the exact date she had a tetanus shot. So she was probably right about the date. And she was absolutely right that the flowers never came again. Not after that day. Every single day, then nothing. The staff and residents missed them almost as much as Dolores did."

Nell looked over at Birdie's notepad. "What's that?" She pointed to a name written out and underlined.

Birdie looked down. "That's the name of the florist. The staff loved the flowers so much that they remembered where they came from and started using the florist for holiday events."

Birdie looked up to see Mary Pisano and Nancy Hughes, weaving their way between the tables. Their faces were somber. Nancy said something to Mary, then walked toward the restroom. Birdie waved Mary over to the table.

"How are things going?" Nell asked. It was one of those things you say, but you already know the answer. *Things are fine—as fine as they can be.*

Not so fine at all.

"It's not been a great day," Mary began.

"What?" Cass asked.

Mary sighed. "Jerry Thompson had us come down to the station again. He's trying to tie up some loose ends, he said. It's distressing."

"What kind of loose ends?"

"Random questions. And repeating the same things we've told him before. Nancy and I each talked to him this morning, separately, as if we'd have different stories, imagine. They've talked to family members again. And Kevin just texted me that he's headed down to the station now."

"Kevin?" Izzy said. "Why?"

"He doesn't know any more than we do. Just confirming what we don't know, I guess."

"But on the up side of things, Kevin has a month's worth of breakfast menus made up. And as soon as the police nail this, maybe I'll actually have overnight guests to enjoy them."

"I think they're close," Izzy said.

Mary's smile was slow to come. "You do?"

"We hope so. And I know you do, too." Birdie's calming voice brought a genuine smile to Mary's lips. "And I wouldn't worry about the questions. It's just what they do. Dotting i's and crossing t's."

"There may be a connection between the married man Pamela was involved with that summer and the murder," Nell said.

"Married? I didn't know he was married," Mary said.

Nell nodded.

Mary was quiet, frowning. "Married," she said again, as if processing its significance. "What would Troy's connection be?"

"Maybe he knew who murdered Pamela; at least that's a possibility."

"So . . . blackmail?" Mary said slowly. "That's plausible. Troy was different after Pamela died—but not in a grieving way. He was even cockier, more arrogant than before. And it would explain all that money. I often wondered why he even stuck around to paint the eaves for us, but somehow Nancy talked him into it. Do you think the man Pamela was involved with still lives on Cape Ann?"

Nell started to shake her head but was saved from answering by Nancy's return and the arrival of the beefy deli owner.

Harry Garozzo wedged himself in between Nancy and Mary, wrapping an arm around each of them. "How am I so blessed?" he said. "Six of Sea Harbor's most ravishing ladies in my deli at the same time. God is good."

"You're just a lucky man, Harry. A heck of a lucky man," Cass said.

"Come, come," Harry said, and he ushered Mary and Nancy to the front of the deli, his arms still around their waists, guiding them toward a festive display of cheeses, wines, and flatbreads. "The perfect welcome for Ravenswood-by-the-Sea guests," they heard him say. "A beautiful guest basket—"

They pulled their attention back to the table, trying to bury their increasing anxiety beneath slices of Harry's strawberry cheesecake. A married man. A wife. In hushed tones and with heavy hearts, they tugged at the loose strands.

Izzy was the first to stand up. "I have a class to teach. But it's Thursday—knitting night. Will I see you later?"

"Knitting night," Nell repeated, startled at the loss of time.

Birdie checked her watch. "I think Nell and I will do a little investigating. But we'll be back in time. We've tossed all these things in the air. We need to bring them down calmly. One by one."

Nell nodded. "But I'm not sure I'll have time to fix food for us."

"No problem," Cass said. "We'll order lobster rolls from Gracie, if need be."

"That would be lovely," Birdie said.

They bundled up and hurried off in different directions, with promises to meet at the usual time. But it wouldn't be a usual Thursday night. They all knew that.

Nell and Birdie sat in the Endicott CRV with the engine running, forcing heat into the car and gathering their thoughts.

"The florist?" Birdie said. "It's a long shot, but maybe they'll have some record of Dolores Pisano's flowers."

Nell nodded. The address Birdie had found for Flowers by Frances was in Gloucester, a short drive along the coast. An odd request like theirs would be better asked in person. Credibility could be questioned over a phone line, but people rarely—if ever—denied Birdie Favazza anything when standing in front of the diminutive matron, face to face.

"Parking karma, as always," Birdie said as Nell pulled into a space in front of the florist shop. It was long and narrow, as was Frances, the owner, who greeted them just inside the door. She wore a flowery name tag on her thick gray sweater and a sprig of holly in her hair.

Birdie breathed in the fragrant air. "In my next life, I want to be you, Frances," she said.

Frances smiled back.

Birdie explained their mission, while Nell walked to the side of the store and made a quick call to Ben. When he didn't answer, she left a short message, trying to squeeze the new information into a few sentences. It was all beginning to fit together, the conclusion she knew Ben would come to, as well.

In the safe confines of the car, she and Birdie had laid out all the bits and pieces of information that they'd gathered for days now, moving around the pieces of information as if they were in a heated Scrabble game. An obsessive man. A wife. And Mary's bed-and-breakfast planted right in the middle of it all.

Nell frowned as the red light on her cell phone indicated a low battery. A distracting couple of days, she thought. If forgetting to charge her battery was the biggest thing she'd done—or not done—she'd be fortunate.

Frances didn't remember the exact dates they were asking about, but she certainly remembered the daily deliveries to the nursing home. The deliveries were arranged over the phone, so she'd never met the sender, but after a couple of weeks of daily deliveries, she had asked him about the occasion for sending the flowers.

"Did you get an answer?"

Frances nodded. The woman had had a setback in the nursing home. "Apparently she was almost adjusted to living there, but her daughter had to leave suddenly, and she relapsed. For some strange reason, the man felt responsible for the setback and thought the flowers might help her recover. He was a sweet man."

Nell wondered how the man knew about Dolores' setback, but a sensible answer came quickly. An obsessive person would have attempted to track Pamela down in New York. And never one to mince words, Pamela probably accused him of affecting her mother's health. The man was kind, the old chief had said. A good person. It worried him. Hurting his wife worried him. Like an alcoholic, destroying a family he loves.

"Do you have the man's name?" Nell asked.

Frances scratched her head. She was sure she did somewhere because it was a credit card order. But it might take a while. "I keep careful records," she assured them. "But that was a few years ago, you understand. Three or four."

And then she'd smiled, took Birdie's number, and promised to call if she found the name.

When they got back to Sea Harbor, the sky was dark.

"One more stop," Nell said, checking her watch. She pulled into the *Sea Harbor Gazette*'s parking lot.

They hurried through the cold, their coat collars pulled up to their ears, and found the records room and a bank of computers.

Obituaries, Nell typed in, and together, counting on their fingers, she and Birdie came up with the year. Then Nell typed in *September 15*.

They held their breath as they pounded the last nail in the coffin.

Chapter 28

$\mathcal{M}$ae had already locked down the day's receipts and left for the day when Birdie and Nell finally hurried through the front door of the Seaside Knitting Studio.

Izzy and Cass came in from the back. "Where've you been? We were worried."

"At the library, the newspaper. A florist over in Gloucester," Nell said, attempting to lighten the tension, but there was nothing light about how she felt inside.

Birdie leaned against Mae's counter, catching her breath. "We've pulled together what we need to know. The dates. Names. The coincidences that weren't really that at all."

Birdie held out the notes she had jotted on the pad of paper that afternoon while Nell had driven from place to place.

Dolores Pisano's surprise flowers had been sent to assuage a guilty conscience, Birdie explained to Cass and Izzy. The deliveries were stopped suddenly without an explanation.

"Why?" Izzy asked.

As if in answer to her question, Birdie's cell phone rang. She looked down at the unfamiliar number.

"The florist?" Nell suggested.

Birdie pressed the button, and Frances began talking. She'd

found the records they were interested in, the dates. And the name of the generous, thoughtful sender.

He had stopped sending the flowers September fifteenth, just as Dolores Pisano had remembered.

Birdie hung up.

"That was the day he killed himself," Nell said.

They stood in stunned silence.

The dots. The connecting lines. All the loose strands of yarn that had been dangling for days were being knit together tightly—and making horrible sense.

All the way down to Mary's dog, Georgia, who had enough trust to follow the murderer out to the porch.

Nell tried again to get Ben, and again left a message. She managed to get the important words out before the battery went dead, this time for good. "Ben is very good about taking his phone. He just doesn't remember to turn it on," she murmured, as if somehow the phone was partially responsible for Ben's lack of attention.

"I almost forgot," Izzy said. "Mary Pisano called, looking for you, Birdie. She was upset. She wanted you to call."

"The police questioned her today," Birdie said, frowning.

"Nancy and Kevin, too," Nell added.

Birdie quickly dialed Mary's number.

Mary started talking without a hello.

Finally Birdie hung up and faced the others. "After Kevin was questioned by the police today, he went back to the bed-and-breakfast looking for Nancy. He was furious, Mary said, an anger so black she was almost afraid of him. He tore out of her house, mumbling something about Nancy and this being the last straw." Birdie paused. Then she said quietly, "Mary was afraid he might harm Nancy."

They piled into Nell's car and headed east toward Canary Cove.

Izzy called Sam, pulling him out of a meeting with the Sea

Harbor Arts Council. She gave him the short version of the day and asked him to find Ben, to call Jerry Thompson, and to meet them.

Birdie and Cass sat in the backseat, suggesting that Nell slow down—the road was narrow and they didn't want to miss Christmas.

Lights were shining brightly on the trees lining the Hughes' drive. Nell pulled in and parked behind Kevin's beat-up Volkswagen. Inside, every room was lit, as if a holiday party was about to begin.

The front door was open, and Nell spotted Kevin through the storm door. His jacket was open, his brows pulled together tightly, his face beet red. His anger masked the Kevin she knew, distorting his features. He was walking across the family room, calling out Nancy's name.

Nell slipped through the open door. Cass, Izzy, and Birdie followed.

"What the hell were you thinking, Nancy?" Kevin's voice, thick with anger, rumbled through the house like a freight train.

They couldn't see Nancy at first, but from another room, her voice traveled to the front hallway, calm and controlled, as if the museum board were sitting in front of her, waiting for her monthly report.

"What do you want, Kevin? You shouldn't be here."

Her voice was coming from Dean's den.

"I want to know why you're crucifying me. You know I didn't kill Pamela Pisano. The police told me what you said, questioned me like a criminal—"

"I only told them the truth."

"That I hated her? That I threatened her? That she knew I was gay and was going to use it to destroy my family?"

"I had to tell them the truth, Kevin."

Kevin moved through the door of the den.

From the hallway, Nell watched Nancy's shadow as she moved to the glass case against the wall. Her breath caught in her throat. The hunting wall, the glass case filled with Dean's guns. Then she heard the click of the lock and the opening of the glass door.

"You told them I threatened Troy," Kevin continued. "That I was the one who knew where all the garage tools were. That I told the workmen to take the metal ladder away."

"You *did* tell them to take it away, Kevin."

Kevin exploded. "Sure I told them to take it away. I told them because *you* told me to. You said some deliveries were coming. I did what you told me to do. What are you trying to do to me, Nancy? What have I ever done to you?" His voice rose until it vibrated off the walls. "You all but told them I was the one who killed those two people—and you gave them reasons to believe you. Are you crazy? What's Mary going to think?"

"She's going to think that you killed them, Kevin," Nancy said calmly. "And then you tried to kill me."

At that moment, Nancy spotted Nell. The color drained from her face, and she stared at Nell and Birdie as they moved toward the wide den door. Izzy and Cass were a few steps behind them.

Kevin's head spun around, and then he looked back at Nancy. "What's going on . . . ?"

Nell's voice was quiet, a schoolteacher's voice, forcing calmness into an unruly classroom. "It's all right, Kevin. No one thinks you murdered Pamela and Troy."

Birdie took a few steps toward Nancy. "It's over now, dear," she said. "Your nightmare is over." She stopped a few feet away, letting her words fill the space between them.

Nancy stared back at her, then the others, and then her body seemed to shrink, her shoulders slumping forward. The look of a trapped animal filled her narrow face. She stared at the gun in her hand. "This was the gun Dean killed himself with; did you

know that? And this"—she flapped a piece of paper in the air—
"this was the note he left for me. I told the police he didn't leave
one, but he did, a private note, meant only for me." Her voice
dropped, and she stared at the piece of stationery as if it had
suddenly betrayed her.

Nell thought back over the years she had known Nancy
Hughes. The composed, capable woman who did so much for
the museum. She had changed after Dean committed suicide;
they had all seen that. It was understandable, everyone said.
Such a good man doing such a horrible thing, without any reason. But Nell never imagined the depth of Nancy's anguish—
and what it had done to her. A terrible disease, eating away at
her core.

Nancy looked up from the letter. "He said he was sorry. And
he loved me—his smart, pretty wife. That's what he wrote." She
looked down and read slowly, " 'But, my darling Nancy, I cannot
function anymore. I have nothing left to give you. I'm empty.
She's taken it all. I cannot live without her.' "

Nell thought of the words Nancy had written in the snow
beside Pamela's lifeless body, hoping it would seem like a suicide to the police. *I'm sorry.* It's what she wanted Pamela to be
for ruining her life. What Dean was for ruining hers. *Sorry.*

Nancy looked at the people surrounding her, her usual control lost in the confusing moment. Then she lifted the gun again
and looked at it intently.

Birdie started to move, but Nell put her hand on her arm and
pulled her back a step.

Emotion had drained from Nancy's face, and Nell remembered that same look at Dean's funeral. Nancy had never cried.
People said she was brave, holding it together. An amazing, remarkable woman, dealing with terrible loss. A man who had every reason to live but threw it all away.

"Full circle," Nancy said, the words catching in her throat. "There's nowhere for me to go, is there?"

In the distance, Nell heard the sounds of cars on gravel, but Nancy seemed not to notice. She cradled the gun, as if it were a special gift.

"Nancy," Nell managed to say. "Don't . . . "

Nancy didn't seem to hear. It was as if she were alone in Dean's room. Just the two of them, talking as lovers. Her words were whispered. "I kept your gun, my darling. And I finally rescued you from her, just as I promised. You're free now, my love."

"Nancy, why don't you give it to me?" Birdie said softly. "You don't need it any longer."

Nancy looked at it. "She ruined people's lives. I've done a good thing. People will thank me."

Close by, Nell felt Ben's presence. And Sam's. Out of the corner of her eye, she saw a sea of blue uniforms walking past the window, making their way into the hallway.

Nancy's hand was unsteady, but her voice was clear.

"Troy DeLuca thought I would support him for the rest of his self-indulgent life to hold his silence. He watched it all from the carriage house, waiting for Pamela to come to him that night. But instead of getting Pamela that night, he thought he'd gotten the mother lode. He rejoiced. He demanded a little bit one day, a lot more the next. And on and on and on. I had to keep him close, to watch him, until I figured out what to do. It would never have stopped." Her forehead furrowed as if it pained her to think about it.

"I'm truly sorry it had to be at Enzo's house; that's a deep regret. Ravenswood-by-the-Sea is a wonderful place. Pamela didn't deserve to die there." Her voice dropped, and she seemed to be speaking to herself. "And she didn't deserve my husband. . . . "

Nell saw the slight movement of Nancy's hand as she turned the gun toward herself. But before anyone could move, Kevin lunged toward Nancy.

The pistol clattered to the floor, the blow causing a bullet to explode and tear through the leather cushions of Dean Hughes' favorite chair.

Nancy's body began to weave, a hollow reed unable to support skin and bones and muscles any longer. In one swift movement, Kevin's arms grabbed her, cradling her shrinking body as she collapsed to the floor in a torrent of wrenching tears.

He stayed there for a moment, his arms holding her as her body shook with grief.

For the first time since Dean Hughes' tragic death, his wife grieved his loss.

Chapter 29

*I*t was a sad group that caravanned to 26 Ravenswood Road, to the comforting warmth of Mary's kitchen.

Tears fell copiously as they took turns filling Mary in on Nancy's terrible, heartbreaking story. All the deceits.

They laid the facts out on the kitchen island, one following after another, small invisible lines connecting the flowers, Dean's death, Nancy's vigilance over the goings-on at the bed-and-breakfast.

"Mary," Nell asked presently, after the facts of the day had been lined up along the island like cups of tea, "why were you so late meeting us the night that Pamela was murdered?"

"Nancy had planned for us to meet at the Ocean's Edge. But then she was late getting there. She called and said to wait; she'd be there soon."

"So she made sure you stayed away."

"And the night Troy was killed, it was Nancy who decided we needed a night off. She had Ed and me over for dinner that night."

"After she'd made sure the ladder would collapse beneath his weight," Izzy said.

"She was handier than any of us," Kevin said. "She knew

how to use those tools better than I did. But she made sure I was the one who moved them around, who carried out the ladder, who sent the good ladder back with the work crew."

"I wanted to fire Troy after Pamela died," Mary said. "Kevin and I didn't trust him, but Nancy convinced me we needed him."

"She needed him close, where she could watch him," Nell said.

"I always thought her insistence on Troy painting the eaves was a bit silly, but she paid such close attention to detail, I bought it."

Kevin sat at the island, listening to Mary, his eyes offering what comfort he could. But they had both befriended Nancy. And in the end, her betrayal was too enormous to get their arms around immediately.

"In time," Ben said, seeing emotion cloud Kevin's face.

He nodded.

Sam arrived then, his arms filled with platters of Gracie's special lobster rolls, a heaping salad, and several bottles of wine.

"Fortification," Mary whispered, pulling herself up as high as she could to embrace the tall photographer.

"Nancy was a victim, too," Nell said. She took the platter of lobster rolls from Sam's bag and passed them around, encouraging everyone to eat.

"Imagine losing your husband because he couldn't live without another woman," Izzy said.

"I think Dean cared deeply for Nancy—but he was . . . "

"Obsessed," Izzy said. "How many times did we hear that word these past weeks?"

Cass nodded. "Obsessed . . . it was like an addiction."

"So terribly sad."

"It's hard to understand unless you've walked in those shoes." Ben passed around glasses of wine. Outside, the sky was dark, and the wind picked up.

"I think Nancy sensed we were beginning to pull it all together. Trying to focus the blame on Kevin was a last-ditch effort," Cass said.

"She was frightened," Nell said. "Nancy is such a bright woman. She must have known that things were closing in on her."

"She overheard one of you talking about the man Pamela had an affair with," Mary said. "She told me it was absurd. But I sensed concern in her voice."

They finished off the platter of lobster rolls and the arugula salad, surprised at themselves that they enjoyed the food so thoroughly.

And then the group of friends began to slowly drift off, first Cass to meet Danny at the Gull.

She glanced at her phone message. It was the third time he'd texted her in the past hour. "The news is traveling along Harbor Road. Danny just needs to see my gorgeous face." She laughed roughly and sorted through the pile of coats, finding her jacket.

Sam stood next, stretching his arms above his head.

Nell watched his movements. She'd seen the great relief that had flooded his face when he entered the Hughes house earlier and found Izzy all right. Now she saw something else.

Resolve.

"Hey, Iz," he said, looking across the island where she sat on a leather stool. "Any chance I could give you a ride home? It's been a long day. I could use a cup of your horrible coffee."

Izzy looked up. Her face lacked the grin Sam seemed to be hoping for.

The day had affected them all in different ways, Nell thought. Thoughts tumbled over thoughts. Emotions grasped for meaning. Lives were examined.

"Okay," Sam said, shrugging. "How about a glass of wine and a fire? I need some time with you. Please?"

Izzy didn't answer, but she slipped on her boots and shrugged into her jacket. The two of them walked silently out the back door, along the porch. Nell watched as Sam pulled her close, lowered his head. And then they disappeared into the blackness of the night.

Ben drew her attention back.

"Let's polish off these last couple inches, Kevin," he said, emptying the bottle of cabernet into the glasses. "Better than Nyquil."

Kevin took the wine with a half smile.

Weariness spread through his body as he drained his glass. His expression was grave and thoughtful at once.

"I suppose I was the likely person for her to try to divert attention to," he said. "The police already had reason to suspect me because Troy had planted that wallet in my locker. He wanted them looking at me, not him, so he could go about his business of blackmailing Nancy. I guess he wouldn't have wanted them looking at Nancy, either. She was his ticket out of here."

"You were around all the time. It was easy to assume you'd know where tools were, what people's schedules were," Nell said. "She was frightened. Nancy so rarely couldn't control things. She was beginning to unravel."

Ben reached for their coats and handed one to Nell, then Birdie.

Birdie slipped hers on and walked around the table to Kevin. She stood between Mary and Kevin and wrapped Kevin in a hug, her arms barely circling his shoulders.

"It happens to all of us, sweet Kevin," she whispered in his ear. "It's been a long haul. But it's over."

Chapter 30

Nell stood next to Ben in front of the fireplace, looking up into Enzo Pisano's wide gray eyes. A roaring fire crackled, heating their legs and arms.

"You're blushing," Ben said, wrapping an arm around her shoulder.

Nell lifted a hand to her warm cheek. "The fire. The evening. You."

"It's good to know I can still bring fire to your cheeks."

Nell smiled and leaned into his side. "Enzo would love all this."

"Every minute of it."

"It's good, isn't it? All of it."

Ben looked down at his wife of nearly forty years. He nodded. "Yes, it is." Ben understood the touch of sadness in his wife's voice, intrinsically mixed with joy.

It had been a long week, from putting a murder behind them—to celebrating the living. With the Pisanos' tragedy put to rest, they could concentrate more fully on those they loved.

Ben had known about Sam's journey for a few days, but Sam had asked him not to talk about it. It was the way Sam handled things, Ben said. He was careful. But it was probably more about caring than anything else. Caring for Izzy. Once you see your life taking a turn, he'd said to Ben, you check all directions to make sure there's nothing bad around the corner. Surprises you don't want in your life—or in someone else's.

He loved Izzy, he said, although no one needed to be told that.

And if they were ever to consider an honest future, he needed to know more about himself. History, medical things, like the genes he carried. So he'd gone back to Kansas and Colorado, pulled out records, asked lots of questions. He found out little about his birth parents. Hippies, he was told. Lived in communes. Came from California. But nothing that answered the pressing questions in his head.

So he'd checked himself into Boston General and subjected himself to every test known to man. Hereditary predispositions. Carrier testing. Sperm counts. All sorts of things he'd never thought about, not until Izzy became the center of his life.

"Why didn't you tell her what you were doing?" Nell had demanded, her relief tangled up in Izzy's anguish.

Ben had shushed her and told her to listen.

"Because I know your niece so well," Sam had answered quietly. "Izzy would have said it didn't matter. That she only cared about me. And she would have believed it. But I needed to know for myself what I had to offer her. Alone. It's my way."

It wasn't the words, really, but the emotion behind them that convinced Nell he was right. We all needed to be true to ourselves, whatever that meant or how it worked. She thought of Izzy's love for babies, the look in her eyes when she held them. Maybe Sam knew a part of her that even she hadn't been privy to.

When the final tests came back, he'd sat Izzy down and shared his journey. He didn't know his parents, but he knew he had good, decent genes, as far as medical science could report, anyway.

Nell brushed her head against Ben's shoulder. She could stay right here in Enzo Pisano's living room, the flames crackling, the music playing, for a long, long time, and be happy.

Mary had flung open the doors to Ravenswood-by-the-Sea to the whole town. It was a joyous Christmas Eve. Soon guests would begin filling the rooms of the bed-and-breakfast. Tonight it was all about friends and neighbors, about the holidays, and Mary had pulled out all the stops.

Across the room, the Scaglias sat with the Wootens, Mayor Stan Hanson was there with his wife, Roberta. Willow Adams and Pete Halloran were engaged in deep conversation, their heads inclined toward each other. A lovely sight, in Nell's mind.

They waved to the Garozzos and Brandleys, to Annabelle Palazola cradling her grandbaby as her daughter Liz and husband Alphonso looked on, not letting the baby get far from their sight. Mary Pisano moved from group to group, welcoming everyone, thanking people for the cards and generous housewarming gifts they'd sent—the dozens of poinsettias filling the hallways, silver and crystal ornaments dripping from the branches of the enormous tree. But it wasn't the gifts; it was what they meant, why they'd been sent; that's what Mary said.

Nell and Ben moved through the crowded living room, through the halls, and beyond the winding staircase. They spotted Ham Brewster in the den, and he met them at the door, kissing Nell beneath the mistletoe hanging from the wide doorway. Jane, holding Henrietta O'Neal's arm, waved at them from a table across the room. It was filled with Kevin's bacon-wrapped figs and enormous mushrooms stuffed with crab and arugula, fruit plates and Christmas cookies, tiny roast beef sandwiches with horseradish dressing, and heaped platters of lobster rolls.

The paneled room had been Enzo's library, and still held his comfortable leather chairs and collection of books. The eight-foot-high ceiling had walnut beams crossing from side to side. French doors opened up to the porch.

A waiter appeared, a tray of champagne glasses balanced in his hands.

Jane beckoned them over to the food table. "An amazing spread. Ham and I went to the kitchen to tell Kevin as much, but we left when Danny Brandley and Kevin began discussing which one of them makes the best chowder. It looked like it might turn into a duel."

"It's fortunate Cass has found a man who cooks," Nell said.

"I heard my name," Cass called out, weaving around Elliott Danvers, heatedly discussing football play-offs with Jerry Thompson.

"Of course I found a man who cooks. It was the number one priority—well, next to being witty and good-looking and charming and kind to dogs and an amazing mystery writer." She lifted one shoulder in a shrug and grinned. "They're a dime a dozen."

"So where are the other kids?" Henrietta asked, causing another chorus of chuckles.

"The kids? Wellllll," Cass drew out the word for effect. "Two of the kids have disappeared." She turned and looked through the French doors, waving her arms dramatically. "I think they've gone off into the winter night. Two lost souls."

Beyond the windows and the porch, the lawn's pathways were lit with low lights, a winding maze from the porch all the way back to the woods. Spotlights beneath the enormous trees cast beams up into the snow-crusted branches. It was a winter wonderland.

As her eyes adjusted to the night, Nell spotted two figures walking toward the house, their arms looped around each other, their gait as slow as if it were the sunniest of summer days.

At first, taking in the scene playing out in front of her, Nell was oblivious to the weather. But then the white flakes grew plump, dancing in the icy air, twirling around, touching the ground.

"It's snowing," someone behind her said.

And then the flakes began to fall in earnest, growing in size and number, until the sky was white with wonder.

The couple drew closer to the house. Sam and Izzy, their hair flecked with snow, their faces lifted to the sky, tongues catching dancing flakes. Rich laughter.

Jubilant laughter.

Nell opened the French doors, and they all crowded in the opening, caught up in the wonder of the night—the snow falling in front of them, the crackling fire at their backs. In the distance, the bells of Our Lady of the Seas began to ring, rolling down the hills and narrow streets, filling the town with joy.

Izzy and Sam walked up onto the porch.

Izzy walked over to Nell and wrapped her scarf around her aunt's neck. "You're crying, Aunt Nell."

Nell brushed the moisture away, oblivious of the cold. She held Izzy's gaze fast. "Izzy—"

Izzy's laugh was as light as the snowflakes and as rich as the emotion swirling around inside Nell. "I'm crying, too."

She lifted one hand in front of Nell's brimming eyes. A deep blue diamond sparkled. "Do you think Mary would like to have a wedding here? They say it brings good luck. Peace and prosperity. But then, I'd always thought your backyard would be nice. . . . "

And then she melted into her aunt's arms.

Sam stood beside Ben a few steps away. He watched the two women for a minute or two. And then he crossed the distance in an easy stride, and his big arms collected Izzy and pulled her close as if he'd never let go.

In the distance, the music changed. The CD quieted, and live guitars, drums, and the keyboard of the Fractured Fish filled the rooms and hallways of the bed-and-breakfast.

The partygoers hushed as Pete's and Merry's voices blended together, and their hearts belted out the familiar words, words about friendship, about being together. Magical words. And by the song's end, a chorus of robust voices, young and old, joined in and filled Mary Pisano's Ravenswood-by-the-Sea with holiday joy:

> *Hang a shining star upon the highest bough.*
> *And have yourself a merry little Christmas now.*

The Seaside Knitters
Knit-a-Square Projects

Nell, Izzy, Birdie, and Cass and dozens of Sea Harbor knitters joined together to knit hundreds of eight-inch squares for orphaned (and vulnerable) children in South Africa who have been infected with AIDS. They found they could knit the colorful squares easily and anywhere—in Harry's Deli, at Coffee's, or sitting on Nell's deck. Then they sent them off to Aunt Ronda and her team of volunteers from Soweto to make into warm blankets for the orphans. The project is one of many created by KasCare, a wonderful nonprofit begun by an amazing Australian family, the McDonalds. Please visit their Web sites to learn more about their projects, to see photos of blankets, and to see the beautiful children they keep warm. The Web sites will also provide information on how to send your own squares or other knitting projects to South Africa.

http://www.kascare.org/
http://www.knit-a-square.com

Simple Knit-a-Square Pattern

(But you can be as creative as the Seaside Knitters and their friends, adding cables, patterns, borders—as long as your finished piece is an eight-inch square. Have fun!)

Materials
- Worsted wool and wool blends or acrylic. One square usually uses a 3.5-ounce ball of yarn or mix-and-match scraps
- 1 pair size 10 needles
- Darning needle

Instructions
1. Cast on 32 stitches. *(Measure your gauge to be sure this equals 8 inches. Adjust as needed.)*
2. Row 1: knit.
3. Row 2: knit. These two rows form the garter-stitch knitting pattern for your square.
4. Continue knitting as per these two rows until you have knitted a square.
5. To ensure that your knitted piece is 8 inches square, either use a tape measure or form a triangle by folding one corner of your square over to meet the opposite corner. If all sides are equal—then you have a square!
6. Cast off. (Be sure to leave a 1¼-yard length of yarn attached to the square to be used to join your square to other squares.)
7. Sew in yarn ends using a darning method.

Knit-a-Square Bunting

• *Courtesy of Anne Powell* •

These tiny buntings will keep infants warm and cuddled. Experiment with color and stripes, but use a close weave, such as a garter stitch, to avoid gaps and guarantee warmth.

Finished dimensions: 25-inch circumference, 25-inch length, including ribbed cuff

Materials
- 14 ounces (4 skeins) soft worsted-weight yarn
- 1 29-inch size 13 circular knitting needle
- 1 stitch marker
- 1 pair size 13 straight knitting needles

Instructions
Knit with 2 strands of yarn held together.
1. Using circular needles, cast on 68 stitches.
2. Knit 2, purl 2 for 5 inches.
3. Place stitch marker on needle for beginning of first round.
4. Join the ends of the ribbing together and knit in the round (garter stitch) until KasCuddle is 24 inches long from top edge of ribbing.
5. Using straight needles and beginning at marker, knit 2 together onto straight needles to end of row (34 stitches on needle).
6. Knit next row to marker.
7. Next row: knit 2 together on the straight needles to end of row at marker (17 stitches on needle).

Remove stitch marker.

Cut yarn, leaving a 10–12-inch tail. Thread yarn needle with tail and pull through remaining 17 stitches.

Draw up tight and secure. Sew in loose ends.

Check http://www.knit-a-square.com for mailing instructions and more ideas.